BROKEN RULES

MICHAELA GREY

For Aaliya. We'll always have Pine nuts.

AUTHOR'S NOTE

This is not a how-to manual for BDSM. If you're interested in exploring the lifestyle, please consult a professional, and always kink responsibly.

1

"I'm just *saying*, I would bang that like a screen door in a hurricane."

Sterling flinched and covered by reaching for his whiskey as Jackson grinned at his companions around the table. Their waitress retreated. She'd almost certainly heard him, although she gave no sign.

"Classy, man," Colby commented.

The dancer on the stage a few yards away spun in place, the lights reflecting off her dark skin in rainbow fractals. The music was a heavy, insistent thump Sterling could feel in his teeth.

He hadn't wanted to come, not really. But given a choice between sitting at home in his sterile apartment or being distracted from his brain by going out with friends, it hadn't been that difficult to decide.

Jackson was laughing, arms slung over the back of the low couch, head craned sideways to ogle their waitress as she returned to the bar with their latest drink order.

"You telling me you *wouldn't*? Fox, man, tell me you'd hit that."

Sterling hunched his shoulders and took a sip of whiskey. "She's pretty," he hedged.

"*Pretty*," Jackson echoed. "That ass should be in a museum! What's wrong with you, man, you can't appreciate art?"

"I appreciate art just fine," Sterling snapped. He entertained the thought—however fanciful—of telling Jackson he preferred a set of broad shoulders and maybe some stubble, but dismissed it with an internal shudder. All hell would break loose the second he did. "She's just not my type."

"She's *my* type," Jackson said. He licked his lips as the waitress came back with a full tray.

There was tension all through her slim body as she set the tray down and handed out the drinks, and Sterling accepted his fresh whiskey and avoided her eyes.

"When do you get off work, sweetheart?" Jackson asked.

Sterling took a long swallow and turned away.

"What are you doing this weekend?" he asked Colby.

Colby shrugged. His blue eyes were troubled, watching Jackson over Sterling's shoulder. "Anneliese wanted to go to the market, I think. Our anniversary's coming up, you know. What about you?"

"Same thing I always do," Sterling said, stretching elaborately. "Enjoying not having a nine-to-five job, the usual."

The waitress hurried off to another table. Jackson said something, and Braden laughed, that nasal snigger Sterling loathed.

"Your dad still hasn't got his hooks into you?" Jackson asked, leaning forward.

Sterling pretended to shiver. "The day I set foot inside my father's brokerage with gainful employment in mind is the day I'm given a lobotomy."

"She's coming back," Jackson said, nudging Braden as the waitress approached again. "Watch this."

Sterling stifled a sigh and stared at the dancer onstage.

2

Sanyam Desai loved destroying people. Hearing the sobs, the pleas, running a hand over skin and feeling it quiver beneath his palm—he lived for it.

His target right now was a middle-aged woman. She knelt in the middle of his room, hands clasped on her nape and eyes downcast demurely as he'd instructed, but twitchy, looking for a reason to disobey, to be punished.

Well, Sanyam could oblige. He paced around the small room, the floor cool beneath his bare feet, running the cat-o'-nine-tails through his hand.

The swish of the leather made the sub shiver, but she didn't move. Sanyam took another turn around her. He undid the top button of his shirt, exposing the brown hollow of his throat, aware that her attention was on him, hungry and wanting, as he moved.

The room was empty, just the two of them, alone and secure in a safe space where no one could see or hear them.

Sanyam passed behind her as she knelt, clad in nothing but sheer satin panties and bra.

What was her name? Eleanor, right. Sloppy, Sanyam chided himself.

He ran a hand across her shoulder blades, scratching lightly with one nail so that a faint welt appeared, and she shuddered.

Trinity's music from the main room was a steady thump and growl filling the space, but Sanyam barely heard it, focused on Eleanor.

She had love handles, stretch marks on her thighs, and a little belly. From the way she hunched her shoulders and tried to curl in on herself, she was self-conscious about her appearance. Sanyam needed to work on that before he went any further.

He dropped the whip, catching a handful of hair and tilting her head back so that her neck was exposed, wrapping his free hand around it. Eleanor swallowed, her brown eyes huge, and Sanyam squeezed, just enough that her air was briefly restricted.

"You are beautiful," he said.

Eleanor shook her head, silently refuting his words, and Sanyam released her, picking up the whip to strike her sharply across the buttocks, just once. She cried out in shock as the welt rose, but didn't move.

Sanyam caught her chin, forcing her gaze up. "Rule number one—never argue with your Dom."

Eleanor nodded fractionally, eyes on Sanyam. He let go and paced around her again, considering.

The hard floor had to be hurting her knees by now, but she made no noise of complaint, not even shifting her weight. Sanyam's estimation of her rose.

Her friend had knocked on his door and pushed her forward. "There will be no fucking," Sanyam had told her bluntly after the door closed. "I do not have sex the first time someone subs for me, and I do not fuck women in any case. Do you still wish to continue?"

Eleanor had gulped but clutched her handbag and nodded earnestly. "That's fine," she'd said, her voice so quiet Sanyam had to strain to hear it. "I just want...." Her voice had trailed off, and Sanyam had felt a rush of pity for her.

"Strip," he'd said, and turned away.

"What do you want?" he said aloud, moving around in front of her again.

Eleanor dropped her head. "I want... I need to be punished. Spanked."

Sanyam arched a brow. "What have you done that is so heinous?"

At that, Eleanor tucked her chin into her chest. "I—" She squeezed her eyes shut. "My husband left. It was my fault."

"Get up," Sanyam ordered. He made a selection from his wall of toys and sat down on the couch opposite the door as Eleanor stood, awkward and crossing her arms over her stomach.

Sanyam patted his knees. "Facedown."

Eleanor's eyes shot wide. "Oh... I'm too heavy—"

Sanyam let his expression speak for him, and Eleanor gulped and moved awkwardly toward him. She settled herself over his knees, all breathless apologies and hands fluttering unhappily, and Sanyam shut her up by smoothing a hand over the curve of her ass.

Eleanor squeaked and stopped talking, across his lap with her face in the couch cushions.

Sanyam picked up the whip and trailed it across her thigh. "Do you have children, Eleanor?"

Eleanor's face was still buried in the couch, but she managed a nod. "Three."

"How old are they?"

"The youngest is… twelve," she said faintly. "Oldest is sixteen."

"Why did your husband leave?"

Eleanor tensed. "I—he met someone else. Someone… prettier."

"And so it is your fault," Sanyam said, understanding dawning. "Because you are not the perfect size four he married, is that it?"

"Size two," Eleanor mumbled into the cushion, and Sanyam fought a smile.

Without warning, he struck a blow, the thin satin of her underwear no protection at all against the sting of the leather.

Eleanor bucked and cried out, and Sanyam steadied her with a hand on her thigh.

"That is for aging," he said.

He hit her again.

"That's for the stretch marks."

Eleanor's body was tense, and Sanyam rubbed a gentle palm across the weals.

He struck her three more times in quick succession.

"The children you bore for this man."

Eleanor sagged and began to weep, her shoulders shaking.

Sanyam swung the whip again, then again, the

harsh *cracks* loud in the small room even over the music.

"For not being perfect," he said between swings. *Crack.* "For having a mind of your own." *Crack.* "For wanting more to your life than serving him."

Eleanor was limp across his knees, her body wracked with sobs, and Sanyam hesitated, whip raised.

"For being human," he said softly, and brought the crop down.

He tossed the whip to the side and pulled Eleanor upright, her tears still shaking her frame, face red and eyes puffy. Sanyam thumbed a tear off her cheek.

"You are not to blame," he said, looking into her eyes. "Do you understand me?"

Eleanor choked on another sob but managed a nod.

Sanyam patted her shoulder. "Get dressed. Scene over."

He waited, back turned to give her privacy, as she struggled into her clothes, but shook his head when she reached into her purse. "Pay Kimi in the main room, behind the bar," he said. "She handles that."

"What about tipping?" Eleanor asked.

Sanyam smiled. "She'll take that too, if you're

so inclined. It's not necessary, but it is appreciated."

Eleanor opened her mouth, shutting it again abruptly. "Can I—would you—can I see you sometime? Not… here? I know you said you don't… see women, but—"

Sanyam smiled, letting her down easy. "It is against club policy to date clients, but I am flattered."

"They wouldn't have to know," Eleanor pointed out. She looked shocked at her own audacity, and Sanyam's smile widened.

"I like your spirit, Eleanor," he said, taking her by the shoulders. "Get someone to rub some cream into those welts, if you can. And you may experience a sub drop at some point over the next few hours or even tomorrow. Stay hydrated, make sure you eat something, and if you get terribly irritable or depressed, reach out for help to someone you trust. Do you have one such?"

Eleanor nodded. "My best friend, Nanette. She's—this was her idea. She'll… stay with me."

"Good." Sanyam opened the door and ushered her through. Shutting it behind her, he leaned against it for a minute and took a deep breath.

Finally, he could go home.

He'd been at the club all evening, seeing client

after client, and he was exhausted. All he wanted to do was go home, change into comfortable clothes, and not have to deal with people again for at least a full day.

He stepped into his shoes and slung his coat over one arm, leaving his shirt loose at the collar. The music hit him like a physical blow in the hall outside his room, and he grimaced.

There weren't many people in the hall, and all were clients, meaning no one made eye contact, too embarrassed by the reality of where they were and what they were doing to actually look at Sanyam as they scurried past.

That was just fine by Sanyam. Human contact was the last thing he wanted at the moment.

He turned down the hall toward the back entrance and swore under his breath as he remembered that the bartender had sent a message that she wanted to talk to him after his shift.

Two minutes. Then he was gone.

Even at 4:00 a.m., the main room of the Honeytrap was full of people, crammed into booths, sprawled on long, low sofas, many of them casually making out in various stages of dishabille. Trinity was onstage, finishing up her last set, long legs made even longer by the six-inch heels and general lack of clothing.

Sanyam threaded his way through the crowds,

ignoring the gazes trained on him. He knew he was eye-catching. He didn't particularly care.

He spotted his friend Farid lounging in one of the booths, foot up on the seat and arm on his knee as he watched the customers. A young man was on his back, head in Farid's lap, eyes closed as Farid ran fingers through his hair.

Sanyam lifted a hand, and Farid smiled at him but didn't invite him over. That worked for Sanyam, who was far too tired to be sociable, even with one of the few people whose company he actively enjoyed.

Kimi was at the bar, deftly stirring, mixing, and pouring drinks. Her long black hair was pulled up in a knot at the back of her head, held there by hairpins that could be—and had been, on more than one occasion, she'd told Sanyam—used to fend off overzealous admirers.

She was wearing a black leather corset that looked painted on and matching leather pants. *How does she breathe?* Sanyam wondered briefly.

Kimi glanced up and saw him, a smile lighting her slanted eyes. "Drink?" she asked, gesturing to the stool.

Sanyam shook his head but sat down. "Soda is fine."

"Give me a second," Kimi said, sliding a Coke down the mahogany bar toward him. "Gotta deal with the preppy brats down there." She gestured with her chin. "They're handsy, the assholes, and they'd better tip Delfia like it's their last night on earth or I'll castrate them myself."

Sanyam popped the tab on the Coke and took a long drink, unfazed. He watched out of the corner of his eye, elbows on the bar, as Kimi took the drinks to Delfia, the diminutive Cuban beauty who had just been hired the week before.

Delfia dimpled at Kimi and scooped the tray up onto her shoulder. Kimi turned back to Sanyam, a blush staining her burnished skin, and propped her elbows on the bar.

"So. Been thinking."

"Dangerous habit," Sanyam observed over his drink.

Kimi threw a peanut at him. "Shut up, talking."

Sanyam muffled a snicker in his soda and waited for her to continue.

"How are you enjoying your job so far?" she asked.

Sanyam lifted a shoulder. "It's fine. A few hiccups here and there, nothing to complain about."

"You've been here, what… a month?"

"Five weeks," Sanyam said.

"Canada's pretty different from India, huh?"

"Did you call me over for small talk?" Sanyam asked.

Kimi bristled. "I'm being *nice*, asshole. I'm told that's what people *do*."

"When they want something, perhaps. What do you want, Kimi?"

Kimi propped her elbows back on the bar. The light glanced off her high cheekbones as she tilted her head. "Those hiccups you mentioned."

Sanyam said nothing. Shouting reverberated through his head. The man who'd claimed he wanted to sub but refused to submit had fought Sanyam at first mentally and then physically, until security had to be called.

He touched the spot under his eye. It was still tender where the man's fist had connected.

"It happens," he said. "He won't be back."

"No, but someone like him might. Here's what I'm suggesting. Crap—hang on." Delfia was back with another order, and Kimi swung into action, mixing and pouring while Sanyam waited.

Delfia was tiny but voluptuous, dimples and dark eyes and heavy black hair, and Sanyam could see why Kimi was so enamored. If he was attracted to women, he might be too.

Delfia loaded her tray with drinks, and Kimi turned back to Sanyam.

"Sorry about that. So what I'm proposing is this—I vet your clients for you."

Sanyam raised an eyebrow.

"Hear me out!" Kimi said. "I'm in the perfect position here. I've talked to Delfia, and she's in, she'll be my eyes and ears on the floor. We'll find you subs who *want* to sub, who'll take what you give them and not fight you. And who'll tip like it's going out of style."

"What's in it for you?"

Kimi shrugged. "Split the tips fifty-fifty?"

Sanyam narrowed his eyes. "Seventy-thirty."

"Done," Kimi said, so fast it was clearly what she'd been hoping for.

Sanyam couldn't help the laugh, and Kimi grinned at him.

Shouting erupted from the table Delfia was serving, and they both spun as glass shattered and people shoved their chairs back.

"*Fuck.*" Kimi grabbed her baseball bat from under the bar and charged into battle as Sanyam followed.

They dove into the knot of people who'd gathered and pulled them apart. Delfia was on the lap of one of the patrons, struggling to get away as he laughed and tightened his grip around her waist, his other hand on her breast.

"*Let her go,*" Kimi snarled.

The man rolled his eyes but released her, lifting his hands in mock surrender, and Delfia scrambled off his lap and dashed away. Kimi dropped her bat and went after her as security arrived then in the form of the bouncers Logan and Elijah, muscles straining their tight T-shirts.

"Back away, please," Sanyam said to the onlookers. "This doesn't concern you." He turned back to the table. Where was the club owner? Why hadn't she shown up to put this particular fire out?

Logan leaned in. "Ava went home early," he said in what passed for a whisper. "Want I should text her?"

Sanyam shook his head and focused on the clients.

There were four young men sitting there, and from the looks of them, they'd been drinking awhile. Sanyam's first instinct was to call the police, and he knew Ava would back him if he did, but he also knew that a police presence tended to discourage cash flow. If he could handle this in-house, it would be better all the way around.

The antagonist was white, rich, and clearly spoiled. His polo was open at the neck and his blond hair disheveled. He lounged against his seat, slinging one arm over the back of it as he looked down his patrician nose at Sanyam.

"What's the problem?" His tone was insolent, and Sanyam disliked him just a little more.

"The problem is you harassed and molested an employee, and your friends are complicit," Sanyam said. "What are your names, please?"

"Jackson, and she was into it. This is Colby, Braden, and Fox." He gestured at his friends, who all looked like variations on a theme. Tall, slim, expensive haircuts, and even more expensive clothes—Sanyam detested them immediately.

"Jackson, I am acting manager Sanyam Desai," Sanyam said. "It is clearly stated in many visible locations that touching the employees in any way is not permitted. Even if she *was* 'into it,' which she clearly was not, you violated our policies. You are not welcome back at this club."

Jackson's face darkened, and he shot to his feet. "Do you know who my father is, you jumped-up little prick?"

"Does *he* know you like to frequent BDSM clubs?" Sanyam fired back, stepping into Jackson's space. "I will be happy to tell him. What's his number?"

"Fuck you," Jackson hissed. "Let's go, guys. This place is stupid anyway."

Sanyam took a step back as the young men

filed past. Braden glowered at him, shoulders up and fists clenching, but Elijah stepped forward, and Braden flinched and scuttled after Jackson. Colby looked faintly ashamed, but Fox just seemed bored, as he flicked his hair out of his face and checked the time.

"Good riddance," Logan rumbled as they left. "Are they all blacklisted or just Jackson?"

Sanyam considered. "Just Jackson, for now. Put the others' names on the list, and if they return, let them know they're on probation. I'm going to check on Delfia."

He found her and Kimi in the dressing room behind the stage. Delfia was curled up in Kimi's arms, her eyes blank, as Sanyam knelt beside them.

"He pinched her breast and put his hand down her pants," Kimi said, her mouth taut with fury.

"I should have called the police," Sanyam said as remorse washed over him. "It's not too late, Delfia. Do you want to file a report?"

Delfia shook her head, burrowing closer to Kimi. "*No.* No cops. I just... want it to go away."

"Jackson is gone, and he will not be allowed back," Sanyam said gently.

Kimi rubbed Delfia's back. "See, honey? You're

safe." She glanced up at Sanyam. "I'm going to take her home."

"Good idea," Sanyam said, standing. "Let Kimi take care of you, Delfia. I'm going home too. Kimi, call me if you need anything."

Kimi just nodded, her body curved protectively around Delfia's.

SANYAM LET himself into his apartment, and the tension leached from his muscles. Door shut and locked, he took his shoes off and padded into the kitchen, where he started the kettle.

"Polly?" he called.

He heard a thump and the pattering of paws down the hallway, and he smiled.

Polly was talking to him before she even made it into the kitchen, a rapid-fire volley of tiny squeaking meows, and Sanyam laughed and bent to pick her up.

"Hello, my darling. How was your day?"

Polly snuggled in under his chin and began to purr thunderously. Sanyam rubbed his cheek against her long, creamy brown fur and turned to take the kettle off the heat and pour it over his tea one-handed.

"We had some assholes at the club tonight," he told her as the tea steeped.

Polly trilled inquisitively.

"Mm, yes. Someone molested Delfia, and there was quite the commotion. Not to worry, though—Kimi is taking good care of her, and that particular person won't be returning."

He carried his tea and armful of furry cat to the table and sat down. Polly rearranged herself on his knees and settled in, kneading his thigh as her purring redoubled.

Sanyam glanced around the apartment, stark walls and open spaces. He'd been drawn to the emptiness of it when he first saw it, the exposed beams in the ceiling and the posts scattered throughout the kitchen and living room area, but—

"I need to decorate," he murmured. He'd been in Vancouver for six weeks, but his time had been so taken up by the club that he hadn't had a chance to make his apartment a home.

"Tomorrow," he told Polly, now fast asleep. "Tomorrow I will go out and perhaps find some furnishings. Some wall hangings would be nice, don't you think?"

That settled, he finished his tea and gently dislodged Polly from her perch to wash out his cup and get ready for bed.

3

He had a leisurely breakfast and then spent the morning curled up in bed reading, Polly a warm lump in the crook of his elbow. Around noon, he stretched and stood up as Polly protested.

"Apologies," he told her as she grumbled and rearranged herself in the warm spot he'd left behind. "I will bring you back a delicacy from the market, I promise."

Dressed in slacks and a sweater befitting the autumn chill, Sanyam ventured out into one of Vancouver's bustling open-air marketplaces.

He took the bus to Granville Market and stepped off into a swarm of people all talking, laughing, and shopping busily. Sanyam pushed his hands into his pockets and allowed himself to be swallowed by the flow of the crowd, wandering the aisles and admiring the colorful produce and wares.

Not quite Crawford Hall, he mused as he walked, *but it has a charm all its own.*

A little girl darted in front of him, and Sanyam stopped dead to avoid tripping over her.

"Deedee!" The girl's mother dashed by, apologizing breathlessly, and Sanyam smiled at them both.

Deedee couldn't have been more than four, fair hair pulled up into two high ponytails, her eyes big and blue, nose pink with the chill. She stopped and stared at Sanyam as her mother scooped her up.

"He has a beard like Daddy," she said in a high, clear voice. "Why do his eyes do that?"

Her mother put a horrified hand over Deedee's mouth. "Deedee, *shh.*"

Sanyam's smile widened, and he bent to address the little girl. "I am Indian. That is why my eyes are slanted. Not all of us have it, but I am one who does."

Deedee popped her thumb in her mouth and considered him around it. "I like it," she announced. "You're very pretty."

Sanyam laughed out loud and bowed to her. "Thank you," he said. "You're prettier."

Deedee giggled and hid her face in her mother's coat as Sanyam straightened.

Sorry, her mother mouthed.

"It's quite all right," Sanyam said. "I hope both you lovely ladies have a wonderful day."

Deedee waved to him, and Sanyam waved back as they left. He was still smiling as he turned away and bumped into a tall, slim man, jostling his arm and spilling the coffee he was holding all down his front.

"Oh fucking *hell*," the man snarled, stumbling back as he pulled his drenched shirt away from his stomach. "Why don't you watch where the fuck you're going, you clumsy asshole?"

"I'm so sorry," Sanyam said, horrified. "Are you burned?"

"Well, it was really fucking hot, so you do the goddamn math," the man snapped. He looked familiar, but Sanyam couldn't place him. He spun before Sanyam could figure out how he knew him and stalked off down the aisle. Sanyam followed, some vague idea of paying for his shirt or the coffee at the very least driving him.

The man ducked into a stall halfway down the row, where a girl glanced up, clearly startled. "Fox? What happened?"

Fox. He'd been with Jackson the night before, Sanyam realized, and disgust welled inside him.

He turned to go, but Fox flung a hand toward him.

"This moron managed to knock my coffee all over my shirt," he said. He jerked his coat off and peeled his shirt over his head, hissing through his teeth. His abdomen was reddened where the coffee had splashed him, and he prodded at the skin with one finger.

"I really am sorry," Sanyam said reluctantly. "Can I pay for your shirt?"

"I don't know, can you?" Fox retorted. "It cost two hundred dollars."

"For a *T-shirt?*"

Fox sneered at him. "Just fuck off already. You've done enough damage." He turned away, presenting a pair of sharply bladed shoulders as he bent and rummaged through a bag on the floor of the stall.

The girl stood and held out her hand. "I'm Cricket, and I apologize for my brother's rudeness."

Sanyam accepted it. "Sanyam Desai. It's quite all right; it was entirely my fault."

"Goddamn right it was," Fox muttered.

Sanyam gritted his teeth and pulled out his wallet. Peeling off two hundred-dollar bills, he held them out to Cricket, who shook her head.

"Oh no, it's really not necessary."

Fox leaned across her and snatched the money. "Says *you.*"

Cricket glared at him and turned back to Sanyam. She was a female version of her brother, tall and slender with long, dark hair and pale skin. Her jade-green eyes were apologetic.

"I'd like to say he's not usually this awful," Cricket said, "but honestly, this is pretty standard behavior."

Fox dragged a shirt over his head and scowled down at the pink unicorn that now graced his chest. "What the *fuck*, Cricket?"

Cricket glanced at him and burst out laughing as Sanyam's lips twitched.

"Serves you right for going through the donation bag, you idiot!"

Sanyam glanced around the stall, realizing for the first time that it offered a variety of crystal and glassware. A tall, blue glass vase caught his eye, and he picked it up, caressing its smooth curves with reverent fingers.

"Oh, this is lovely," he said. He knew exactly where he would put it—on the high shelf in front of the windows that faced the rising sun, where the glass would catch the light. "How much?"

"That one's seventy-five," Cricket said.

"But for you, it's an even hundred," Fox

chimed in. He collapsed in a folding chair on the side of the booth and stretched his long legs out.

Cricket ignored him as Sanyam counted off another seventy-five dollars and held them out.

"Do you make these pieces yourself?" he asked.

Cricket dimpled. "No, I go to yard sales and flea markets and buy them, clean them up, and then sell them here."

"Slumming it," Fox said, sotto voce.

Sanyam's lips tightened. Cricket flinched but said nothing as she took the vase back and wrapped it in paper, tying it with twine before slipping it into a small bag and handing it to him.

"You have exquisite taste," he told her.

"Come back anytime," Cricket said, smiling.

"Preferably on a day I haven't been roped into helping," Fox said. He dropped his head back and gazed up at the ceiling, revealing his long neck.

"My God, you're no better in daylight, are you?" Sanyam said. He regretted his words instantly, but it was too late. Fox jerked his head up, eyes narrowing.

"You. I *do* know you, you're that asshole from —" He glanced at Cricket and cleared his throat. "From last night. What are you doing *here*?"

"Shopping," Sanyam said dryly. "Normal, ordinary stuff that most people do."

Fox curled his lip, but a couple walked up before he could reply. Cricket turned to help them, and Sanyam took a step nearer to Fox.

"If you ask me," he said, his voice pitched low, "you need to be taught some manners."

Fox's mouth went flat, his eyes dangerous. "Are you offering?"

Sanyam pulled a card from his wallet and handed it over. "Ask for me tonight and find out."

He walked away without looking back.

4

Fox wasn't there when Sanyam started his shift that evening, and by the time the night was half over, Sanyam had nearly forgotten about him, engrossed in teaching a new submissive the joys to be found in rigging, and indulging another in some pain-play.

His phone buzzed as he was ushering a client out with a warning to stay hydrated and watch for a sub drop.

It was Kimi. *Someone here wants you for the rest of your night. Says you gave him your card. Paid up front.*

Sanyam straightened as electricity tingled through him. *Send him back.* He put a few supplies on the small table in the corner and settled in to wait.

He was sitting on the sofa when Fox walked in, eyes wary and slim body taut with evident nerves.

"Shut the door," Sanyam said.

Fox's lips tightened, but he obeyed before turning back to look at Sanyam, his fingers twitching at the seams of his pants.

Sanyam gestured with his chin at the table, and Fox took a hesitant step in that direction, then another.

"What…?" Fox picked up the sheaf of papers and riffled through them. "What the fuck is this?"

"Standard contract, lasting one night only. If you want to become a permanent or even semiregular client, then you'll sign a different form. This one states that you're a submissive, that you wish to be dominated, and that you accept my authority over you for the specified length of time. There's a space for you to fill in your hard and soft limits."

Fox's chin jutted. "I'm not a submissive."

Sanyam lifted an eyebrow. "Then what are you doing here?"

"I—" Fox shifted his weight, crumpling the papers in his hand. "I don't kn—"

"Sit down," Sanyam ordered.

Fox sat instantly. His mouth fell open in

shock as he realized what he'd done, and Sanyam hid his amusement.

"Read the contract. We don't have to do anything you don't want to do. But if you're here, it's because you need something, consciously or otherwise. Perhaps I can give it to you."

Fox swallowed hard and smoothed the papers out. His hands were trembling, Sanyam noticed, and he stood up and straightened his vest. Fox watched him out of the corner of his eye, his head down as he ostensibly studied the contract, as Sanyam moved up behind him. Fox needed to be taken out of his head, shown the peace that could be gained through surrendering control, and Sanyam could help with that.

He said nothing, standing still as Fox forced himself to read the contract, and waited until Fox's attention was fully on the page and the tension in his shoulders had relaxed. Then he slid a hand into Fox's hair and dragged his head to the side.

Fox dropped the papers, and they fell in a looping flutter to the floor as he reached up and back to catch Sanyam's wrist.

Sanyam leaned down and nosed at the crook of Fox's elegant neck, corded with tension. "This throat of yours is criminal," he murmured. "It's *begging* to be marked up."

Fox dragged air in through his nose, clutching at Sanyam's wrist. His eyes were closed, mouth soft and lax, and Sanyam couldn't resist nipping—gently—at the skin under Fox's ear.

Fox jerked and made a needy, helpless noise.

"That's what I thought," Sanyam said. He let go of Fox's hair and straightened. "Pick up the mess you made, and then decide if you want to be here or not."

He sat down again and crossed his legs, watching as Fox fought an internal battle, his mouth working and his eyes angry. Sanyam draped his arms across the back of the couch and waited him out.

Finally, Fox bent and picked the papers up. He dropped them onto the table with little regard for neatness, then grabbed the pen, signed his name, and glared at Sanyam when he was done.

Sanyam held out a silent hand.

Fox's glare intensified, but Sanyam didn't move. It was several more minutes of Fox fighting with himself before he picked up the contract and shoved it at Sanyam, who accepted it graciously.

He clicked his tongue as he looked through it. "No limits at all? That's rather dangerous." Fox's signature was sharp, jagged lines, and Sanyam looked closer. "Your name isn't Fox?"

Fox lifted his chin. "I—it's Sterling. Sterling

Reynard. My friends call me Fox because of my last name."

"And your limits?"

"I don't have any," Fox said. He sounded equal parts terrified and defiant.

Sanyam looked up. "Everyone has limits, Fox. Have you ever subbed before?"

Fox shook his head silently.

"I will not fuck you tonight," Sanyam said, standing in a fluid movement to set the pages on the table. He signed under Fox's name in his neat, contained handwriting, and straightened.

Fox looked outraged. "I didn't—"

"You didn't what?" Sanyam said. "You didn't ask? You have no idea, do you?"

"About what?"

Sanyam tilted his head. "You're desperate for it. You would beg if your pride allowed." He smiled and moved closer. "Don't worry." He spoke so low Fox had to lean in to hear him. "You'll beg eventually."

Fox's throat bobbed as he swallowed. This close, Sanyam could see that his eyes were olive green, with a ring of gold around the pupils.

"Before we go any further, what's your safeword?" Sanyam asked.

Fox frowned. "I—I don't need one."

"Yes you do," Sanyam said flatly. "And if you refuse to pick one, you will be shown the door."

Fox took a step back, hands opening and closing. "I don't understand. Why is it so important?"

"It is your guarantee of safety while under my care," Sanyam said. "Your safeword ensures that no matter what we're doing, once used, we will cease all activities with no questions asked and no judgments made."

"What if I don't—want to stop? Does it mean—"

"It does not mean we can't start again," Sanyam said. He took Fox's chin in his hand and turned his head as Fox's eyes fluttered shut. "It simply means we stop and renegotiate." Sanyam ran a thumb across Fox's lips, pressing lightly until Fox opened his mouth.

Sanyam pulled away, dropping his hand, and Fox opened his eyes, awareness filling them. His brow knit, and he clenched his fists as frustration flickered across his face.

"Kneel," Sanyam said, and turned his back. There was furious silence behind him but Sanyam didn't look, selecting a length of rope from the wall. Finally, Fox's knees hit the floor with a thump and Sanyam smiled.

When he turned, sober, Fox was glaring up at him.

"So angry," Sanyam murmured. "So desperate to be dominated."

"I *don't*, I told you! I'm not a submissive!" Fox snarled.

"So you said, indeed." Sanyam stepped behind Fox and pulled his arms behind his back. "And yet… here we are." He tied Fox's arms in a figure eight pattern, keeping the loops of rope even and taut, and stepped back. "Safeword. Right now."

Fox was breathing hard, spots of color high on his cheeks. "I—I can't—I don't know—"

"Not something you would use in casual conversation."

"I—Calypso," Fox managed.

"Very good," Sanyam said. "Mine is Crawford." He stepped in between Fox's spread knees and looked down at him. Fox was pulling on the bonds, lip caught between his teeth, but he stilled as Sanyam traced the curve of his jaw. "You are beautiful," Sanyam said.

Fox sneered wordlessly.

"Oh, you already know that, do you?" Sanyam tilted Fox's head up and wrapped a hand around his throat. "You're also incredibly spoiled, petulant, and awful. Do you have any redeeming characteristics, besides your looks?"

"Fuck you," Fox spat.

"Perhaps someday," Sanyam said, unmoved.

He bent until their lips were a scant inch apart. He could feel Fox's breath warm on his face, puffing in sharp, short gusts. Fox's pupils were blown wide, his lips bitten red, and Sanyam closed the distance and covered Fox's lips with his own.

He took his time, licking into Fox's mouth in slow, gentle sweeps. Fox was utterly still at first, and finally he groaned deep in his chest and surged up to kiss back with a wild desperation.

Sanyam tightened his grip on Fox's throat and pushed him down onto his heels without breaking contact with his mouth, holding him there as he kept control of the kiss.

When he broke away, they were both breathing hard, and Fox looked dazed, swollen lips and the dark hair falling forward over his brow giving him a debauched air.

He pulled again at the rope, whining in the back of his throat. "I need—"

Sanyam glanced down. Fox was desperately hard, his erection straining his pants as a damp patch formed.

"You do, don't you? But you won't get it. Not tonight."

Fox whimpered, squeezing his eyes shut, and Sanyam leaned down to cup his crotch. Fox jerked and pushed against Sanyam's hand, looking for friction.

Sanyam rubbed the hardness through the fabric for a minute, eyes steady on Fox's face, but when Fox's breathing quickened and his hips lost rhythm, Sanyam pulled away.

Fox moaned, nearly overbalancing. "You *asshole*," he managed.

"Watch that mouth," Sanyam warned. "Or we'll get started on the manners a little earlier than I intended." He took a step back, tapping his bottom lip in contemplation. "We need to figure out what your hard limits are, first of all." He sank down on the couch and crossed his legs again.

"I don't *have* any," Fox snapped.

"So you're all right with me pissing in your mouth or attaching electrodes to your testicles?" Sanyam said.

Fox blinked and fumbled for words, his mouth opening and closing. "I—no."

"Then you *do* have hard limits." Sanyam danced his fingers along the back of the couch, not looking at Fox's disheveled form. "Hitting?"

"Yes," Fox said instantly.

Sanyam hummed approval. "Pain in general."

"*Yes.*"

"I'd ask if you like being restrained but it's

fairly obvious you do." Sanyam glanced at Fox's crotch, his lips twitching. "Cross-dressing?"

Fox hesitated, and a variety of emotions flickered over his mobile features. Interest, Sanyam thought, but also a knee-jerk repulsion.

"Tabled for later, perhaps," Sanyam suggested. "What about breath-play?"

Fox looked confused. "What's that?"

"It can take various forms," Sanyam said. "But the general idea is that I restrict your breathing in order to heighten your pleasure. It's incredibly dangerous, but consider—I hold your throat for a few seconds while fucking you so that you can't draw in air. Or perhaps I pinch your nostrils shut while my cock is buried in your throat—*don't come.*"

Fox had doubled over, his face pressed to his knees as he fought off the orgasm, body heaving.

"Perhaps we can explore that at a future date," Sanyam murmured. "With adequate preparation and research on the subject and full consent, of course."

Fox lifted his head. His sallow cheeks were flushed, his breathing unsteady, and Sanyam smiled at him.

"On the one hand, making you come in your pants and then wear them out of the club after has a certain... appeal," Sanyam mused. "On the other… I think—yes, I think it would be best for you if you were not to come at all until our next session."

Fox's mouth fell open. "You can't—you can't do that."

"Can't I?" Sanyam said. He stretched, letting his shirt ride up as he rolled his neck to get the kinks out. "And yet that's exactly what I'm going to do. Fox, you are not to touch yourself in any pleasurable way until you come to see me again. If you do, I will know, and you will be… punished."

Fox looked outraged, his mouth working. "You don't own me—you can't tell me what to do!"

Sanyam surged to his feet and caught Fox's face in an iron grip, forcing his head back. "I do not own you; that is true. I don't hold with owning people. But I think you'll find I *can* tell you what to do. And when you walk out that door, it will be your choice whether you walk back in or not."

He bent and nipped lightly at Fox's bottom lip. "But if you do come back, it will be the best orgasm of your life to date. I can promise you that."

Fox was utterly still. He seemed to have stopped breathing entirely.

Sanyam let go and stepped away. He moved

around behind Fox and untied his arms quickly. As soon as Fox was free, Sanyam turned to begin tidying the room.

"Get out," he said over his shoulder.

He could hear shuffling as Fox climbed to his feet. There was silence for a moment, but Sanyam didn't look, putting the rope in a hamper to be cleaned later and sorting through his supplies. *Do I have what I need for tomorrow? I'm getting low on lube and condoms. Better ask Ava to restock tonight.*

The door slammed, and Sanyam finally let himself smile. Tomorrow was going to be *fun.*

5

Sterling wasn't entirely sure how he made it out of the club, in retrospect. He came back to full awareness in his car, sitting silently behind the wheel in the dark parking lot.

He lifted his hands, examining the marks the rope had left on his wrists. His mind wouldn't let go of the image of Sanyam prowling around him, feet silent on the hard floor, dark, slanted eyes predatory and sharp on Sterling's kneeling form.

Sterling took a shuddering breath and started the car. The Lamborghini roared to life, the engine settling into a steady growl that vibrated through his seat as he pulled out and turned for home.

He parked in the garage of his high-rise and acknowledged the doorman's greeting with a vague flip of his hand. The elevator rose swift and smooth to the forty-seventh floor, and Sterling stepped off, still dazed, and fumbled for the key to his apartment.

Inside, he closed the door and leaned against it, running a hand through his hair. His living room was cold and stark in the moonlight that poured through the floor-to-ceiling windows, Vancouver spread below him in glittering splendor, like jewels strewn on black velvet. The white puzzle Cricket had given him for his most recent birthday gleamed in pearlescent pieces on the coffee table, waiting for him to finish it.

Sterling kicked his shoes off and dropped his keys in the bowl by the door before padding into the spotless kitchen that gleamed with silver appliances and marble countertops.

He pulled a Utopias from the refrigerator and leaned a hip against the stove as he took a swig.

"But if you do come back, it will be the best orgasm of your life to date. I can promise you that."

Sterling groaned as his cock stirred.

"Fox, you are not to touch yourself in any pleasurable way until you come to see me again."

Sterling scowled at the sink. "I'm not your slave, asshole," he said aloud, his voice echoing through the empty apartment. "If I want to jack off, I'm going to jack off." He pushed the heel of his hand against his erection, biting his lip as sparks skittered through him. *It's not like he'll* actually *know*, his subconscious pointed out.

Sterling set the beer on the counter and stumbled for the bedroom, unzipping his pants as he went.

He sank onto the bed and wrapped a hand around himself. Sanyam was the most beautiful man Sterling had ever seen, with those tilted eyes and black curls. He kissed like a god, strong and commanding and focused, and Sterling couldn't wait for him to put those big hands all over his body. It took only a few quick pumps of his fist before his toes curled, and his back arched, and he came with a choked noise.

———

HE WOKE up the next morning and stared at the ceiling as the memories of the night before rushed over him. Sanyam circling him, looking at him like Sterling was a dessert he couldn't wait to take a bite out of, and Sterling wishing he *would* already.

He rolled out of bed, and things immediately began to go wrong.

He nicked himself shaving as Sanyam's words

floated through his mind. *"This throat of yours is criminal."*

He stubbed his toe and swore viciously as he stepped out of the shower and grabbed a towel.

He dropped his bottle of aftershave, and it shattered on the floor, filling the bathroom with a choking miasma of evergreen and clove. Sterling snarled and escaped into the bedroom to dress. He'd clean it up later, when he wasn't quite so ready to commit murder.

He grabbed the first pair of jeans and—expensive, designer—T-shirt that came to hand, and stomped barefoot out of the bedroom to do something about breakfast.

Astrid was in the kitchen, humming to herself as she cleaned. "Good morning, Mr. Sterling!" she sang as he stalked in.

Sterling muttered something and poured a glass of orange juice. Turning, he froze at the sight of the child seated at his dining room table, coloring busily.

"Uh…. Astrid," he said. "What is he doing here?"

Astrid dried her hands on her apron, clearly unhappy. "I'm so sorry, Mr. Sterling," she said in her soft Danish accent. "Dag's school had burst pipes. It was closed for the day for repairs. I had nowhere else for him to go. It won't happen again, I promise."

Dag looked up, and Sterling suppressed a shudder at the grape jam smears on his mouth. He did a double take when he realized Dag was wearing what was undeniably a pink tulle tutu over his navy-and-white school uniform.

"Why is he wearing a skirt?" Sterling asked, unable to look away.

Astrid smiled fondly at her son. "He is in a ballet class. I have told him—only the girls wear the tutus, but nothing would do but that he wear one too."

"Is he a boy or a girl, then?" Sterling snapped.

Astrid tilted her head, confusion on her face. "He is a boy, Mr. Sterling. He just likes to wear the tutu sometimes."

"Mama, look!" Dag chirped and brandished a drawing, nearly knocking over his glass of milk.

Sterling flinched and set his orange juice down. "I'm going out."

"But your breakfast is almost ready!" Astrid protested.

"Give it to Dag," Sterling said over his shoulder, and escaped.

He grabbed a coat on the way out the door and shoved his arms into the sleeves, muttering as he rode the elevator down and stalked out through the lobby. The doorman, wisely, said nothing as Sterling stormed past.

Outside, Sterling stopped and considered his options. He wasn't really hungry, but there was no way he was going back in his apartment while a child was in there.

It was Sunday, he realized. Cricket would be at Granville Island for the day. Maybe he'd go bother her—that always made him feel better.

He set out on foot, hunching his shoulders and pushing his hands into his pockets as he walked. It was a lovely autumn day, with a crispness to the air that warned of cold to come.

If he was being honest with himself, it wasn't the child in his home that had him so on edge. It wasn't even Dag wearing a skirt, although that bothered him too for some reason he couldn't pin down yet.

No, his irritability stemmed from something deep inside him, something ugly and small, and Sterling was afraid to look at it directly, afraid to even acknowledge it for fear of it growing.

You're not worth anything. You never will be. You're hateful and mean, and no one likes you. No one wants *you.*

He stopped at the little coffee shop on the edge of the market and got coffee for himself and

Cricket before braving the crowds that already clogged the aisles.

Sterling slithered through the throng, muttering imprecations under his breath. Why did people have to exist in his general vicinity, anyway? Someone stepped on his foot, and Sterling snarled, making the offender cower backward.

Finally, he won through and ducked into Cricket's stall. She looked up, startled.

"Fox, what are you doing here? It's not your day to help me."

"I needed fresh air," Sterling said, handing her the coffee. He flopped down in the camp chair and heaved a sigh of relief. "I just wish the fresh air didn't come with so many *people* attached to it."

Cricket snorted. "We live in Vancouver, dearest big brother. Did you get Dorian coffee too?"

Sterling lifted his head. "Dorian is here?"

Cricket sighed. "You are the most airheaded idiot. Of course Dorian is here. *You're* not supposed to be, remember? And Daddy won't let me do this without *one* of you tagging along, which is still stupid—"

Sterling held up a hand to forestall the rant. "Save it, know it by heart. Shut up and let me get some caffeine into my bloodstream. Where *is* the Dodo, anyway?"

"He went to get some breakfast," Cricket said, smiling at a customer who was admiring a Depression-era bowl. "He'll be right back."

Sterling took a gulp of coffee and settled into the chair. He didn't have long to wait before Dorian showed up, yet another perfect example of Reynard genes, with his long limbs, still coltish with adolescence, pale skin, and dark hair. His emerald-green eyes narrowed at the sight of Sterling in his chair.

"The fuck are you doing here?"

Sterling saluted him lazily with his coffee. "Had nothing better to do; thought I'd come harass my favorite sister and her twin."

"I'm your only sister, you ass," Cricket said. She accepted the customer's payment and wrapped the bowl for her, handing it over with a smile before shooting Sterling a glare. "You be nice."

"I'm *always* nice!" Sterling protested, stung. "*He*, on the other hand—" He let his hand gesture in Dorian's general direction encompass everything he didn't say.

"Fuck you," Dorian snapped, and sat down on the trunk where Cricket stored her unsold wares.

Sterling gave Cricket a pointed look, and she sighed.

Dorian pulled his phone out and began texting.

"Did you finally meet a nice girl?" Sterling asked.

"None of your business," Dorian said without looking up.

"Ooh, you did!" Sterling said, straightening. "Let me see, little brother."

"Fuck *off*," Dorian growled. "Crick, if he's here, I don't need to be, do I?"

"Sterling, how long are you staying?"

Sterling lifted a shoulder in elegant indecision. "Absolutely no clue. I go where the wind and my whims take me."

Dorian scowled at him and slumped back onto the trunk.

"Come on, what's her name?" Sterling cajoled.

"Tatum," Cricket offered.

"And do our parents approve of her?"

"Doubt it," Dorian muttered.

"Tatum's a little… unconventional," Cricket said.

Someone else approached the booth, and Cricket turned her attention to them. Dorian went back to his phone and Sterling pouted, deprived of his target.

He sulked into his coffee for a while, as Cricket sold several more pieces of glassware, her smile never slipping.

"Fox," she said during a lull, "there's an estate sale in Shaughnessy on Wednesday. Will you go with me?"

"I'm busy," Sterling said instantly.

Cricket gave him a disillusioned stare. "You don't have a job. You don't have a life, you barely even have any hobbies, and it's not a flea market, so you can't claim we're slumming it, so no, you're *not* busy. Don't give me that shit."

Sterling glowered. "I *could* be busy," he mumbled.

"Pick me up at seven," Cricket told him.

"In the goddamn *morning*?" Sterling yelped.

Dorian snickered.

"Stay out of it," Cricket said without looking.

"Fine." Sterling sighed. "You'd better make it up to me, though." He stood up, flicking dust from his jeans. "I'll see you next time I'm forced to."

"Dinner on the hill Tuesday night," Cricket said. "Mom and Dad want to meet Tatum. We're all summoned."

Sterling groaned and escaped.

HE SHOWERED TWICE MORE before he was due at the club, somehow afraid that Sanyam would know about the masturbation, maybe by smelling it on his skin. He changed his outfit four times before swearing and going back to the first one, a black button-down shirt and a pair of dove-gray slacks.

He considered himself critically in the mirror.

"You look like a fucking accountant," he told his reflection, and yanked the clothes off.

In the end, he chose a long-sleeved silk T-shirt the exact color of his eyes and a pair of leather pants he'd never quite had the courage to wear in public before. They hugged his ass and made his legs look even longer, and Sterling swallowed hard and left his apartment before he could change his mind.

He drove to the club, the roar of the Lamborghini's engine somehow soothing, and found Kimi at the bar.

She winked and slid a drink down the polished wood to him before picking up her phone.

Within a minute, she set it back down and nodded at Sterling. "Go on back. He's yours for the night. Or maybe I should say… you're his for the night." She grinned, and butterflies stirred in Sterling's stomach.

He gulped his drink down and threaded his way through the crowds, ignoring the show being performed on the stage, and stepped into the hall that led to Sanyam's room. It was quieter, the passage lit with soft white light, and Sterling's breath was loud in his ears as he stopped in front of Sanyam's door and lifted a hand to knock. He hesitated, chewing his lip.

Don't be a fucking idiot, he told himself. *Just knock already.*

6

There was a knock, and Sanyam straightened. "Come in, Fox."

The door swung open, revealing Fox, shifting his weight and looking ready to bolt at any second.

"Shut the door behind you," Sanyam said and stepped away to give him breathing room. After a minute, the door closed, and Sanyam turned back to inspect Fox from head to toe.

He was wearing an olive-green shirt that made his eyes even greener and tight leather pants that cupped his crotch and clung to his long legs.

Sanyam hummed approval. "Very nice. Come here."

Fox took a step forward, hands opening and closing at his sides, and another, until he was right in front of Sanyam. They were almost the same height, but Sanyam outweighed him by close to thirty pounds. Sanyam decided he liked Fox's willowy build and lean frame, even though he was too slender. He needed feeding up.

He ran a finger along Fox's jaw. "Kiss me."

Fox hesitated, then leaned in and pressed their lips together in a chaste, dry kiss. Sanyam regarded him with dissatisfaction as he pulled away.

"That was not a kiss. That was a tragic disappointment. Kiss me properly."

Fox's eyes tightened, and he took a deliberate step forward, so their bodies were flush. He cupped the back of Sanyam's neck and tilted his head, slotting their mouths together.

This time the kiss was filthy, wet and hungry, and Sanyam made a noise of contentment as Fox pushed into his mouth with dirty sweeps of his tongue.

"*Much* better," Sanyam said when he broke away.

Fox was breathing hard, his pupils dilated, but he still said nothing.

"Contract is on the table," Sanyam said. "It's another temporary one. After tonight, if you wish to see me again, we will negotiate a more permanent agreement. Sign it before we go any further."

Fox turned to the table and picked up the pen. He signed without looking at the papers, and Sanyam tsked disapprovingly.

"Someone is going to take advantage of you someday, if you keep doing that. *Look* at the papers, Fox. Fill out the hard limits, at the very least."

Fox's mouth flattened, but he turned back and bent over the table, writing in quick, jagged letters. When he was done, he shoved the papers at Sanyam, who took them and sat down on the sofa.

"Electricity, fecal play, watersports, sounding," he read aloud. "Very good, Fox. These are all things I prefer to do without too."

Fox's rigid stance eased slightly.

Sanyam pointed at the floor between his own feet. "Knees."

He signed under Fox's name as he waited for Fox to obey, and didn't look up until Fox had knelt in front of him, his knuckles white with tension.

Only then did Sanyam set the papers aside and lean forward to rest his elbows on his knees. "Did you obey my order, Fox?"

"Yes," Fox said immediately, tipping his chin up. His eyes were defiant and guilty, though, and Sanyam sucked in a breath.

"You're lying to me."

"I'm not!" Fox protested, dropping his gaze to his knees.

Sanyam caught him by the throat and lifted him up effortlessly as Fox choked and grabbed at Sanyam's wrist. "You jerked off; it's written all over you." He let go, and Fox sprawled backward. "Strip. Or I will strip you and you will leave here with your clothes in pieces."

Fox's throat worked, and he fumbled at the waist of his pants, then shoved them down and off with his shoes in a tangled mess. His shirt followed as Sanyam stood up and pointed at the rack in the corner.

"Facing the wall. Arms up next to the cuffs."

Fox stood and stumbled toward the rack. Sanyam caught his left arm and strapped it into the cuff. He repeated that with the right arm and knelt, pushing Fox's feet apart and cuffing them in place so that Fox was spread-eagled.

Fox teetered, and Sanyam skimmed his hand down the curve of his spine.

"Remember those manners I spoke of?" he said. He stepped close and nipped at Fox's earlobe. "You're about to be taught some."

Fox shuddered, his eyes closed.

"Actions have consequences, Fox," Sanyam

said, stepping back to choose a riding crop from his wall. "What's your safeword?"

"C-Calypso," Fox managed. He was trembling, and Sanyam hesitated before taking a blindfold out of the drawer. The second it was in place, Fox sagged, tension visibly leaving his body.

"We can stop at any point if you need to," Sanyam reminded him.

"Don't coddle me," Fox snapped.

Sanyam smiled and struck the first blow.

Fox jerked and cried out. A red welt rose on the fair skin of his buttocks, and Sanyam ran his finger along it admiringly as Fox shivered under his touch.

"Do you know what sub space is?" Sanyam asked.

Fox's mouth worked as if he was trying to remember what words were. "A-are you going to punish me or talk me to death?"

"I can't do both?" Sanyam said mildly.

"Fuck you," Fox hissed.

Sanyam hit him again. "Answer the question."

Fox's head fell back, and he opened and closed his mouth. "I—don't know. Wh-what it is. I d-don't—"

Sanyam caressed the stripes he'd made, and Fox shivered, hips bucking.

"It's a feeling of euphoria, of safety and trust,"

Sanyam said. "You may lose awareness when you hit it, feel like you're floating or in space."

"What's your p-point?" Fox managed.

"My God, you're a brat," Sanyam said, and brought the crop down three more times in quick succession. He waited until Fox was still again, quivering in the restraints, before he continued. "You may experience it tonight. It's important to understand that it's normal and you're safe with me. I am going to punish you, but you can still safeword at any time."

"Get *on* with it," Fox said through his teeth.

"With pleasure," Sanyam said, and went to work in earnest. Fox's pale skin showed every mark, and Sanyam lost himself in the joy of striping him from hips to upper thighs, each blow placed with careful precision.

He stopped after a few minutes and reached around to catch Fox's shaft in his hand and stroke him, rough and careless. Arousal careened through his bloodstream at Fox's helpless state.

Fox sobbed, head falling forward blindly as he bucked into Sanyam's fist.

"Don't come," Sanyam said. "You are forbidden to come, do you hear me?"

"I have to," Fox said, pulling at his bonds. "I have to—"

"You have to obey me," Sanyam said flatly. "If

you come, you will *not* enjoy the punishment that follows. Do you understand?"

Fox was still for a long moment and then nodded jerkily.

Sanyam stepped back and turned to his drawer of toys, pulling out an adjustable ring and then fastening it in place around Fox's cock.

Fox sucked in air through his nose but said nothing, his head turned to track Sanyam's movement.

Sanyam leaned in and kissed him, nipping Fox's lower lip as he skimmed a hand over the curve of Fox's ass. He slipped under to press a finger against his hole, and Fox tensed and pushed back, seeking more, but Sanyam pulled away.

"Not right now," he said. He picked up the crop and counted off the blows as he struck them.

He was only halfway to his goal when Fox went limp, his head falling against his chest as he hung in the restraints.

Sanyam kept going. He knew what sub space looked like when he saw it, and if he stopped now, he'd just pull Fox back out of it. That was the last thing he wanted.

Finally he tossed the crop to the side. He was painfully aroused himself, so hard it hurt, but it wasn't time for that. Instead he took off the cock ring, knelt and undid the ankle cuffs, then stood and removed the wrist restraints.

Fox fell against him, head lolling, and Sanyam half dragged, half carried his unresisting form to the couch. He sat and arranged Fox on his side, long limbs tucked in neatly. Then he took the blindfold off and settled Fox's head in his lap, stroking the hair off his forehead.

Fox's eyes were blank and unaware, his mouth soft. He looked desperately young and vulnerable, and Sanyam felt a startling surge of protectiveness.

"No one's ever taken you in hand, have they?" he murmured. "You're dying to be dominated, to be pulled out of your head, but you don't know how to ask for it." He laughed quietly. "You're not a fox, you're a kit. You put up a good front, but you're just a frightened pup, underneath the bluster."

Fox's eyes closed, lashes thick and dark against his pale cheeks, and he rubbed his face against Sanyam's thigh dreamily.

Sanyam stroked his hair. "Rest, kit."

IT WAS close to an hour before Fox stirred. He turned his head a fraction and froze as he clearly realized where he was.

Sanyam smiled down at him, gently pushing his hair away from his face. "Welcome back."

Fox jerked away and sat up so fast he nearly overbalanced. "What—"

"You hit sub space," Sanyam said, watching him carefully. He leaned over and pulled a bottle of water from the minifridge by the couch. "Drink this."

Fox batted his hand away. "Not thirsty."

Sanyam narrowed his eyes. "We're not done scening, Fox, which means that you're still mine to command. *Drink.*"

Fox glared at him but snatched the bottle and drained it, his throat working.

When he was done, Sanyam took the empty bottle without comment and tossed it in the recycling bin. "How do you feel?"

"Horny," Fox snapped. "Are we going to have sex or not?"

"No," Sanyam said, unruffled. "You're not coming tonight either."

Fox's mouth fell open. "But—"

Sanyam raised an eyebrow. "You disobeyed me. Did you think a simple spanking was enough to get you off the hook? It's not that easy. I'm not going to reward your disobedience with an orgasm. You must be taught to *obey.*"

Fox scrambled to his feet, clenching his fists.

"Fuck you," he spat. "I don't need this—this is *stupid*."

Sanyam didn't move. "You know where the door is."

Fox dragged on his clothes, hissing as he drew the pants on over the welts.

"This is your last chance," Sanyam said as Fox fumbled into his shoes. "If you can prove to me that you have the self-control to keep from touching yourself before tomorrow evening, I promise it will be worth it when you return."

"Or?" Fox snapped.

"Or you walk out that door, and you never come back," Sanyam said.

Fox spun away and slammed the door behind him.

It wasn't until he was done cleaning the room that Sanyam realized he hadn't warned Fox about the possibility of a sub drop.

He swore and ran for the front, but Fox was nowhere in sight.

Kimi raised an eyebrow at him. "'Sup?"

"Fox—my client for tonight," Sanyam said. "Did he already leave?"

"Oh yeah, he blew through here a while ago looking like eighteen different kinds of murder," Kimi said. "He's long gone."

Sanyam pushed his hands through his hair, blowing out a frustrated breath. "How's Delfia?"

"See for yourself," Kimi said, gesturing with her chin. "She was a little shaky yesterday, but she's a lot better and back to work today."

Delfia was serving a table, handing out drinks with a smile on her face.

"Ava talked to her," Kimi continued. "Told her that she didn't have to put up with that, that if it happens again, Delfia's welcome to break the guy's wrist in self-defense and Ava would back her every step of the way. That helped a lot."

"*Good*," Sanyam said. "I guess I should warn you, so you can tell her, but my… client, Fox… he was with the boy who did that."

Kimi tensed. "I thought he looked familiar, but I didn't—you're still letting him in here? What the fuck, San?"

"He's not like Jackson," Sanyam said defensively. "He's—okay, he's an asshole, and incredibly spoiled, but… there's good in him. Somewhere. I think… he just has to learn it's okay to show it."

"Fine," Kimi said. "But if he gets near Delfia, *I'll* break his wrist. And possibly his nose."

"Fair enough," Sanyam said. "Do you have the client list? I need to find him. He took off too quickly."

Kimi produced the client list, and Sanyam

scanned it for Fox's name. There—he'd put his address but no phone number.

Sanyam swore under his breath. "It's too late tonight—I'll have to go round in the morning. Thanks, Kimi. Give Delfia my love."

7

———

Sterling woke up and stomped to the bathroom in a foul mood. He stepped on the mess of aftershave he'd forgotten to clean up and cut his foot, swearing violently. He hopped on his other foot as he rocketed from angry to furious in a heartbeat.

He took a scalding hot shower, scrubbing until his skin was bright red and felt like it was about to peel off as tears prickled his eyelids. He felt filthy, more useless and pathetic than usual, and he couldn't get *clean*.

The red swirled away down the drain from the cut on his foot, and he pressed his forehead against the glass of the shower stall as the hot water pounded his shoulders.

Finally he gave up and stepped out, avoiding

the glass this time, and dried off, flinching as the towel scraped against the bruises from the night before.

Digging out his softest pair of pajamas, he pulled them on and hobbled into the kitchen, then swore yet again when he remembered that it was Astrid's day off and there was no breakfast waiting for him.

On the plus side, there were no jam-sticky hobgoblins sitting at his dining room table, either, so maybe it wasn't all bad.

Sterling rooted around in his fridge half-heartedly, but when a cursory search failed to turn up anything besides the casseroles Astrid made ahead of time to cook for him, he gave up and limped back to his room.

He flopped onto the bed facedown and buried his face in a pillow. The day was going to be a total wash, he could already tell. Better for everyone—especially him—if he just stayed in bed all day.

When the doorbell rang a few minutes later, Sterling jerked his head up with a snarl, ready to do battle.

"Fuck off!" he shouted in the direction of the door.

The bell rang again.

"Go *away*," Sterling roared.

The bell somehow sounded even more insistent this time.

Sterling rolled to his feet. He landed on the open wound and snarled under his breath as he limped for the door, prepared to eviscerate whoever had the *nerve* to talk to him today.

He was entirely unprepared to be faced with Sanyam, wearing a gray, cabled sweater and carrying two cups of coffee.

"What the *fuck* are you doing here?" Sterling sputtered.

"Your doorman let me up," Sanyam said, holding out one of the cups and stepping around him into the apartment as Sterling accepted it, dumb with shock.

Sterling closed the door and turned to face him. "Why are you *here*, though?"

Sanyam was in the middle of his living room, looking around critically. The morning sun haloed his curly hair, and he smiled, white teeth flashing against the black of his beard. Sterling was suddenly acutely aware of what a wreck he himself was, and he set the coffee on the counter and crossed his arms over his bare stomach.

"You left so quickly last night that I didn't get a chance to warn you about the possibility of sub drops," Sanyam was saying, unaware of Sterling's internal dilemma. He turned to admire the view of the city and sighed appreciatively.

"Of… what?"

"Sub drops," Sanyam said, turning back.

"I don't know what those are, but I don't have them," Sterling said. "Go away."

Sanyam arched an eyebrow. "Are you feeling irritable? Weepy? Moody?" His eyes lit with a smile. "More than usual, I mean, because I already know what a stellar personality you have."

"Fuck *off*," Sterling snapped. "I'm fine. Now go *away*." He stomped for the bedroom as Sanyam took a startled breath behind him.

"Fox, you're bleeding."

"I stepped on something; it's not a big deal," Sterling said over his shoulder. "The door's over there. See yourself out."

Sanyam followed him into the bedroom instead as Sterling fell onto the bed again. "Let me see." He gripped Sterling's ankle in one big hand, stopping him easily when Sterling tried to jerk away. "Be still," he said, and Sterling growled but stopped fighting.

Instead he lay on his stomach and sulked as Sanyam gently wiped the skin around the cut with a tissue from the box on the nightstand.

"Is there a first aid kit in your bathroom?" Sanyam asked.

Sterling shrugged, face still buried in the pillow. "Might be. I don't know."

"Don't move," Sanyam said.

"Where would I go?" Sterling muttered, not expecting an answer.

Sanyam's footsteps disappeared into the bathroom, followed by rustling as he rooted through the cupboards.

"You're in luck," Sanyam called. "There's a very nice one. What happened in here, by the way?"

"Tragic aftershave suicide," Sterling mumbled as Sanyam came back in and knelt beside the bed again. "It couldn't take the pressures that a heteronormative society put on it any longer."

Sanyam laughed, sounding startled. "I had no idea you had an actual sense of humor," he said as he gently cleaned the cut.

Sterling scowled into the pillow. "I don't. Why are you still here?"

"Because I didn't tell you about sub drops, remember?" Sanyam taped the bandage in place and patted Sterling's ankle before he stood. "It's very important that you take care of yourself during one, because they can cause you to experience very strong negative emotions. And since it's obvious you're dropping fairly badly right now, well… that's why I'm here."

"I'm not dropping, and I don't want you," Sterling grumbled. "Go 'way."

Sanyam just laughed again, and any other time, Sterling might have liked the sound. It was open, easy, and honest, just like Sanyam himself. As it was—

He rolled onto his side, flinching as it put pressure on the bruising. "You're just here because you don't trust me not to touch myself."

Sanyam was picking up the mess he'd made, and he straightened, eyebrows going up. "Is that really what you think? That I'll follow you around all day to make sure you don't put your hand down your pants?"

Sterling glowered at him and rolled back onto his stomach.

"I will afford you some leeway because you're dropping," Sanyam said, "but kindly give me *some* credit." His footsteps receded toward the bathroom again as Sterling lay silently and hated the world. After a minute, glass shards clinked, and Sterling realized Sanyam was cleaning up the aftershave death scene.

Worthless, waste of space, can't even clean up your own messes. Sterling pushed his face into his elbow and took a shaky breath.

Sanyam came out of the bathroom and

climbed onto the bed to kneel next to Sterling's motionless form.

"Take your pants off," he said.

Sterling jerked away. "What? *No!*"

Sanyam rolled his eyes. "We're not having sex—I brought some arnica cream. I want to attend to your bruises."

"Go fuck yourself," Sterling snarled.

"Fine," Sanyam said, and got off the bed.

There was silence after he left the room, and Sterling spent a minute deliberating on whether he'd chased him away for good. Probably. He wondered idly if he could lie still long enough for his skin to graft with the bedspread.

Gross, he decided. He couldn't hear anything from where he was, so he got up and limped out to the kitchen.

Sanyam was turning on the oven. "You have an impressive selection of frozen casseroles here," he said without looking. "I'm assuming you don't do the prep for them yourself?"

"Do I look like I cook?" Sterling sniped. He flopped on the sofa and yelped as he made contact. He'd forgotten about the bruises, and he was pretty sure his ass and upper thighs were suddenly on fire. He rolled onto his side and fumbled for the remote.

"The arnica cream would bring down the

swelling and ease the pain," Sanyam said offhandedly. "Just an observation."

Sterling's glare was half-hearted. He pillowed his cheek on his hand and tried to watch the news.

He dozed off somewhere in the middle of a report about how awful the world was, and awoke to the smell of sausage and eggs as Sanyam pulled a tray from the oven, enticing scents wafting from it.

Sterling lifted his head and sniffed the air.

"Stay there; I'll bring some to you," Sanyam said.

"Wasn't planning on moving," Sterling muttered.

Sanyam put the food on plates and brought them to the couch. "Your best options are probably going to be eating standing up or lying on your stomach," he said, setting Sterling's plate on the coffee table, careful not to disturb the half-done puzzle.

Sterling glared and grabbed the plate, very deliberately still on his side as he took a big bite of fluffy eggs and potatoes.

Sanyam sighed and sat down on the other end of the couch. Sterling jerked his feet away, but Sanyam didn't seem to notice, focused on his food.

After a few minutes, Sanyam nodded at the coffee table. "You like puzzles?"

"No, I do them because I hate them."

Sanyam rolled his eyes again but took the hint. They ate in silence, and when Sterling had cleared his plate, Sanyam stood up without speaking and brought him more, along with a glass of orange juice.

Sterling propped himself on his elbow and drained the juice in thirsty gulps. He set the glass down with a satisfied sigh.

Sanyam immediately got up and refilled it.

Sterling applied himself to his food, watching Sanyam out of the corner of his eye as an idea occurred to him. *How much can I get away with?*

He shivered, still bare from the waist up, and rubbed his arms for effect.

Sanyam glanced around the living room and frowned. "Why isn't there a blanket on the back of your couch?"

"Ruins the aesthetic of the room," Sterling said, lifting his nose in the air.

Sanyam snorted rudely and stood. He headed for the bedroom and reappeared a minute later with one of Sterling's sweaters.

"I'm not cold," Sterling said.

Sanyam narrowed his eyes and set the sweater

on the armrest without comment as Sterling took another bite, hiding his glee.

When he'd finished his second helping, Sanyam carried the plates into the kitchen and began cleaning up. Sterling rolled onto his stomach to watch him.

Sanyam was well worth watching, his sleeves pushed up on his muscular forearms, white teeth set in his lower lip and a tiny furrow on his brow as he concentrated. His curly hair was perfectly in place, and Sterling had the sudden impulse to muss it all up, dishevel *him*, see what he looked like wrecked and exhausted. He had a feeling it would be a rewarding experience.

A thought struck him, and he straightened. "I, uh… changed my mind."

Sanyam looked up. "About what?"

"The arnica cream. You can put it on me if you want."

Sanyam smiled. "Let me finish this, and I'll do that."

Sterling got up, wincing, and shuffled for the bedroom.

"Where are you going?" Sanyam called.

"Bed," Sterling said over his shoulder. "I don't want to get anything on the couch. It's new."

In the bedroom, he crawled onto the mattress and face-planted again, sighing with relief. It wasn't long before Sanyam joined him, and the bed dipped.

"I'm going to pull your pants down, okay?"

"You mean you can't put it on while I'm wearing clothes?"

There was an annoyed silence, and Sterling snickered into the pillow.

Still, Sanyam's fingers were gentle as he took hold of the waistband and tugged the pants down to Sterling's midthighs, careful to avoid the welts.

The cream was cold when it landed on Sterling's skin, and he gasped.

"Sorry." Sanyam's voice was amused, and Sterling rolled his head to glare at him.

"No, you're not."

"No, I'm not," Sanyam agreed. He began to work the cream in, and Sterling stiffened as nerve endings awoke and fired in protest. "Easy," Sanyam murmured. "It'll feel better in a minute."

Sterling closed his eyes and pushed his face into the pillow. *God*, it felt good, both to be touched and to be hurt, to *feel* something instead of the emptiness that usually gnawed at his insides.

Okay, he acknowledged after a moment, *that was angsty even for me.*

Still. Sanyam wasn't being rough—was, in fact, being very gentle, and Sterling wanted more.

He pushed back against Sanyam's hands, seeking contact, and Sanyam stopped abruptly.

"What are you doing, Fox?"

Sterling slanted a look over his shoulder that said he didn't think much of Sanyam's intelligence if he had to ask, and rolled his hips lazily against the bedspread, shuddering as his cock dragged along the satin.

Sanyam slapped his ass hard, and Sterling bucked, stifling a moan.

"I told you not to touch yourself," Sanyam said flatly.

"Technically, I'm not," Sterling pointed out. "Besides, if *you* touch me, that's not breaking the rules."

It was Sanyam's turn for the unimpressed look. "It still counts, and I'm not here for sex. I'm here to take care of you during your sub drop because I didn't warn you about it beforehand."

Sterling fought the desire to beg. He *wouldn't*. No matter what Sanyam had said that first night, no matter what they ended up doing, he would never beg.

Instead he tucked his face into his elbow and sighed. "Whatever."

Sanyam hesitated and finally began rubbing the cream back into the welts.

Sterling closed his eyes and let go of the frustration and sick irritability, the miseries of the day, and drifted, lulled into security by Sanyam's steady hands.

When he woke up, he was alone in the apartment. He could tell by the absolute stillness of the air that surrounded him.

Sterling propped himself on his elbows and glanced at the clock. It was close to dinnertime. He'd slept right through lunch, he realized, surprised.

"Sanyam?"

There was no answer. Of course there was no answer. Why on earth would Sanyam have stuck around?

Rolling off the bed, Sterling limped to the bathroom, which was spotless. He used the toilet, washed his hands, and shuffled his halting way out to the living room just as Sanyam pushed the front door open and stepped inside.

"Oh," Sterling said blankly. "I—thought you'd gone."

Sanyam hefted the bags in his hands. "I did, briefly. I had a craving for some Thai curry. I hope you like spicy food."

Sterling followed him to the table, and Sanyam set the food on it before turning to inspect Sterling, who blinked and drew back a pace.

"What are you doing?"

"Trying to get a gauge of your mental state," Sanyam said. "How are you feeling?"

Sterling twitched away from Sanyam's probing gaze. "I didn't jack off, if that's what you're asking."

Sanyam's eyes creased as he smiled. "I know. Sit. Let's eat."

Sterling sank into a chair as Sanyam gathered silverware and plates from his cupboards.

"How do you know?"

"Hmm? Know what?"

"Whether I've jacked off," Sterling clarified. He shifted in his seat and winced. "You knew… at the club, that I had. And today, you knew I hadn't. So… *how*?"

Sanyam straightened with plates in his hands. "It's in your bearing, for one thing. I can't really put a finger on it, but it's a combination of tension or lack thereof, as well as—" He laughed as he put the plates on the table. "You looked ridiculously guilty when you lied to me last night. You're a terrible liar."

Sterling scowled. "I'm a *great* liar, excuse you. My parents still think I'm straight, for one thing."

Sanyam's eyebrows went up as he went back to the kitchen to get Utopias from the refrigerator. "Oh dear. Are they homophobic?"

"Dad is," Sterling said, hunching his shoulders and twirling a fork between his fingers. "Mom… doesn't care."

"About you being gay or in general?"

"Yes," Sterling said flatly. "What kind of curry did you get?"

"Massaman and red," Sanyam said. His eyes were sharp, but mercifully, he dropped the subject of Sterling's parents. "If you can't handle spice, stick with the massaman; I'll take the red."

Sterling bridled and snatched the red curry. "I can handle spice just fine, asshole."

Sanyam's lips twitched. "If I'd said I preferred the massaman, you'd have taken that instead, wouldn't you?"

His eyes danced with amusement, and Sterling floundered. No one had ever found his dickish behavior *funny* before.

Sanyam's smile widened. "Enjoy your spice, Fox."

Sterling hesitated.

"What is it?"

"I… actually like massaman better," he admitted.

Sanyam laughed out loud and handed him the container. "Good, because I prefer the red."

Sterling's lips curved as he took the curry and began to ladle it over his rice.

WHEN THEY WERE DONE, Sanyam cleared the table as Sterling watched.

"You can leave those," Sterling said.

Sanyam was running water in the sink, and he glanced up. "I don't mind. You should stay off your feet."

"No, I mean Astrid will do them in the morning."

Sanyam's lips flattened, but he said nothing, turning his attention to the dishes as Sterling tried to figure out what he'd said wrong.

"Look," he tried, "I didn't mean—"

"It's fine," Sanyam said abruptly.

"No, I just… it's her *job*, and I pay her really well, I'm not—"

Sanyam drained the sink and dried his hands on the towel by the stove. "I know, Fox." He came back around the counter and stepped in between Sterling's knees as he sat in the chair looking up at him.

Sterling swallowed hard. Sanyam was so *close*, and he smelled so good, like vanilla and red curry and dark beer, as he put a finger under Sterling's chin, drawing it up and over the dimple there.

"Have you decided whether or not I'll see you tonight?" he said quietly.

Sterling struggled to marshal words. "I—"

Sanyam smiled. "Don't leave it too late. I tend to fill my bookings rather quickly, even on a Monday night."

He thumbed Sterling's chin, and Sterling shivered. It was too close, too intimate, too *much*, and he opened his mouth to say something biting and sharp, something to keep Sanyam from getting any ideas, but Sanyam beat him to it.

"I'm going to kiss you, Fox. And then I'm going to leave."

Sterling forgot what he was going to say as Sanyam bent, one warm hand cradling his jaw, and fitted their lips together.

He tasted good, so good, heat and spice and that kick of *want* that terrified Sterling with how badly he needed more as Sanyam claimed his mouth, slow and easy and confident.

When he drew away, Sterling swayed in his seat, dazed.

"Goodbye, Fox," Sanyam said. He walked away without looking back and let himself out the door silently as Sterling watched.

8

That evening, Sanyam found Kimi at a table that Delfia was bussing.

"That asshole tried to come back," Kimi said before Sanyam could speak. "Jackson what's-his-name. Logan stopped him, turned him away at the door. But I figured you'd want to know."

"Are you all right, Delfia?" Sanyam asked as alarm spiked through him.

Delfia set a plate in the tub and nodded, brushing her hair out of her eyes. "I didn't actually see him," she said in her soft Cuban accent. "And I have Kimi and her baseball bat."

"Goddamn right you do," Kimi said, patting Delfia's arm.

"That client of mine may come in," Sanyam

said. "If he does, I won't be accepting anyone else tonight."

"Oh, you like him that much, do you?" Kimi tapped the side of her nose. "I got you, big man."

Delfia snickered, and Kimi pivoted, hair flying out around her, and marched back to the bar before Sanyam could muster a reply.

"It's not like that," he protested to the room at large.

Trinity was on the stage, warming up for her set, and she flipped a hand at him. Sanyam waved back and headed for his room.

He couldn't stop thinking about Fox's eyes, wide and dark and vulnerable when he'd kissed him. Sanyam scared him, that much was obvious. He also fascinated him, a moth to flame, and it was going to be up to Sanyam to make sure Fox didn't scorch his wings off.

"Foxes don't have wings," he said aloud, and laughed at himself.

HIS FIRST CLIENT was a man in his fifties, thin and nervous and stooped.

"Roger," he said, shaking Sanyam's hand. "I'd like to explore some role play."

"Certainly," Sanyam said. He gestured to the

table. "What kind of role play did you have in mind?"

Roger looked at the contract, flipping through the pages. "I'm a big fan of Rudyard Kipling," he said finally.

Sanyam stiffened. "Please leave."

"What? But we haven't even started!"

"I don't do race play," Sanyam said flatly. "Get out."

Roger drew himself to his full height, eyes turning venomous. "You're nothing," he hissed. "You're a crawling little ant, a… a—"

"Say it and I will punch you in the face before calling security," Sanyam said, taking a step closer. "Go ahead. *Say it.*"

Roger's mouth twisted around the slur he clearly wanted to spit, but in the end, his nerve failed him, and he deflated like a weak balloon.

Sanyam stepped aside, and Roger scuttled for the door.

Alone, Sanyam sat down on the couch.

He missed India sometimes, the bustle and seething humanity, the sprawl of beautiful buildings and shanties crammed up against each other, and it was true that they had their own form of racism over there and it was just as toxic and ugly.

It was still a shock to be hit with it here, when he was least expecting it.

Someone knocked, and Sanyam jerked his head up. He hadn't heard his phone go off—

Fox stepped inside, looking wary, and Sanyam sighed with relief.

"I never thought I'd say this, but I'm very glad to see you," he said.

Fox frowned, obviously trying to figure out if he'd been insulted or not.

Sanyam stood and crossed the room, slipping an arm around Fox's waist to pull him close.

"Your character flaws are many and multifaceted," he said, putting a finger over Fox's mouth when he tried to speak. "But at least you've never been racist to me."

He removed his hand and kissed him, soft and welcoming, and Fox relaxed against him, mouth sweet under Sanyam's.

"So," Sanyam said when they broke away. "Does this mean you're interested in something more permanent?"

Fox nodded, looking unsure, and Sanyam hid his smile and turned to pull out the appropriate contract.

"Here," he said, handing it over. "This is the semipermanent contract. You'll still have a place to put in your hard limits, and it will be binding for any amount of time that we agree on, up to three months. At the end of that period, we will renegotiate."

Fox eased himself into a chair, perching on the edge of it, and began to read the paperwork.

Sanyam sat back on the couch and watched him, the elegant curve of Fox's body as he bent over the table, the wrinkle on his forehead as he studied the words. Sanyam itched to touch him, to explore him all over, to take him apart and put him back together again in perfect, excruciating detail.

His cock stirred, and Sanyam crossed his legs, willing it back to sleep. *Not yet.*

Fox glanced up. "If I change my mind and want to renegotiate sooner, can we do that?"

"Yes, of course," Sanyam said. "We can overhaul the contract at any point that either of us desires. The main thing is that you are protected and feel safe in this relationship."

Fox nodded and turned back to the pages, hair falling into his face.

"Oh," Sanyam said. "Your friend. Jackson."

Fox stiffened and lifted his head. "What about him?"

"He came to the club tonight. Logan turned him away, and he left before the police arrived. Did you know he was planning to do that?"

Outrage flashed across Fox's face. "Of course not!"

Sanyam held up his hands. "I had to ask. After all, you were with him that night."

"I didn't *do* anything!" Fox protested.

"No, you didn't," Sanyam said softly. "That's part of the problem, don't you see?"

Fox stared at him. "I don't—what do you mean?"

"I mean, you didn't stop him. You said *nothing* to prevent him from molesting poor Delfia, who he outweighs by at least fifty pounds. You seemed bored by the whole affair, honestly."

"It wasn't my business," Fox said, but his voice was unsteady.

Sanyam stood up, and Fox shrank into his chair. "When someone weaker than you is being hurt, and you're in a position to stop it and you *don't*, you're as bad as the person committing the atrocity."

Fox's throat bobbed and shame flitted across his face. "I—"

"Enough for now," Sanyam said. He stepped closer and cupped the nape of Fox's long neck. "We can discuss it another time, but tonight is for you." He bent and looked into Fox's face. "For now…." He smiled. "You've been good. You obeyed my order, and that means you've earned a reward."

"Oh, thank Christ," Fox breathed, and Sanyam laughed out loud.

"Sign the contract, Fox, so I can give it to you."

Fox signed in his quick, jagged handwriting, filling in his hard limits with a hand that trembled slightly before he pushed the contract along the table for Sanyam to sign.

Sanyam accepted the pen and signed below Fox's name. When he was done, he turned back and stepped between Fox's knees.

"What do you want, Fox?"

"To come, mostly," Fox admitted.

Sanyam choked on laughter, and Fox's lips curved up. "Well, yes," Sanyam managed when he'd sobered. "But specifically, I meant."

Fox lifted a shoulder. "I don't—I hadn't thought that far ahead."

"So we'll wing it," Sanyam said. He tugged lightly on Fox's earlobe, making him shiver. "Strip."

He sat down on the couch and leaned to the side to retrieve a few things while Fox took his clothes off and left them in a careless heap on the floor. Naked, he stood before Sanyam, fingers twitching by his sides.

Sanyam sat back to admire. Every bit of Fox was elegant, curve of bone and muscle under skin that looked satin-soft, the fall of his hair—even his feet were graceful, long and slender and high-arching.

"You really are lovely," he said, almost to himself.

Fox shifted his weight but kept his mouth shut.

Sanyam held out a hand. "Come here."

Fox took it. He slid into Sanyam's lap and settled his weight across Sanyam's thighs. His eyes were uncertain, but his cock was thickening, clearly interested in the proceedings.

Sanyam tapped his lips and Fox got the message and bent until their mouths met as he slid his arms around Sanyam's neck.

He kissed like there was nothing else worth doing, sweet and hot and wanting, with that hint of teeth that underscored everything he did, sharp and demanding but somehow needy at the same time.

Sanyam tasted peppermint toothpaste, and it made him like Fox better, somehow, knowing he'd brushed his teeth before their session, like a nervous kid on a first date.

He couldn't get enough, running his hands over Fox's thighs and feeling the lean, corded muscle under skin that was as soft as it looked. He caught Fox's hip and pulled him closer, squeezing and rubbing his buttock, and Fox gasped against his mouth.

"Sorry," Sanyam said breathlessly, breaking away. He'd forgotten about the bruising, but Fox didn't look upset. If anything, he looked even more aroused, a flush crawling up his neck and his cock dribbling precome onto Sanyam's pants.

Sanyam was painfully hard himself, and he smacked Fox's ass, making him jerk again. "Off," he said. "Knees."

Fox scrambled to obey, slithering to the floor with a thump.

Sanyam gestured to his pants. "Take them off." He stopped Fox when he reached for them, though. "Without your hands."

Fox's eyes went wide, and he licked his lips. "Can—I won't have any leverage—"

"You can brace yourself on my knees or the couch," Sanyam said. He reached out and brushed the hair off Fox's forehead, and Fox shivered.

He leaned forward, hands on either side of Sanyam's hips, and bent to nose at his zipper.

Sanyam draped his arms along the back of the couch to watch. Fox concentrating on his assigned task was somehow both adorable and hot as hell. His brow was furrowed as he studied Sanyam's pants, chewing on his lip. He lowered his head and tugged on the placket until the button popped free, then caught the tab of the zipper with his teeth, pulling it down in careful stages.

Sanyam raised his eyebrows. "Dexterous, aren't you?"

"When it suits me," Fox said, looking up with a gleam in his eye. "Gonna need your help getting them over your hips."

Sanyam obliged, lifting himself and scooting his pants down just enough that he wasn't sitting on them. "Carry on," he said.

Fox huffed a laugh against the silk of Sanyam's underwear, his breath warm and wet, and rubbed his cheek along the underside of Sanyam's shaft.

Sanyam muttered a curse in Hindi, stuffing his knuckles in his mouth, but when Fox tried to take him in his mouth through the silk, Sanyam stopped him.

"As much as I would love that, and *believe* me, kit, I would—safe sex." He held up a condom and Fox glowered but accepted it. Sanyam ran his thumb along Fox's cheekbone. "Can you put it on with your mouth?"

"Not *that* dexterous," Fox said as he ripped the foil.

"Yet," Sanyam said, grinning, and Fox snorted.

He bent again, and Sanyam caught his shoulders. "What are you doing?"

"Still wearing underwear," Fox said. "Or hadn't you noticed?"

"Mouthy," Sanyam said, letting him go. "Have to do something about that."

Fox just hummed and leaned in, catching the waistband of Sanyam's underwear in his teeth and pulling. His nose tickled Sanyam's skin, and his breath puffed in hot gusts as he worked on getting the left side down as far as possible before switching to the right.

"How do you feel about hair-pulling?" Sanyam asked, trying to keep his voice steady.

Fox glanced up. "Yes *please*."

"And marking?"

Fox dropped his face to Sanyam's abdomen. "Oh God, yes." His voice was muffled against Sanyam's shirt.

"Biting?" Sanyam inquired. He cupped the back of Fox's skull and ran his fingers over the bumps of bone.

Fox shuddered all over and reached for his cock.

Sanyam caught a fistful of Fox's hair. "I didn't say you could touch yourself, kit."

Neck cranked back, Fox sagged in his hand, eyelashes fluttering. "I'm—I won't."

Sanyam let go and petted his hair back into place. "You're not done," he said mildly.

Fox steadied himself with his hands on the cushions and went back to work.

Sanyam enjoyed the view until a thought occurred to him. "What are your thoughts on penetration?"

Fox stiffened briefly and glanced up. His eyes were uncertain. "I—in theory I like it, but... it's been years."

Sanyam hummed and touched his cheek. "We'll take it slow. Feel free to continue."

The room was silent except for the distant bass growl of Trinity's music, and Sanyam focused on Fox's breathing, the way the soft strands of hair curled behind his ears, the tension in his shoulders as he worked Sanyam's underwear down until his cock fell free.

Sanyam stretched as it slapped his stomach, sighing. "Oh yes, that's better."

Fox fumbled for the condom. "Can I—"

"By all means," Sanyam said.

Fox's fingers were deft and gentle as they rolled the condom down his shaft, sliding it into place. He didn't wait for permission when he was done, either—his mouth followed his fingers, hot and wet around Sanyam's cock and making Sanyam gasp, his hips bucking up helplessly.

Fox gagged as Sanyam hit his soft palate, but didn't stop, sinking impossibly even farther, cheeks hollowing and tongue busy on Sanyam's frenulum.

"Ah, *mashalla*," Sanyam said. He hunched forward and slipped his hands into Fox's hair, the strands fine like spun silk, as his entire body woke, and tendrils of heat licked out from his core.

Fox kept going, head bobbing, eyes closed, and a furrow on his forehead, until Sanyam tightened his grip on his hair and pulled him off.

Fox growled, fighting it, but Sanyam held him in place easily.

"Nowhere near done with you, kit," he said, "but if you keep that up, I will be."

Fox stopped struggling, and Sanyam let him go.

"Up," he said. "My turn."

Fox scrambled backward and stood in one easy, fluid motion as Sanyam kicked his pants the rest of the way off and dragged his shirt up and over his head before standing.

"On the couch. On your back; arms above your head."

"But—"

Sanyam arched an eyebrow. "Are you really going to argue with me?"

Fox gulped and lowered himself gingerly to

the couch. He flinched as his bruised body made contact but obediently stretched his arms out. Sanyam bent and pulled the soft restraints on the end of the couch up and into place on Fox's narrow wrists.

He turned then, and pulled out a blindfold. Fox's breath whooshed out of him as Sanyam put it in place, and he visibly relaxed.

"You like that, don't you?" Sanyam murmured. "Not being able to see. Takes your choices away from you, doesn't it?"

Fox turned his head toward him and tilted his face blindly up. Sanyam indulged the unspoken request, bending to sip lightly from Fox's mouth, slipping his tongue between Fox's lips and tasting sweet peppermint again.

Finally he drew back and surveyed Fox's long body, limbs pale against the dark fabric of his couch.

"Have you ever come untouched?" he asked as he leaned across and retrieved another condom, tearing the foil.

Fox tensed and shook his head. "I—no."

"I think we'll have to explore that at some point," Sanyam said. He touched Fox's hip to let him know he was there, then rolled the condom down over Fox's shaft.

Fox made a strangled noise, and Sanyam

obliged by stroking him for a minute, enjoying the way every movement rippled through Fox's body, abs taut and hips rolling into Sanyam's touch.

"So responsive," he murmured. "Any rules for marking?"

Fox's mouth opened and closed. "Dinner with my parents—tomorrow."

Thrown, Sanyam looked up. "What?"

"Nothing… above the collar," Fox managed.

Sanyam snorted a laugh and drew a finger down Fox's sternum. "As sad as I am that your throat is off-limits for now, there's plenty of other… real estate." He flicked Fox's nipple, and Fox whined, twisting in his bonds. "Well, if you insist," Sanyam said, and proceeded to take him apart.

He savored the salt-bitter taste of Fox's skin as he played with the nub, swirling it around on his tongue until it was hard and stiff. He reached over and gave Fox's erection a couple of quick strokes, until Fox was shaking all over, bucking against Sanyam's hand.

Every time Fox got close, though, his rhythm faltering and breath short in his throat, Sanyam stopped and turned his attention to another part of Fox's body, sucking livid marks into the skin with almost cruel precision.

He took his time, working his way across Fox's chest. He gave him a necklace of bruises and then concentrated on his hip, scraping his teeth lightly over the bone until Fox squirmed, his movements slowing like treacle on a cold day, limbs gone soft and pliant. It was obvious he was deep into sub space, in the perfect dimension of trust and utter surrender that Sanyam loved inducing.

He moved down the couch and sucked the tip of Fox's shaft into his mouth, humming as Fox made a helpless, quiet noise.

He spent several leisurely minutes working him over, until Fox's abs tightened again, thighs quivering. Sanyam pressed a thumb into the bruise on Fox's hip bone and took him to the hilt, and Fox sobbed a breath and filled the condom, cock spasming on Sanyam's tongue in long throbs as he curled forward as far as the ropes would allow.

Sanyam eased him through it as Fox collapsed back onto the couch. Only then did he pull off, wiping his mouth, to turn his attention to himself.

It took almost no time at all before he felt the familiar tightening in his balls, and he groaned and bent forward to press his forehead to Fox's still-heaving rib cage to come quick and hard.

Silence fell in the room. Sanyam closed his

eyes, Fox warm and sweet-smelling against his face, heart rabbit-fast in Sanyam's ear.

Finally Sanyam sighed and pushed himself to his feet. He padded to the cleanup station in the corner and came back with wet wipes from the warmer. He cleaned them both in gentle strokes before pulling Fox's blindfold off.

Fox's eyes were open but dreamy and unaware, still lost in his head, and Sanyam dropped a quick kiss on his lips before getting dressed. He folded Fox's clothes, set them on the arm of the couch, and turned back.

"I would hold you until you return from wherever you are," he said, undoing Fox's wrists and lifting his head so he could sit down. "But I think if you came to in my arms, you might bite me."

Fox turned on his side and rubbed his face against Sanyam's thigh, heaving a quiet sigh.

Sanyam pushed his hair off his forehead. "See you when you wake up, kit."

When Fox woke, Sanyam was reading quietly on his phone. He set it down as Fox stirred and lifted his head.

"Welcome back," Sanyam said, careful not to touch him.

Fox rolled to a sitting position, wincing, and glanced down at himself. His eyes widened at the bloom of bruises that littered his skin, and he touched the one on his hip with a cautious finger.

"How are you feeling?" Sanyam asked.

Fox looked up. "Um. Better."

"I'll bet," Sanyam said, smiling. "That was a pretty spectacular orgasm."

Confusion flickered across Fox's face. "I don't —why can't I remember?" Gooseflesh pebbled his arms, and he hunched his shoulders, uncertainty in his bearing.

Sanyam held out a hand, but Fox shied away. Sanyam dropped it, keeping his expression neutral.

"Memory loss during sub space is fairly common, especially for newcomers to scening. As you get more comfortable with relinquishing control, you'll begin to remember more of what we did."

Fox seemed to suddenly realize he was naked and wrapped his arms around his rib cage, looking for his clothes.

"Behind you," Sanyam said.

Fox turned and saw his neatly folded clothes, nearly falling in his haste to stand up and get them on. He was wobbly like a newborn foal, and Sanyam tensed, discreetly scooting forward on the couch, ready to catch him.

"Are you all right to drive?" he asked.

Fox dragged his pants on, flinching as he buttoned them. "I'm fine," he said, but he avoided eye contact as he reached for his shirt.

"What about tomorrow?" Sanyam persisted. "Do you have anyone to stay with you?"

Fox hesitated. "Cricket—no, she has class all day. It's not a problem."

"Don't you have *anyone* who can come over and help you through the drop?"

"I'll be *fine*," Fox snapped. "How many times do you want me to say it?"

"Part of being a good Dom is making sure my subs are cared for," Sanyam said evenly. "Be unpleasant all you want; it won't stop me from helping you through this."

Fox snarled, lip curling. "Fine. I'll call Colby —will that make you happy?"

"Ecstatic," Sanyam said. "Do it right now."

Fox glared. "It's too late now. He's asleep."

"First thing in the morning, then," Sanyam said, implacable.

"Are you like this with every sub?" Fox demanded. "Do you go around to every single one's house and make them breakfast and rub *arnica cream* onto their ass after you've scened with them? Do you insist they eat their vegetables and kiss them stupid and make them want more, or am I *special?*"

Sanyam stood up so quickly that Fox stumbled back a step, clearly startled. Sanyam closed the gap between them and caught Fox's shoulders, shoving him back until he hit the wall.

Sanyam pinned him there, and Fox caught his breath. He grabbed Sanyam's wrists, fingers loose and his eyes dark, lips parting.

"Never doubt that you are special, Fox," Sanyam whispered.

Fox's mouth twisted, but Sanyam lowered his head and kissed him before he could speak, and Fox sagged in his hands as he opened for Sanyam's tongue.

Sanyam let go, and Fox made a quiet noise of protest. But Sanyam had turned away, straightening his shirt.

"Call Colby first thing," he said. He bent to pick up the condom wrappers and began tidying the room, half his attention on Fox's motionless form.

After a minute, Fox shook himself and grabbed his shoes. After stepping into them, he hesitated, but finally he dragged the door open, and it slammed behind him.

Sanyam straightened, gazing after him. "Kiss you stupid?"

HE PUSHED his door open and set his groceries on the counter with a relieved sigh, then rolled his shoulders. He heard Polly hit the floor and the rapid patter of her feet as she hurried to greet him, and he smiled.

"Hello, my darling," Sanyam said as she skidded around the corner, squeaking happily at the sight of him.

He bent and picked her up, and Polly snuggled in under his chin, kneading his sweater with her front paws.

"Fox and I had our first real scene today," he told her as he put groceries away one-handed. "He puts up a good front, and I even bought it at first, but he's actually terrified underneath. Of what, I'm not sure yet. Perhaps just life in general."

Polly *mrrp*ed encouragingly, and Sanyam set her down to pick up the milk and put it in the fridge.

"The scene was intense," Sanyam said, straightening. "He's going to drop badly tomorrow. But he'll be all right. I told him to call his friend. He said he would."

Polly wrapped her tail around her dainty feet.

"He'll be fine," Sanyam said.

Polly blinked crystal-blue eyes and yawned, displaying sharp white teeth.

Sanyam sighed. "I know."

9

———

Sterling slept late, his dreams filled with anger, bitter voices raised in disappointment and betrayal.

When he woke, his phone told him it was close to 10:00 a.m., and he had no missed calls or texts.

Sterling got out of bed and dragged himself to the bathroom, still limping. In the shower, he braced an elbow on the glass and stared unseeingly out over the cityscape.

He didn't feel angry, unlike the last drop. He was just… empty.

He stood under the spray until the water ran cold and finally sighed and stepped out. He couldn't be bothered to do more than pull on a pair of soft pants before he shuffled back to the bedroom. Astrid was still off, so he wouldn't have food waiting, not that he could eat.

Facedown on the bed, he realized he hadn't called Colby.

Sterling rolled onto his side and groped for the phone.

It rang until Colby's voicemail picked up. "If you're calling, you must have a good reason. Make me want it, baby."

Too much effort to roll his eyes. The phone beeped, and Sterling groped for words.

"Hey…. Col…. Could you—call me back at some point? It's not a big deal, I just—" Feeling suddenly stupid, he hung up and dropped the phone on the bed, burying his face in the pillow. He'd try again later. Maybe.

He dropped into a fitful doze and was jerked out of it an hour later by someone ringing the doorbell.

Sterling lifted his head, blinking sleep from his eyes. A quick look at his phone confirmed Colby hadn't called him back.

The bell rang again, and Sterling heaved a sigh and pulled himself to his feet.

He wasn't really surprised to see Sanyam standing there, paper bag in one hand and coffee in the other. Sterling moved back silently, and Sanyam stepped inside. He put the food down and turned to look into Sterling's face, eyes concerned.

"I left a message," Sterling said. "He didn't—I did try."

Sanyam smiled and brought a hand up to thumb Sterling's dimple. "I'm sure you did. Have you eaten?"

Sterling forced himself not to lean into Sanyam's warmth and shook his head, hugging himself.

"You don't take care of yourself," Sanyam said. "You need to eat, Fox, or you'll just feel worse."

Sterling couldn't find the energy to come up with a snappy retort.

"Sit," Sanyam said. "I brought you breakfast."

Sterling shuffled to the table and sank into a chair, shifting in an attempt to get comfortable.

Sanyam set the bags on the table and pulled out several croissants filled with ham and eggs.

"Perhaps not the healthiest," he said, sitting opposite. "But right now you need calories more than you need health food."

Sterling picked at the croissant in front of him.

"Eat, Fox," Sanyam said, his voice leaving no room for disobedience.

Sterling managed a half-hearted glare as he picked up the sandwich and took a bite.

"I don't know how you like your coffee," Sanyam said, "so I got one black and one with cream and sugar. I'll drink whichever you don't."

Sterling chewed and swallowed, lifting a shoulder. "I don't care."

Sanyam leveled a look at him.

"Black," Sterling sighed. He shifted his weight again, wincing.

"When you're done with breakfast, I'll put some more cream on," Sanyam said.

"Why are you here?" Sterling immediately regretted the words, but it was too late.

Sanyam lifted a shoulder. "I… had a feeling you'd need me."

"You didn't trust me to call Colby."

"That's not it at all," Sanyam said. He leaned forward and held Sterling's eyes. "I came prepared to give Colby the food I'd brought and leave. But I thought—there was a possibility he wouldn't be here. And you shouldn't be alone right now."

Sterling broke first, looking down at his lap.

They ate in silence, and Sterling watched Sanyam out of the corner of his eye as Sanyam took neat, even bites. His hair was perfectly brushed, curls in place, short beard only serving to emphasize the strength of his jaw. Emptiness yawned within him, and Sterling put his food down.

"You're not done," Sanyam observed.

"I'm—I can't," Sterling said. He pushed away from the table and stood. "I'm going to lie down."

Sanyam stood too. "Let me put the food away, and I'll be right there."

Sterling just headed for the bedroom, footsteps slow and dragging on his hardwood floors. He crawled into his bed and pulled a pillow to his chest, staring at the wall.

After a minute, the bed dipped.

"I'm going to pull your pants down," Sanyam said, his voice quiet.

Sterling said nothing, closing his eyes as Sanyam gently worked the pants down over Sterling's thighs. The cream was warm this time, like he'd held it in his hand before applying it to Sterling's skin, but Sterling didn't know how to thank him.

So he lay still and let the tears come as the emptiness rolled over him in a great, crashing wave, disgust with himself following hard on its heels. *Men don't cry. Stop bawling, you useless, pathetic waste of oxygen.*

Sanyam worked the cream in thoroughly, fingers deft and gentle. Then he leaned across Sterling to set the tube on the bedside table and sat back to pull his pants into place.

"Oh, Fox," he said, wiping a tear from Sterling's cheek. "It's okay. This is normal. You'll feel better soon."

Sterling couldn't figure out how to tell him that this was how he always felt, that he just usually hid it better, and Sanyam cupped his face.

"Will you do me a favor?" he asked quietly.

Sterling looked at him.

"Would you let me hold you?"

Sterling pulled away. "Don't—patronize me," he said, hating how thick his voice was.

"I'm not," Sanyam said, his voice still quiet and his eyes serious. "I'm a very tactile person, and you would be helping me out a lot if you'd let me hold you, even if just for a few minutes."

"Bullshit," Sterling said. He hid his face in his elbow, but Sanyam didn't stir.

"I haven't had a partner in nearly three years," Sanyam said. "My boyfriend and I broke up because he had so much internalized homophobia he couldn't handle it anymore. Last I heard, his parents had found him a sweet Indian girl. I'm… lonely, Fox."

"You're a *Dom*," Sterling said. "You have sex every night."

"Not the same thing," Sanyam said. He moved around and sat back against the wall, his thigh warm and solid near Sterling's face.

"Besides, we don't have sex nearly as often as you might think."

Sterling lowered his elbow and considered Sanyam's leg in front of him. Sanyam didn't move, his head against the wall and his almond-shaped eyes closed.

Sterling chewed on his lip and finally scooted closer, until his face was pressed against Sanyam's hip. He felt Sanyam settle one big hand on his bare back, warm and comforting.

"This means nothing," Sterling said.

"Of course not," Sanyam agreed gravely. "Thank you, Fox."

Sterling closed his eyes and fell asleep.

***

WHEN HE WOKE UP, he was alone in the bed. He sat up and stretched, his stomach growling, and realized there was a note on the pillow beside him.

It was a phone number.

Had errands to run. Text me when you wake up, and hydrate, please.

Sterling scowled.

Not thirsty, he sent.

Sanyam's reply was almost immediate. *Don't care. Drink something. How are you feeling?*

Sterling rolled off the bed. He landed on his

good foot and padded for the bathroom. It was midafternoon, he realized—he'd slept through lunch, and it was time to get ready for his parents' dinner. He felt oddly good, like he'd had a week-long nap, energized and ready to wreak havoc.

I'm fine, he texted after he was done in the bathroom. He hesitated, deliberating on what to say. "When will I see you?" seemed too needy, and he had no idea how to actually thank Sanyam for what he'd done.

Sanyam took the dilemma out of his hands. *Have a good dinner with your family. Tell Cricket I said hello, and her blue vase is on a shelf below my favorite window.*

Sterling headed for the kitchen to get a bottle of water and then back into the bedroom to get ready.

He went with the olive-green shirt again, although he chose pants that were more conserva-tive—black linen, with knife-sharp creases.

Sterling surveyed himself in the mirror. The shirt hid the marks Sanyam had sucked into his skin, a secret testament to the side of Sterling his parents knew nothing about.

He stepped into his shoes and grabbed his wallet and phone.

His parents lived in one of the wealthier

districts of Vancouver, huge houses hidden by tasteful walls, trees lining all the streets.

Sterling pulled into the driveway and punched in the code. He waited for the gate to slide back in its stately majesty, and then rolled up the gravel drive and parked in front of the white-columned house.

Humphrey was waiting for him, turned out as perfectly as ever. He bowed slightly as Sterling climbed the steps to the front door.

"Good evening, Mr. Reynard."

"Hump, you've been this family's butler since I was three," Sterling said, tossing the keys to him. "How many times do I have to tell you to call me Fox?"

Humphrey's nostrils flared. "Yes, Mr. Reynard. Your parents are in the drawing room."

Sterling sighed and headed that direction.

Alice Reynard, tall and willowy and lovely, rose to greet him. Her dark hair was swept up in a sleek chignon, cheekbones prominent under her porcelain skin, and the cheek she offered for Sterling to kiss was rose-petal smooth.

"Hello, darling," she said. "How have you been?"

"Can't complain," Sterling said. "How are the charities?"

"Oh, they're wonderful," Alice said. "We're

doing a golf tournament next month, would you like to play a round for a good cause?"

"Outdoors," Sterling pointed out. "Couldn't pay me enough. Hi, Dad."

His father had his nose buried in a newspaper, and he just grunted something.

Sterling glanced around the room as Humphrey brought in a tray of drinks. "Where are Cricket and Dorian?"

"On their way," Alice said.

Yates slapped his newspaper down. "God-damn stupid liberals are ruining this country. Can't even read a paper in peace without getting slapped in the face with their stupid political bullshit."

"Hi, Dad," Sterling repeated.

"Hmm?" Yates glanced up. "Oh. Sterling. What are you doing here?"

"Family dinner, mandated appearance," Sterling said. "I don't want to be cut out of the will, so…." He spread his arms. "Ta-da."

Alice made an irritated noise. "Behave, Sterling."

Sterling opened his mouth to point out that he never behaved, that in fact he took great pride in how regularly he *mis*behaved, but Yates spoke first.

"How much are you costing me this month?"

Sterling flinched. "What are you talking about?"

Yates scoffed disbelievingly. "What, no antics for me to try to keep out of the press? No hookers or blow I have to cover up?"

"*Yates*," Alice hissed.

Yates ignored her. "I'm already paying for Cricket's and Dorian's educations, and Cricket's after me to buy her a Land Rover of her own so she can go to her stupid estate sales, and of course Dorian's hounding me for 'extracurricular' classes, so let's have it, how much am I looking at this time?"

"*Nothing*, Dad, Jesus! I haven't done anything wrong, I swear!"

Yates looked at him. "Are you still doing those stupid puzzles instead of going out and finding a real job?"

Sterling turned his flinch this time into a step backward. "They—help me focus."

The twins arrived before Yates could speak again. Cricket breezed in first, looking chic in her green minidress and tights, hair loose and flowing down to her shoulders. Dorian was on her heels, firmly clasping the hand of someone who could only be Tatum.

Sterling blinked, tilting his head. Was Tatum a girl or a boy? He honestly couldn't tell. They were dressed in black from head to toe, big brown eyes ringed in eyeliner and a silver hoop in one delicate nostril, with soft, messy brown curls that reached their shoulders.

"Mom, Dad," Dorian said, his voice too loud, "this is Tatum. We're dating."

Yates looked as confused as Sterling felt, but Alice spoke first.

"We've heard a lot about you, Tatum," she said as she held out her hand. "I'm Alice, Dorian's mother. I'm sure you've met Cricket, and this is our oldest, Sterling. We're very glad to have you."

"Good to see Dorian finally got himself a girl-friend!" Yates said, shaking Tatum's hand in turn. "We were beginning to wonder if there was some-thing wrong with him!" His laugh invited Tatum to share the joke, but they just looked flatly at him.

"I'm not a girl," they said, voice calm and brooking no argument.

"You're... a guy?" Yates said.

"No," Tatum said pleasantly. They looked around the drawing room. "You have a lot of books. May I look at them?"

"Of course," Yates said. He glanced at Dorian, who was watching Tatum and refused to make eye contact with either of his parents. Yates cleared his throat, obviously determined to be a good host. "So, Tatum, how do you know Dorian?"

Tatum was trailing a finger along the shelf, gamine chin tilted up as they inspected the books above their head. They glanced over their shoulder at Dorian. "You can tell him, baby."

Baby? Sterling mouthed at Cricket.

Cricket just shrugged and sat down on the sofa, crossing her long legs and pulling out her phone.

"We, ah… met playing minigolf," Dorian said.

Tatum made a noise that sounded somewhere between a laugh and a cough but just nodded soberly when Alice glanced at them.

"Since when do you minigolf?" Sterling demanded.

"What? I'm not allowed to have fun now?"

"Were you *ever?*"

"Boys," Alice said mildly. "Please." She stood, straightening her linen pantsuit, and Sterling was struck with the memory of Sanyam tugging his shirt into place after kissing him. "Dorian, a word?"

Sterling sat down on the couch next to Cricket as they left. "At some point, you're going to have to tell me how they really met," he said under his breath.

"Porn shop," Cricket said, equally quietly, and Sterling choked on his tongue.

He coughed and spluttered as Cricket pounded him on the back, muffling her giggles in faux-concern for his plight. When he was able to draw breath, eyes streaming, he looked up to see Tatum sitting on his other side, regarding him. Those brown eyes were disconcerting in their intensity, and Sterling gulped, trying for a smile.

"I'm Sterling, but call me Fox," he said, holding out his hand.

"Oh yes, Dorian has told me all about you," Tatum said. They accepted his hand, skin warm and smooth. "Spoiled rotten, thinks he owns the place, overinflated sense of self-worth—I could go on."

"Aw," Sterling said, pressing a hand to his heart. "He's being *nice*. Dodo's in love, Cricket!"

Tatum raised an eyebrow. "He didn't mention you were funny."

"I won't tell if you don't," Sterling said.

To his surprise, that won him a smile, setting Tatum's eyes dancing.

"I like you," they announced.

"Thank you," Sterling said. "I have to admit, you're not Dorian's usual type. Which is a compliment, I should point out."

Tatum laughed. "Dorian's more open-minded

than you might think." They glanced at the wall and the framed snowflake puzzle hanging there, and their eyes widened. "Whoa, who did that?"

"Me," Sterling said.

Tatum glanced at him, clearly reassessing their opinion of him. "You like puzzles?"

"Difficult ones, yeah," Sterling said. "The kinds without edges or a cover image so I don't know what I'm making—those are fun. You know, if you ever need birthday or Christmas gift ideas."

Tatum grinned. "Noted."

Sterling fidgeted, uncomfortable with being so close. "So... can I ask?"

"They and them pronouns," Tatum said. "I'm not a boy *or* a girl."

"How does that work, exactly?"

Tatum shrugged. Their fingernails were painted dark, iridescent blue, with swirls of violet throughout. "I'm bi-gender."

"I don't understand," Sterling admitted, scooting an inch away.

Tatum gave him a pitying smile. "Not many people do. It's okay. Basically, I don't identify with either gender. I'm both... and neither. I'm just me. Calling me she isn't accurate because I have male aspects, but calling me he is equally problematic and dismisses my feminine qualities." It had the practiced ring of something they'd said often, patient and rehearsed.

"I thought it was one or the other," Cricket added. "Tatum set me straight. Did you know that there are actually a lot of genders?"

"Are you okay with this?" Tatum asked.

Sterling squirmed, unable to make eye contact. "Sure. Why wouldn't I be?"

"Maybe because you're having a hard time looking at me?" Tatum said. Their voice was calm, like they'd had this conversation more than once, and a bubble of guilt welled under Sterling's breastbone.

"I'm—I guess I'm having trouble wrapping my head around the concept." He managed to look at them, and Tatum gave him an encouraging smile. "For Dorian, though, I'll try," Sterling said, and Tatum's smile widened.

I feel like I'm standing in the middle of a rose.

Sterling closed his eyes as scraps of memory floated through his mind.

"But... I'm a boy."

The memories fled as Alice and Dorian came back into the drawing room, high spots of color burning on Alice's cheeks. Dorian mostly looked irritated, and he made a beeline for Tatum, who held out a hand and pulled him down onto the couch.

Humphrey stepped inside, discreetly clearing his throat. "Dinner is served."

The meal was a reserved, chilly affair, with Alice obviously upset and Yates getting more and more annoyed throughout the courses, sneaking glances at Tatum, who was calmly eating and talking to the siblings.

The tension in the room only grew, though, and over dessert, Yates set his spoon down and leaned forward to address Tatum. "So tell me the truth, are you a boy or a girl?"

"*Dad*," Dorian snarled.

Yates ignored him, and Tatum put a hand on Dorian's arm.

"It's okay. I'm neither, Mr. Reynard."

"Okay, whatever, I don't even know what that means, but what's between your legs?"

"Yates!" Alice hissed.

Tatum didn't seem fazed. "Dorian, if I'm lucky," they said, lips curving.

Sterling choked on his sorbet, and Cricket snorted and hastily stifled it as Dorian turned bright red, and Yates glared.

"What were you *born as*?" he insisted.

Tatum regarded him, Dorian nearly vibrating with fury beside them. "If I tell you that, you'll use those pronouns to refer to me, won't you?"

"It's what you truly are," Yates said. "None of

this 'part boy, part girl' bullshit. What you are when you're born is the gender you should be."

Tatum nodded gravely. "So transgender people are just confused?"

Yates bridled. "Look, the problem with young folk in this day and age is that they're *coddled*. They're told they don't have to conform, so they all decide they want to be special snowflakes. Your gender at birth is what defines you, and—"

Dorian shot to his feet. "We're done. Dad, when you can treat my partner with *respect*, maybe we'll consider coming back. Let's go, Tatum."

Tatum stood more slowly and held their hand out to Sterling, who accepted it. "It was nice to meet *you*, at any rate." They leaned in. "Nice hickey, by the way."

Sterling glanced down and realized with horror that his shirt had slid to the side, exposing one of the marks. He jerked at his shirt, swearing silently as Tatum winked and followed Dorian out the door.

Alone with Cricket and his parents, Sterling glanced around the room. "So that was fun."

"Eat your sorbet," Alice snapped.

Cricket elbowed him. "Who gave you *that?*" she whispered as Alice and Yates conversed in low tones at the head of the table.

"None of your business," Sterling said.

"Do I know him?" Cricket continued.

Sterling dropped his spoon and stared at her. She blinked big green eyes at him, innocence all over her face.

"You—what—how—"

Cricket rolled her eyes. "Don't give yourself an aneurysm. I've known you were gay since I was eight."

"But… I didn't know until I was fifteen!" Sterling protested.

"Because you have even less grasp of your personal identity than you do others'," Cricket said. "It's painfully obvious to anyone with eyes."

Yates cleared his throat, and the siblings' heads whipped around.

"What are you two gossiping about?" he asked, forcing cheer into his voice.

"Fox's most recent girlfriend," Cricket said instantly.

Sterling kicked her under the table, and she punched him in the ribs, smile still firmly in place.

"*Children*," Alice said despairingly.

"When *are* you going to bring a girl home for us to meet?" Yates asked. "Surely there must be *one* out there you like well enough to keep around for more than a few weeks. Or who likes *you* well enough, I suppose. We could take her out on the Calypso before the sea gets too cold."

Sterling flinched. "No such creature," he said, keeping his tone light. "Mom, as always, it's been a pleasure. Dad, have fun trashing the liberals ruining the country. I have things to do this evening."

He kissed his mother's cheek again and escaped out the front door, the oppressive atmosphere easing as soon as he was outside. He'd been lying, of course—he had nothing to do, no plans to get together with anyone, but he couldn't stay in that house another minute.

He drove home in the gathering twilight as fireflies winked among the branches of the trees that crowded the boulevards.

Sterling had always loved this time of day. There was a peace to it, a feeling of stillness that made him think, impossibly, that things might be all right eventually.

He was eight years old, a blur of constant activity, unable to sit still for even a minute.

"Mom, Mom! Come quick!"

Alice dropped her pen on top of the papers and caught Sterling's slim body before he could launch himself at her. "Sterling, we've discussed your indoor voice," she said, gently holding his wrists away from her perfectly pressed pantsuit.

"I wanna show you something," Sterling insisted, squirming in her grasp.

"I'm busy, darling," Alice said. "Can't you show Cricket or Dorian? Or how about Amparo? I'm sure she'd love to see it."

Sterling pouted. "Cricky's too little, and Dorian is dumb. And 'Paro is doing laundry. It won't take long, Mom, please?"

Alice sighed and stood up, smoothing her hair back as Sterling danced around her. He wrapped his small, grubby fingers around her hand and towed her out into the back garden.

"Look!" he said, gesturing expansively at the fireflies that dotted the garden with streaks of phosphorescence. "Their butts light up, see?"

Alice almost smiled. "Yes, dear. Because they're fireflies."

She ruffled Sterling's hair, and he squirmed away from her to dash out into the garden and spin in a circle, small arms flung wide in the delight that wouldn't be contained.

When he stumbled to a stop, breathless and dizzy with laughter, his mother had gone back inside.

. . .

HE GOT a text from Cricket as he was pulling into his parking spot.

Don't forget about estate sale @ 7. Taking Daddy's Land Rover.

Sterling groaned, the half-formed idea of finding some friends to hang out with dashed on the spot, and instead headed upstairs to shower before bed.

10

He picked Cricket up the next morning, parking as she bounced down the steps, glossy hair swinging in a careless ponytail.

"Good morning!" she chirped as he stepped out.

"Matter of opinion," Sterling grumbled. He stalked for the Land Rover that Humphrey had pulled around, sliding into the seat and starting the engine. Cricket hopped in next to him and buckled, flipping her hair over her shoulder.

Sterling slanted a look at her as she pulled the address up on her phone. "Why are you forcing me into this again?"

"Dorian is busy, and he helped me at the booth most recently," Cricket said. "I mean, I'm nineteen years old, I could totally do this on my own, but Daddy—"

"Do *not* start," Sterling said, holding up a hand. "I haven't even eaten. I can't take your rants on an empty stomach."

Cricket shook her head. "You don't take proper care of yourself, Fox. It's not healthy. Have you ever even exercised?"

Sterling shuddered delicately and pulled out onto the boulevard, following the directions through Vancouver to Shaughnessy.

Cricket regarded him, and Sterling pretended not to notice.

"Are you going to do this for the rest of your life?" she asked.

"What?" Sterling asked, caught off guard.

"Act like you don't care," Cricket said.

Sterling bridled. "What's *that* supposed to mean?"

"You know exactly what that means," Cricket said flatly. "You're above it all, aren't you? Too good to mix with the unwashed masses? No, I mean it"—as Sterling tried to protest—"you turn up your nose and you sneer at us 'plebes,' you laze around and spend Daddy's money—isn't there anything you *want* to do? It's a serious question; I want to know."

Sterling swallowed the affront and tried to

consider the question. "I'm—I don't know," he finally admitted. "I'm not good at anything. There's nothing I like doing well enough to consider doing it as a career. Why should I? It's not like Dad's going to run out of money—he can afford it, and maybe when I hit my thirties, I'll actually join his firm. For now, why shouldn't I have fun? Is that so wrong?"

"It's not *wrong*," Cricket said. "But caring about stuff doesn't make you uncool or whatever. Having a passion is important."

Sterling shrugged this off. "What about you? Is this really what you want to do with your life?"

Cricket glanced at him, her boots propped on the dash. "Is that a serious question?"

"Well yeah," Sterling admitted. "I guess I'm curious. This is what makes you happy? Finding glassware and repurposing it?"

"There's more to it than that," Cricket said. "And I'm hoping to have my own antique shop at some point, but yeah. This is what I want to do with my life. I love glass, I love cleaning it up and making it sparkle again, seeing it come to life, and I really want to branch out into refurbishing and sourcing antique furniture when I can convince Daddy that I'm serious about this. Are you even familiar with the history of Depression-era glassware?"

"Only what you've forced me to learn," Sterling said, slowing to turn into the driveway of a house even more palatial than their parents'. "So who kicked it?"

Cricket snorted a hastily smothered laugh and tried to replace it with a frown. "Really, Fox, for shame, have some respect for the dead."

Sterling grinned and parked in the designated area. "I'll be here when you're done," he said, putting his seat back.

"Oh no," Cricket said. She grabbed the keys from the ignition and scrambled out of the front seat as he lunged to get them back. "You're coming in with me. Come on. I'm not doing this alone."

"Goddammit!" Without the engine running, it was too cold to stay in the car, so Sterling got out, glaring ferociously.

Cricket just smiled and turned to march inside, Sterling trailing behind her and muttering under his breath.

He followed her from room to room, bored out of his head, as Cricket inspected the items and pointed out interesting things.

"Look, Fox, a zoetrope!"

Sterling yawned. "Fascinating."

Undaunted, Cricket kept going. "Oh, oh Fox,

look at the *glassware!*" she said as she dragged him into the next room.

"There's a lot of it," Sterling agreed.

Cricket gasped out loud and pounced on an iridescent bowl. "Oh my God, a Fenton fantail-footed carnival glass bowl, I don't *believe* it! Fox, hold this for me." She shoved it at him, and Sterling swore as he grabbed it.

"Why does it look like rainbows?" he asked, turning it gingerly in his hands.

Cricket was poring over the rest of the collection, making happy noises as she gathered pieces. "The makers would spray a mineral salt solution on the surface before firing it," she said without looking up.

"Kind of looks like an oil slick," Sterling said. He ran a finger over the embossed pattern of grapes and butterflies around the rim of the bowl. "Is this Depression glass?"

"No," Cricket said, putting another piece in his hands—a heavy platter that matched the bowl. "This is carnival glass. Similar era, different style."

"Where'd the name come from? Did carnivals make it?" Sterling asked, following her through the room.

Cricket shot him a glowing smile over her shoulder. "No, they gave it away to customers as incentive to get them to come. Oh, *oh*, elegant glass, this is the best day *ever*!" She picked up a cobalt-blue pitcher and held it to the light.

"That's not Depression glass?" Sterling asked, struggling to keep his armful steady. "I thought Depression glass was blue."

"It can be," Cricket said. She tucked the pitcher under her arm and turned back to the table. "Elegant glass was made at the same time as Depression, but especially if you compare them, you can see the difference in quality. Elegant was fire polished to get rid of flaws, and a lot of the things you'll see in a Depression piece—raised seams, uneven bases, things like that—aren't there with an elegant piece. It's worth more, obviously, and I haven't found many pieces up here."

A small man in a perfectly pressed suit approached, discreetly clearing his throat. "Perhaps sir would like to put his purchases in here," he said, offering a box.

Sterling accepted it gratefully and put the glassware inside, making sure each piece was securely nestled and wouldn't bump into the others. He took Cricket's items and set them inside as well, then locked the lid as Cricket went through the rooms one more time to make sure she hadn't missed anything.

Finally, though, she decided she was done, and Sterling heaved a sigh of relief as she paid for the pieces, and he carried them down the steps onto the front lawn toward the Rover.

Cricket was ahead of him, keys in hand as she cheerfully chattered on about the history of glassware in general, and Sterling hefted the box in his arms and missed the last step, unable to see his feet.

He went sprawling, horror dawning in slow motion as he realized what was happening but unable to stop his forward plunge.

The box hit first, the glass inside shattering like it had been hit by a hammer. Sterling clipped his forehead on the corner of the box as he went down hard, and his wrist turned beneath him. Pain burst in kaleidoscope colors on the inside of his eyelids.

Cricket spun, shock blooming on her face as she took in the aftermath.

Sterling tried to push himself up, sick guilt worming in his stomach, as Cricket went to her knees beside him.

"I'm sorry," he gasped.

"Fox, you're bleeding," she said, stopping him with a hand on his shoulder.

"I'm fine," Sterling said automatically. "Your glass, Crick, I broke it, I ruined it, I'm so sorry, I'll replace it or fix it—"

Cricket smiled, her eyes sad. "You can't 'fix'

this, Fox. But it's okay—you're more important. We need to get you to the hospital, get your head looked at."

Sterling insisted on carrying the box of shattered glass to the Rover, some vague thought of putting it back together pushing him to stow it in the back before Cricket drove him to the hospital.

He put his head back as she drove, pain swimming sluggishly through his bloodstream as he held a hastily salvaged napkin to the open wound to stop the bleeding.

The nurse was sympathetic but brisk, peeling the napkin off to clean the gash thoroughly as Cricket held Sterling's hand.

"You've sprained your wrist and you'll have a very dashing scar," the nurse told him. "You'll be able to impress all the girls with it."

Sterling didn't reply. He wanted, suddenly, desperately, to see Sanyam again. *Pathetic, whiny, crybaby*, a tiny voice sneered. *Be a man.*

IT WAS midafternoon before Cricket drove him home in his Lamborghini, the box of ruined glass in the trunk.

"I'll get a cab home," she said, waving off Sterling's protests.

"I ruined your whole day," Sterling said, floating on misery and the painkillers the nurse had given him. "I'm sorry, Crick—"

"Honestly?" Cricket said, squeezing his hand across the gearshift. "I've had a better time being with you today than I have in years."

Sterling blinked, confused. "But—"

Cricket's lips curved. "You've been *nice* today. Even before you broke the glass, you were asking me questions, you were interested in what I was doing—it was pretty cool, I'm not gonna lie." She pulled into his parking spot and hurried around to help him out of the car.

"I sprained my wrist, not my ankle," Sterling said with a touch of his usual asperity. "I'm not going to collapse."

"No point in risking it," Cricket said, slipping an arm around his waist. "Besides, you hit your head pretty hard."

She stayed next to him up to his apartment and settled him in the bed, taking off his shoes as he lay facedown.

"What'd you do to your *foot*?" she demanded as she pulled his socks off.

"Broke my bottle of aftershave," Sterling mumbled through a yawn. "Then stepped on it."

"This is a nice bandage job," Cricket said. "Did you do it yourself?"

"San," Sterling slurred.

"Who?"

"Complicated," Sterling said, stifling another yawn.

Cricket patted his calf. "Have a nap. I woke you up early and you're high as balls. I'll see you later—maybe this weekend?"

"I'd like that," Sterling said, surprised to realize it was true, and fell asleep.

11

***

Sanyam got an email from Ava on Wednesday.

Can you come in early on Friday? I need to speak with you.

Sanyam pushed down the spike of illogical worry and typed out a quick response.

He arrived early Friday and went straight to Ava's office, knocking on the door.

"Come in," Ava called.

Sanyam stepped inside. Ava was sitting at her desk, busily typing, and she waved one chubby hand at him.

"Sit anywhere, just have to finish this real quick."

Sanyam moved a pile of books and papers

from the nearest chair and perched on the edge of the seat as Ava tapped away on the keyboard.

She reminded Sanyam of a robin, small, round, and cheerful, with a way of puffing herself up when she got upset that was reminiscent of ruffled feathers. Sanyam had liked her immediately when Kali had put him in touch with her, and when she'd offered him the job in Vancouver, it hadn't taken him long at all to decide to accept it.

Ava hit Send and folded her hands, smiling at Sanyam. "Sorry about that. How are you settling in?"

"Fine," Sanyam said.

"You're very popular here," Ava said. "Your nights fill fast, and Kimi reports that she's getting a lot of people specifically asking for you."

Sanyam lifted a shoulder. "It is gratifying," he admitted.

"Gratifying," Ava echoed, and laughed. "I heard about the thing with Delfia that night I went home early. That's what I wanted to speak to you about. I understand you've just signed a semi-permanent contract with one of his friends?"

"I—yes," Sanyam said.

"And you think that was wise?"

"Perhaps not *wise*," Sanyam said. He resisted the urge to squirm, like a schoolboy being reprimanded. "But I… see something in him. Something his 'friend' is lacking."

"A soul?" Ava said, grinning.

Sanyam almost smiled back. "Perhaps," he allowed. "Or perhaps a sense of decency that he himself doesn't know he possesses yet. All I know is that he is not like Jackson."

Ava leaned forward, fixing him with piercing blue eyes. "Are you dating him, Sanyam?"

"No!" Sanyam said, horrified. "That's against club policy. I know the rules, Ava. I'm only seeing him in a Dom/sub capacity, I promise."

"So you haven't been spending time with him outside the club?"

Sanyam opened and closed his mouth. Ava's eyes were sharp and knowing.

"I—went to his place to help him through a sub drop," he admitted. "But I only did it because it was my fault. I did not warn him after our scene that he would likely experience it, and I was… worried."

Ava nodded. "You're a grown man, Sanyam. What you do in your time off is your business, and I don't own you. However, dating a client *is* against club policy, and I just needed to make that explicitly stated, so that there aren't any crossed wires." She smiled suddenly. "Go on, get out of here. Your room was restocked this morning. Have a good shift."

Sanyam closed the door behind him and ruffled his hair as he headed for his room. He couldn't help wondering if he'd see Fox that night. He was honest enough with himself to admit that he wanted to. But they hadn't spoken since Tuesday, and Sanyam had no idea what Fox had going on.

His phone buzzed, and he picked it up. It was Kimi.

Potential client. Sweet kid, wants a daddy Dom, has a lg kink.

Sanyam grimaced. He had nothing against people with daddy/little girl kinks, but it wasn't his favorite. *Anyone else?*

Older couple, he wants to be dominated, she wants to watch. They look like good tippers.

Send them back, Sanyam replied.

"I'm Melody. This is Raul," the woman said by way of introduction. "I want you to *wreck* him."

Sanyam glanced at Raul, who nodded, his eyes eager.

"He's not allowed to speak except to answer

direct questions or to safeword," Melody said, running a fingertip along Raul's jaw. "But we'll sign whatever you need us to."

"It will be my pleasure," Sanyam said, and showed them both to the table and the contracts laid out.

Two hours later, he shut the door behind them. Both Melody and Raul had proven to be old hands at the game, Raul submitting to Sanyam's touch gladly as Melody sat on the couch and made suggestions.

It had been diverting, and Sanyam had the feeling that they would indeed tip handsomely. Still, he couldn't shake the sense that he was… waiting. For something or someone, he wasn't sure, but it niggled at him as he cleaned the room, and he wondered briefly how Fox was.

His phone went off, and he reached for it.

Kimi again. *911, cops called, need you.*

Sanyam ran for the main room, right into chaos. Someone was crying, another person was yelling, rage thick in his voice, and there were policemen everywhere, separating combatants still intent on throwing punches.

Kimi caught sight of him and waved him over

with the hand holding her bat, her other arm around Delfia. She had to raise her voice to be heard over the din.

"Fox came back to see you. His buddies were with him, or followed him, I don't know, but—"

Sanyam spun, scanning the room. There, in the corner, two policemen were talking to Fox, who was deathly pale, blood on his face. Sanyam bolted in his direction as Kimi kept talking.

Fox was unsteady on his feet, his eyes dazed and the beginnings of an impressive shiner developing on his cheekbone. He caught sight of Sanyam and took a step toward him before collecting himself and turning back to the policemen.

He answered a question as Sanyam joined them, his slim body turned toward Sanyam like filings to a magnet even as he listened to the policewoman talking to him, a short, stocky officer with a serious face.

Sanyam held out his hand to the other policeman. "Sanyam Desai. I work here. This is a friend of mine. Can you tell me what happened?"

"Officers Savage and Harwell," the man said. "Harwell's getting your friend's version of events —we'll be done in just a minute."

Fox swayed again, and Sanyam lunged to catch him as his legs buckled. Sanyam eased him to a chair, and Fox sagged against him, soft hair brushing Sanyam's cheek.

Sanyam turned to the officers. "Why hasn't he been seen by paramedics? He's bleeding!"

Fox caught his wrist. "That's old," he said, his voice low. "Jacks… he clipped my temple, reopened the cut. I'm fine."

"You're not fine," Sanyam said flatly. He straightened, a hand still on Fox's shoulder. "Can someone please tell me what happened while my friend gets some *medical attention*?"

Officer Harwell beckoned, and a paramedic hurried over and knelt in front of Fox as Harwell addressed Sanyam, consulting her notebook as she spoke.

"From what we can gather, Mr. Reynard had been here for about an hour when Mr. Whittier showed up and began causing a scene, along with their mutual friend Braden Thompson. Mr. Reynard tried to stop them, Mr. Whittier made an inappropriate comment, and punches were thrown."

"Where is he?" Sanyam demanded, fury blinding him.

Officer Harwell pointed at the far wall. Jackson was on his knees, face contorted, nose swollen and dripping blood as he spat invectives at the burly officer holding him down.

Sanyam tensed, and Fox tightened his grip on Sanyam's wrist. "*Don't.*"

"Your friend is right," Officer Savage said. "Please don't make our jobs harder, sir. I think Mr. Reynard would prefer you stay with him, in any case."

"Did anyone else come with you?" Sanyam asked Fox.

Someone slithered through the crowd and popped out next to the police officers, and Sanyam recognized Farid with a jolt of surprise.

Fox shook his head, squeezing his eyes shut. "I was bored, I started drinking while I waited for you, and then Jacks and Braden showed up, and Jackson said something about the waitress, and I might have, ah…."

"It appears he may have punched him in the nose," Harwell said, amusement in her voice. "Although we can't seem to find any witnesses to that, so we won't be pressing charges."

"I saw it happen," Farid said in his husky, gentle voice.

Harwell swung to face him as Fox and Sanyam tensed.

"Can you tell me what occurred, Mister…?"

"Qadir," Farid supplied. "Farid Qadir. I was a few booths away, and… occupied with something, but—Fox, is it?"

Fox nodded, his eyes still closed.

Farid glanced back at the officers. "Fox was in my line of sight, as was his companion. It was obvious his 'friend' was provoking him, trying to get a rise out of him. Fox was trying to de-escalate the situation, I could tell by his body language, but—"

"What do you know about body language that would give you that information?" Harwell asked.

"He's a Dom like me," Sanyam said before Farid could reply. "Not… professionally, but we're friends, and trust me—he knows body language."

Farid inclined his head, a smile flirting at the corners of his mouth. "At any rate, Fox's companion made a threatening move toward Fox. Fox's actions were self-defense."

Harwell inspected him. "Would you be willing to testify to that?"

"If it goes so far as trial, absolutely," Farid said. He was neat as ever, his hair perfect and his three-piece suit not even wrinkled. He looked professional, competent, and intelligent, and Sanyam could feel the police officers relaxing.

Harwell turned back to Fox. "Mr. Reynard, I think we have all the information we need, but you're in no state to drive. Do you have anyone who can take you home, or would you like us to call you a cab?"

"I'll do it," Sanyam said immediately. He helped Fox to his feet with a hand on his elbow and accepted his keys from him. He nodded at Farid, who smiled at him, and stuck close to Fox's side as they made a more-or-less straight line for the exit.

It was a cold night, and Fox shivered but shook his head when Sanyam hesitated, wondering if he should go back for his coat.

"I didn't bring a jacket. I'll be fine," Fox said. "I just… wanna go home. I parked over there." He pointed, and Sanyam led him in that direction.

The drive was silent, Fox resting his head against the seat, his eyes closed, long throat thrown into relief by the streetlights they passed under.

"So how did you cut your face in the first place?" Sanyam asked as he pulled into Fox's high-rise.

Fox opened his eyes and made a visible effort to drag himself back together. "I was… helping Cricket, couple of days ago. Estate sale. I tripped. Dropped the box I was carrying, cut my forehead on it when I went down."

Sanyam winced in sympathy. "I'm sorry." He parked and stepped out, hurrying around to help Fox to his feet.

"This is getting old," Fox muttered. He refused to elaborate, though, and pulled away when Sanyam tried to put his arm around his waist. "I can walk."

Sanyam directed him through the lobby, waving the doorman's worried exclamations off with soothing comments, and got Fox on the elevator.

Fox leaned against the mirrored wall, his shoulders sagging. "I fuck everything up," he muttered, mostly to himself.

"What do you mean?" Sanyam asked, moving closer.

Fox sighed. "Nothing. I'm drunk. I can take it from here."

Sanyam just smiled. "If you think I'm leaving you in the elevator, you don't know me very well yet."

The elevator rose smoothly, and Sanyam steadied him as the car slowed and stopped on Fox's floor.

Sanyam let them into the apartment and Fox made a vague gesture toward the bowl by the front door.

"Leave the keys there. Thanks… for your help."

I should leave. Instead, Sanyam dropped the keys in the bowl and moved into Fox's space, bringing a hand up to thumb over Fox's dimple. Ava didn't have to know. All he could think about was tasting Fox's mouth again.

Fox swallowed hard and leaned into his hand. "I want—I…. San, I want you—"

"I know," Sanyam whispered. "Me too, Fox." He closed the distance and kissed him, Fox yielding and soft under his mouth, tasting like honey whiskey and peanuts. It took all his self-control to pull away as Fox made a quiet noise of protest.

Sanyam touched his unbruised cheekbone. "May I take you to bed, Fox?"

Fox nodded silently, desperately, and plastered himself against Sanyam's frame. "Yes, yes I want that, I want *you*—"

"Are you sure you're thinking clearly enough?" Sanyam persisted. He wanted, *needed*, all of it, everything Fox could give him, but he had to make sure, he had to *know* Fox was able to give consent.

Fox gave him an annoyed look. "I'm not *that* drunk."

"Not concussed, either?"

Fox pulled away and lifted both hands, middle fingers extended. "How many fingers am I holding up?"

Sanyam laughed outright and reeled him back

in to nip at the column of his throat. "You're such an asshole. Why do I like you?"

Fox wriggled out of his grip, swaying, and kicked his shoes off. "Beats me. Come on, bedroom."

He towed Sanyam through the apartment and pushed him backward onto the bed, flinging a leg over Sanyam's hips and riding him down.

Sanyam ran his hands up Fox's thighs, smiling. "I suppose if you have the physical coordination to manage that, then you have the mental capacity to consent to sex."

"Your dirty talk is *terrible*," Fox said, and kissed him, hot and hungry.

Sanyam laughed into Fox's mouth and rolled them, a flurry of limbs that ended with him on top and Fox looking stunned, eyes dark and lips wet.

"That, uh… that works too," Fox managed.

"Do you have condoms?" Sanyam asked.

"Bedside drawer."

Sanyam leaned across him and fumbled in the drawer, swearing under his breath as Fox worked a hand between them and cupped his shaft through his pants.

"*Mashalla*, kit, you're going to kill me yet." He found the supplies and sat up triumphantly, dropping one condom on Fox's chest and tearing the foil on the other.

"Can't get naked with you pinning me down," Fox pointed out.

"What a pity," Sanyam murmured, scooting down the bed so that he was on Fox's thighs. "Whatever will you do?" He lowered his head and scraped his teeth across Fox's collarbone.

"If you make me come in my pants, I will put itching powder in your—*ah*—" Fox jerked as Sanyam bit down and sucked a fresh bruise into his pale skin, overlapping the faint green-purple of the old marks he'd left.

"I mean it," Fox managed after a minute, when Sanyam showed no signs of letting up. "Goddammit, San, let me—" He pushed futilely at Sanyam's shoulders, and Sanyam laughed against his skin but finally let go with a wet, sucking *pop* and rolled off. "*Asshole*," Fox said, and dragged at his clothes with shaking hands.

Sanyam grinned and pushed his pants down over his hips, then yanked his shirt up and over his head before rolling the condom on and settling back onto Fox's thighs as Fox fumbled for his own condom.

"Need some help?" Sanyam asked, lightly flicking the head of Fox's shaft with a thumbnail.

Fox yelped and dropped the condom, glaring at him.

Sanyam picked it up and winked, scooting back down on the bed. "Not that dexterous, right? Watch and learn, kit." He put the unrolled condom in his mouth and dropped his head, rolling the condom down Fox's shaft in one smooth motion with lips and tongue.

Fox made a strangled noise and clutched at the bedspread, thighs quivering.

Sanyam hummed appreciatively, savoring the weight and feel of Fox on his tongue, the silken slide even through the latex. He spent several leisurely minutes working him over, until Fox's chest was heaving and a flush pinked his porcelain skin under the bruises.

Finally Sanyam pulled off. He grabbed the lube and slicked Fox's shaft before he crawled back up, propping himself on his elbows so they were chest to chest.

Fox's eyes were dazed, his hair rumpled, and Sanyam kissed the end of his nose, making him blink.

Then he rolled them again, stopping on his back with Fox balanced on top of him, hard shaft caught in the groove of Sanyam's hip.

"Ah, *yes*," Sanyam said. Fox rolled downward against him in a filthy grind, spit and sweat and lube making the slide so perfect that Sanyam's toes curled against the mattress.

He grabbed Fox's hips, pulling him closer, fingers biting into flesh. Fox dropped his head on a choked moan, hips in a steady rhythm as he opened his mouth and set his teeth in Sanyam's collarbone.

His breath was hot and wet against Sanyam's skin, teeth skidding along bone, and it was a matter of minutes before Sanyam planted both feet flat on the bed and shoved his hips up, filling the condom thick and fast, brain whiting out in ecstasy.

Fox was still moving in short, abortive thrusts of his hips, eyes hungry, when Sanyam came around, settling back into his body with a deep sigh.

Sanyam flexed his fingers and pulled Fox closer again. "Come on, then, kit," he murmured. "Let me see it. Come for me, beautiful."

Fox obeyed with a muffled whimper, shuddering all over and finally collapsing in a limp heap on top of Sanyam's body.

They lay quietly for several long, delicious minutes, Sanyam running his hand up and down Fox's heaving ribs.

After a while, though, he patted Fox's ass. "Shower time."

Fox made a protesting noise into Sanyam's collarbone.

"Up," Sanyam said, poking him in the ribs. "Come on. You'll feel better when you're clean."

Fox twisted away from his finger, growling, but allowed Sanyam to pull him off the bed and up onto his feet.

They shared a slow, leisurely shower, with Fox leaning a shoulder against the glass and watching Sanyam through sleepy eyes.

When they were done, Sanyam dried them both off and helped Fox into pajamas while he yawned, limbs gone floppy with exhaustion.

"Will you be okay now?" Sanyam asked as Fox curled up on his side and Sanyam pulled the blankets over him.

Fox nodded, shoving his fist against his mouth to stifle another yawn.

Sanyam laughed quietly, affection startling him with its intensity. "You need a minder, you do."

"Do not," Fox said, eyes drooping.

"I'll see myself out," Sanyam said, pushing Fox's hair off his forehead.

Fox was asleep before Sanyam tiptoed from the room.

12

Sterling woke abruptly around 3:00 a.m., sitting up straight in the bed. He yawned and stretched, kicking off the covers, and evaluated. He felt better than he had in a while, and he wandered to the bathroom and from there to the living room.

The box from Cricket's estate sale sat on his coffee table, painted in shades of platinum from the moonlight that streamed through the glass door to his balcony, and Sterling sat down and flipped the lid off.

It was bright enough to easily see the disaster within. Shards of colored glass tumbled together to create a cacophonic kaleidoscope in riotous hues.

Sterling bit his lip, guilt crawling through his

veins again, and lifted one of the bigger pieces out.

It was from the platter that had matched the bowl, the reds and blues and greens spreading over the surface of the glass like oil on water.

Sterling swept the half-finished puzzle into its box, then set the glass shard on the table and began picking out the other pieces, one by one.

After a minute, he put the box on the floor by his knee, stood and turned on the light, and went back to work, separating out each piece with methodic care.

He'd gone to the club to see Sanyam, of course. But Delfia had been his waitress, and she'd been *scared* of him, which made Sterling sick, somewhere deep in a forgotten part of his soul.

So he'd poured on the charm, tipping her generously with every drink she'd brought him, careful not to so much as brush her fingers when accepting his glass, and after about half an hour, she'd lost some of the tightness around her eyes and the stiffness in her posture.

Half an hour after that, Jackson had shown up, all suave swagger, sunglasses in his casually tousled hair and his polo open at the neck. He'd made a beeline for Sterling's table, Braden on his heels, and Delfia had bolted.

Sterling jerked, swearing as blood welled on his finger, and put the digit in his mouth to suck on the cut.

He'd tried to get Jackson to leave, making a subtle motion for Kimi to call the police, but Jackson had laughed in his face.

"Please," he'd said, settling in at the table. "I'm not breaking any laws, and they can't kick me out unless I am."

He'd slung his arms along the low back of the couch, an insolent move reminiscent of the way Sanyam took up the space of any area he was in, and it made Sterling grit his teeth as he fought to keep his temper.

"That's not how it works," he'd said, his voice even. "Your dad's a lawyer, you should know this, Jacks. You're blacklisted. They're within their rights to refuse you service *and* call the cops. The bouncer shouldn't have even let you *in*."

Jackson had openly sneered. "My father could buy and sell this place ten times over. They're lucky to have me."

A young man sashayed past, hair swept up into an elaborate do and slim body on display in a silvery dress that glittered with sequins. His long legs looked even longer with the six-inch heels he was wearing, and Jackson made a noise of disgust.

"This place was great, right up until they started letting the trannies in."

Sterling had swung without thinking, fist connecting with Jackson's nose.

He dropped the piece of glass with a hiss, staring dumbly at the gash on his palm. He'd been gripping it too tightly, he realized. *Stupid.*

Standing, he pressed his thumb against the wound as blood welled around it, and stumbled for the bathroom.

Sanyam had put the first aid kit under the sink, and Sterling fumbled it out one-handed and set it on the toilet lid.

He stared at it for a moment, flummoxed. *What now?*

Maybe he should call someone. Before he could think better of the idea, he'd dug his phone out of his pocket and dialed Sanyam's number.

"Fox? What time is it? Are you all right?" Sanyam's voice was foggy with sleep, sharpening rapidly into concern.

Sterling put the phone on speaker and set it on the sink, ignoring the blood smears. "I... cut my hand."

"How bad is it? Is it deep enough to see bone? Should I come over?"

"*No*," Sterling protested. "It's just a cut, I'm fine, I just… I don't know how to bandage it. Look, I'm sorry, forget it. I'll… go to the ER or something."

"Just a moment."

There were rustling noises, like Sanyam was sitting up in bed and then speaking in a low voice to someone.

Sterling squeezed his eyes shut. Of course Sanyam had a partner. Sterling was an idiot, why had he done this—

He was groping for the phone to turn it off when Sanyam came back.

"Sorry about that," he said. "My cat didn't appreciate being disturbed."

He had a cat. Sterling couldn't figure out if he was more relieved or embarrassed by his own reaction.

"Okay, has the bleeding stopped?" Sanyam asked.

Sterling poked at it with a cautious fingertip. "Mostly?" he said, as blood oozed sluggishly. "I think I just started it again."

Sanyam sighed. "You *do* need a minder. All right, run it under cool water until the water runs clear and your skin is clean."

Sterling turned the water on and hissed through his teeth as it made contact with the wound.

"I know," Sanyam said, his deep voice reassuring through the haze of pain sparking in Sterling's mind. "It hurts, I know, but keep it there. Don't move, kit. Hold your hand steady. You can do it."

Sterling kept the whimper locked in the back of his throat, holding his wrist with his good hand as the blood swirled away down the drain.

"You're doing really well," Sanyam said after a minute. "Just a little longer."

"How—do you know?" Sterling managed through gritted teeth, closing his eyes. "You're not even—*here.*"

"You think I don't know you by now?" Sanyam said, amusement in his voice. "You're running the cut under the tap, and those long fingers of yours are likely wrapped around your wrist to hold yourself in place as you wait."

Sterling was silent, and Sanyam laughed, quietly triumphant.

"It's all right, kit. How's it looking?"

"Water's running clear," Sterling said, peering at the cut. The edges were clean, and it was oddly fascinating to see how the glass had sliced through the layers of skin.

"Good," Sanyam said. "Turn the water off and very gently pat your hand dry with a *clean* towel."

"What kind of slob do you think I am?" Sterling demanded as he obeyed.

Sanyam's laugh was rich and easy and made Sterling's mouth tug upward as he pulled a towel from the linen closet and gingerly dried his hand.

"Now what?"

"How deep is it?"

"It's not the Marianas Trench," Sterling said as he stood in the middle of his bathroom, feeling suddenly ridiculous.

"Can you move your fingers?"

"It *hurts*," Sterling protested.

"I know, kit, but I need to be sure you haven't cut any tendons. Move your fingers for me. Touch each one to your thumb."

Sterling gritted his teeth and obeyed, breathing hard through his nose. His hand ached sharply, but he moved his fingers, touching the tip of each to his thumb before sagging in relief.

"I did it. I—look, I'll be fine."

"Oh no," Sanyam said. "I'm not leaving you to handle this alone now. Do you think you'll need stitches?"

Sterling shrugged before he remembered Sanyam couldn't see him. "I don't… think so? Not exactly a doctor, though."

"Send me a picture," Sanyam ordered.

Why hadn't he thought of that? Sterling

obeyed, grimacing at the blood on the sink as he picked the phone up. He was half tempted to take a picture with his middle finger extended, but it still hurt to move his hand, so instead he just angled the phone and sent the picture.

Sanyam hummed approval. "Good," he said, and why did that make Sterling's chest feel warm and tight? "It looks clean. You did well, kit. I don't think you'll need stitches. Get a piece of gauze from the box and put it in place over the open wound, then wrap a bandage around it. Use a piece of medical tape to secure the end. Don't pull the bandage too tight—losing circulation in your hand would be infinitely worse for you than a scar."

Sterling put the phone back down to obey.

"What were you doing, anyway?" Sanyam asked as Sterling struggled to open the gauze with one hand and his teeth. "How did you manage to cut yourself at nearly four o'clock in the morning?"

Sterling shrugged again as he wrapped the bandage in place. "I was… messing around. Remember that stuff of Cricket's I broke? I guess I was playing with the pieces."

"You're a walking disaster," Sanyam said, and there was, impossibly, affection in his voice. "First your foot, then your forehead, now your hand—what's next?"

"I'm not *completely* helpless," Sterling said, nettled.

"I know you're not." Sanyam yawned, a muffled noise. "Sorry."

"I woke you," Sterling said. "Go back to bed."

"Will you be all right?"

"Yeah," Sterling said, admiring his bandage job. "I'll be fine."

"Fox," Sanyam said, voice suddenly serious. "I didn't say it earlier, and I should have—I'm proud of you."

Sterling was stunned into silence, gawping at the phone. "You what?" he finally managed.

"I'm proud of you," Sanyam repeated. "You stood up for Delfia tonight. You did the right thing at a cost to yourself. You did well, Fox."

"I—" Sterling couldn't think of anything to say as a hot flush crawled up his chest and throat.

"Go back to bed," Sanyam said. "I'll come over and check your bandage tomorrow. How's that? Good night, kit."

Sterling hung up and stared at his phone. He still wasn't sleepy, though, and he'd had a sudden idea what he could do with the shattered glass.

He headed for the living room, already plotting out what he'd need.

— · —

He was fifteen years old, just coming to grips with his sexuality and terrified of what it would mean for his future.

"Happy birthday!" Cricket held out a brightly wrapped package, and Sterling eyed it skeptically.

"What is it?"

"Open it and find out, you idiot!"

Sterling took it and ripped the paper off to reveal a puzzle box inside, the cover proudly touting that it was "the hardest puzzle on the market."

"Edgeless pieces?" Sterling said, looking up. "And how come there's no picture on the box? How am I supposed to know what I'm making?"

Cricket smiled at him. "That's the whole point! You're smart; you'll figure it out."

Yates snorted. "Puzzles. You should be thinking about your college education, where you want to attend university, not playing with puzzles."

Sterling clutched the box to his chest. "Thanks, Cricky. I love it."

— · —

He woke to the sound of his phone ringing and realized he'd dozed off waiting for the craft store to open.

It was his father.

"*Have you completely lost your mind?*"

His voice reverberated through Sterling's head, making his teeth hurt, and he nearly dropped the phone as he sat up.

"I—Dad? What are you talking about?"

"I got a call from Noble Whittier this morning," Yates hissed, fury thickening his words. "Guess what he had to say about you?"

Sterling froze. "Oh."

"Yes," Yates mocked. "'Oh.' What the fuck were you thinking, punching Jackson in the nose? You're *lucky* you're not in jail, you stupid little—" He sucked in air as Sterling closed his eyes.

"I was just—"

"Save it," Yates said. "I don't actually care. The real question is, why were you in a *sex club*?"

"I was… just seeing a friend," Sterling said, hating how small his voice was. "His shift was almost over, and I was waiting to talk to him, and Jackson was saying awful things about one of the waitresses and—"

"*So?*" Yates interrupted. "Who cares what that spoiled brat was doing? He is not my concern. *You*, however, are. You are a Reynard, and Reynards don't frequent *sex clubs*. I've let you run wild long enough. It's time for you to work for your living. Report to my office at 9:00 a.m. Let's see if we can actually get some use out of that degree I paid for, or if your head really is as empty as you act. If you don't shape up, I'm cutting you off without a penny, don't think I won't."

He hung up, and Sterling was left staring at the wall, a yawning pit in his chest.

He was still sitting there when someone knocked on the door. Sterling lifted his head, trying to focus.

Oh no. He'd forgotten about Sanyam coming over. He probably had breakfast and coffee, those damned slanted eyes smiling and kind and seeing way too much.

Sterling shoved himself off the couch and stalked for the door.

The smile slid from Sanyam's face when Sterling confronted him, his fists clenched in abortive fury, the pain from the cut only making him angrier.

"What happened?" Sanyam asked.

"Nothing," Sterling said. "Go away."

He tried to shut the door, but Sanyam put his foot in the opening and it bounced back. Sterling snarled and spun on his heel.

"Fuck off," he said over his shoulder, stalking back to the couch. He knew Sanyam had followed him into the living room, but he didn't look, sweeping the glass he'd arranged so carefully back into the box with one vicious swing of his arm.

"*Fox*," Sanyam said, shock in his voice. "What *happened?*"

"It doesn't matter," Sterling said. "My hand is fine, see?" He shoved it under Sanyam's nose.

"I'm not really worried about your hand right now," Sanyam said, eyes steady on Sterling's face.

"Yeah, well, there's nothing else *wrong*," Sterling snapped. "Why won't you take a hint? Why are you *here?*"

"I'm here because I care about you," Sanyam said quietly. "Because I want to make sure you're all right, and it's quite obvious something's wrong."

Sterling sneered as nauseating self-hate wormed under his breastbone. "Do you honestly think we shared 'a moment' or something? We had sex, pal. Nothing more. You're not my boyfriend. The next time I want it, I'll pay you for it."

Sanyam flinched, and Sterling knew, with a kind of spiteful, sick triumph, that he'd found his target.

"Something's happened," Sanyam said. "You—you weren't like this last night. You were—what changed?"

"What changed is that I came to my senses,"

Sterling said. "I was bored, okay? You were available; I wanted to experiment. I'm not a sub, so there's no reason for you to be here."

"Just like that." Sanyam's voice was flat. "We—after what we shared, you think it was still just sex?"

"I *know* it was." Sterling flung the words like knives and watched as they sliced into Sanyam's skin and burrowed deep. "You really thought someone like me would end up with someone like *you*? That's adorable. It truly is."

Sanyam's eyes were tight. "You're right," he said, his voice even more clipped than usual. "I was mistaken." He took a step away and ran his hands through his hair. "Don't come back to the club, please. You're not welcome there any longer."

Sterling lifted his chin. "As if I was planning to. Get out of my house."

Sanyam nodded sharply and turned. He closed the door quietly behind him, and Sterling sat down hard on the couch. He folded forward and clutched his knees as he struggled to breathe, his eyes stinging. *Don't you dare cry, you pathetic piece of—*

His phone buzzed, and Sterling groped for it, something like hope stirring in his chest.

But it was just his father. *One hour. Don't be late.*

Sterling scrambled to his feet and ran for the bedroom.

13

Sanyam left Sterling's apartment and went straight to the club. He stalked inside, yanking his scarf off and balling it in his fist as he strode through the empty room.

Trinity was onstage, working on a new set as her music echoed, and Kimi was behind the bar.

Kimi's eyes widened and she closed her laptop and ran to catch up. "Hey, hey, San, wait up. What's going on? You look *pissed*."

Sanyam swung toward her, and Kimi took a step back.

"Whoa, okay. What happened?"

"A spoiled, selfish brat happened," Sanyam said through his teeth. "I'm just here to do inventory and the weekly clean of the room."

"Was it that guy you've been not-seeing?" Kimi persisted, following as Sanyam turned away again. "The one from last night?"

"I'm *not* seeing him," Sanyam snapped.

Kimi held her hands up. "Okay, sure, definitely not seeing him. Let me know if I can help with anything."

Sanyam didn't reply, heading for the back with his jaw set, as Trinity let go of the pole and knelt at the end of the stage to talk to Kimi.

He spent an hour cleaning his room from top to bottom, scrubbing at the floor on his hands and knees as he fumed. *Stupid, stupid—Ava told you not to see him and you went and slept with him the same night. And look what happened. You idiot.*

Sitting back on his heels, he surveyed the room. It gleamed, spotless from his attentions, and most of his anger had dissolved. That was good, because an angry Dom was a dangerous Dom.

There had been something in Fox's eyes, a deep hurt under the fury, and Sanyam didn't know what had caused it. He *wanted* to know. He wanted to take Fox apart, dismantle him to his component parts, see what made him tick, and then put him back together. He wanted to know who had hurt him so badly and make sure that person never got close to him for the rest of Fox's life.

He shook himself. *You're never seeing him again,* he told himself. *He's not your concern any longer. He never really was, outside this room.*

His phone buzzed. It was Ava.

My office, please.

Sanyam rocked to his feet and brushed the knees of his pants off. He had a feeling he knew why she wanted to see him.

SURE ENOUGH, Ava was vibrating with fury. "Trinity told me what happened," she said flatly when Sanyam walked in. "I'm writing you up. Be glad I'm not suspending you."

Sanyam said nothing as he sat down and crossed his legs.

"What were you *thinking?*" Ava demanded. "He came to the club to see you, and you went *home* with him? Did you have sex, Sanyam? Did you actually fuck a client the same night I told you specifically not to?"

"Safe to say I wasn't thinking clearly," Sanyam said quietly. "It won't happen again, Ava."

"Better fucking not," Ava said. "You had *glowing* recommendations, a reputation as one of the best Doms in Mumbai, if not all of India. Don't make me regret hiring you."

"Are we done?"

Ava flicked a finger. "Out."

Sanyam obeyed, closing her door softly behind him and taking a deep breath.

14

———

When Sterling presented himself at his father's brokerage, he was shaved, perfectly turned out, and hating the world.

Yates inspected him with a sharp eye as Sterling flung himself into a chair and draped a leg over the armrest.

"Sit up straight, Sterling, honestly."

Sterling slouched harder, doing his best to become one with the chair.

Yates made an annoyed noise and pretended not to notice. "You'll be shadowing Donna today. She'll show you your office—you know, the one you've never even set foot in? If you have any questions, she'll answer them."

"Why can't I shadow you?" Sterling asked.

Yates pursed his mouth. "Because I'm busy."

"And Donna's not?"

Yates glared at him. "Do not make this harder on yourself than it has to be. And let me make myself perfectly clear—if you do not apply yourself to this opportunity that is being handed to you on a silver platter, you *will* find yourself without an inheritance and with as much of your trust fund cut off as I can possibly get away with."

Sterling stiffened. He'd hoped—"You wouldn't."

"Try me," Yates said, voice hard. "Get out of my office and prove to me I didn't waste an Ivy League education on you."

Sterling stood as Yates turned away. Sterling twitched his suit coat straight and stalked out into the atrium, where Donna was holding court on her usual throne.

She was a tall woman, almost Sterling's height, and some fifteen years older, crow's-feet bracketing her deceptively mild brown eyes and smile lines around her mouth.

Sterling throttled back his fury and draped himself across her tall desk. "Donna, my love, queen of my blackened heart, when are you going to give all this up and run away with me?"

Donna tossed her head, flicking dark red hair out of her face. "When you make more than your father does and can support me in the lifestyle I deserve."

Sterling clutched his chest. "Wounded to the core yet again. So where do you want me?"

"As far away from me as possible," Donna said tartly. She stood and smoothed her plum-colored gabardine dress. "Come on."

Sterling trailed behind her as she led him through the building to the opposite corner. *Also as far from Dad as possible*, he noted.

Donna pushed the door open and stood aside. Sterling wandered in, hands in his pockets, and turned in a circle, pretending to admire the stainless steel and glass.

"We'll give you the day to get settled in," Donna told him. "Explore the building, meet people, familiarize yourself with the phone system. Tomorrow, you'll start working in earnest."

Sterling shuddered.

"What did you do, anyway?" Donna asked, honest curiosity in her voice. "We had a pool going that your father would never be able to drag you through the doors of this place."

"I—" Sterling snapped his mouth shut and shrugged. "Decided it was time to grow up."

Something in Donna's expression softened. "I'll keep your father off your back while you find your feet." She patted his shoulder. "I've loaded client spreadsheets on your computer. Yates wants you to look them over, get a feel for the database and how he runs things." She hesitated. "I know you like puzzles. Maybe think of them as giant jigsaws. See how the pieces fit."

STERLING SHOWED up to the office every morning, jaw set. Donna dropped in to check on him several times throughout each day, and Sterling fought the impulse to cling to her Louboutins and beg her to rescue him.

Instead he airily told her he was fine every time she asked, making an effort to look busy when he heard her distinctive footsteps coming down the hall.

He barely saw his father, who came in early and stayed late. Sterling kept his head down and struggled to remember what he'd learned in college as he pored over spreadsheets and memorized client names, learning about slush and hedge funds, all the ins and outs of investment banking that he'd done his best to forget the second he'd received his degree.

About halfway through the second week, a thread stood out in the web he was struggling through, and Sterling reached for it, but it slicked and fuzzed away into nothing as he tried to follow it back to its source.

Intrigued, Sterling dug deeper.

Sometimes he thought he was getting somewhere, the pieces poised to click into place, and then it would all slide out of focus again, the numbers blurring in front of his eyes and other images taking shape—himself, kneeling in front of Sanyam, his hands tied behind his back, or Sanyam prowling around him on silent feet as Sterling trembled with anticipation.

He always pushed those thoughts away with a snarl, forcing himself to concentrate on the data again.

He was hunched over his desk, fighting with the numbers one day when someone knocked.

Sterling looked up, blinking.

Cricket was smiling at him. "Feel like taking lunch?"

"What are you doing here?"

"Seeing how the other half lives," Cricket said wryly. "Daddy wanted me to learn from your example, I think."

"Of a shitty son?" Sterling snapped. He shoved his hands through his hair. "Or of what a terrible worker bee I am?"

Cricket's brows rose, and she stepped inside,

swinging the door shut behind her. "Do you want to talk about it?"

"No. I want to figure out what the fuck I'm doing."

"How so?"

Sterling shook his head. "It's like… you know those 3-D pictures that were so popular a while ago? Where if you didn't look at the individual pieces, if you let your focus sort of… blur, another image would take shape within the pixels?"

"Oh yeah," Cricket said, propping her hip on the edge of the desk. "Like a Seurat painting. Are you studying 3-D art, Fox?"

Sterling pushed away from the computer with a growl, sending his chair flying. "It's *right there*," he said, flinging a hand in the direction of the monitor. "I can *almost* see it, and then I lose it again, I can't figure out what I'm doing *wrong*!"

"For one thing, you're not eating enough," Cricket said. "Your skin is doing that waxy pale thing again and you've lost weight."

"Eating is boring," Sterling said absently, rolling his chair back to the desk and resettling himself. "Go away, Cricky, I'm busy."

Cricket took a startled breath. "You haven't called me that in *years*."

"Hmm?" Sterling said, looking up. "Called you what?"

"Nothing," Cricket said. She bent and dropped a kiss on his cheek. "I'll see you this Friday on the hill for dinner."

Sterling barely noticed as she left, already sucked back into the puzzle. He was so *close*.

WHEN HE FINALLY FIGURED IT OUT, three days later, the tabs slotted into place so neatly that Sterling was left with his mouth hanging open, wondering why he hadn't seen it before.

"You fucking *idiot*," he said aloud, the sound of his voice startling in the empty office.

Sterling put his head out the door and glanced up and down the hall. The sun had set and almost everyone had left for the day. It was nearly 7.00 p.m., which meant—Sterling ducked back into the office, grabbed the thumb drive out of the port, and bolted down the hall.

Donna was at her desk, putting things to rights before leaving, and she jerked in surprise when Sterling burst in.

"What on *earth*—I thought you'd gone home ages ago!"

"Is he still here?" Sterling panted.

Donna nodded, her eyes wide and startled,

and Sterling brushed by and pushed his father's door open.

Yates was in front of the windows, suit coat off, sleeves rolled up and hands on his hips. He was speaking what sounded like Japanese to Sterling's untrained ear, a steady stream of rolling syllables, a tinny voice answering him from the phone on the desk.

Sterling hesitated and Yates turned toward him, expression of surprise melting into faint irritation and annoyance.

He said something else and cut off the speakerphone, looking at Sterling.

"Well? What's so important you had to interrupt a board meeting with Tokyo?"

Sterling squared his shoulders and held up the thumb drive. "Why?"

"Why what?" Yates snapped. "Why do we use thumb drives? Because they're efficient, Sterling."

"Why did you *do* it?" Sterling persisted. "We had enough money, didn't we?"

Yates froze in the act of putting on his jacket and very slowly straightened. "What."

"You've been embezzling," Sterling said. "*Stealing*. I know, Dad. I found the evidence. It's all right there in plain sight if you know how to look for it. The decimal points transposed, the fractions of fractions of pennies shifted into another account, one under *Mom's* name. You lied and you cheated and you *stole*, Dad. Millions of dollars. How could you?"

Yates's eyes were dangerous. "You don't know what you're talking about."

"Don't I?" Sterling challenged, taking a step forward. "Tell that to the board of directors at their next meeting, when I show them the data I've collected." He barked a laugh, the sound harsh and brittle. "I guess that degree you paid for *did* come in handy after all."

"Give me that drive," Yates said, one hand outstretched.

Sterling recoiled. "Oh no. No fucking way. It stays with me. *Why?* We were fine. We had more than enough money, and you had to go and *steal?* What is wrong with you?"

"That's *precious*, coming from you," Yates snarled. "You have no idea what it's like, running a business such as this, staying at the helm all these years when the board tries to force you into early retirement. I've been *good* to this company. I've made *profits*. Do you have any idea how much you and the twins cost me? All you've done is be an embarrassment to me, to my family name. The *money* I've spent keeping your stunts out of the press." His voice rose. "*I deserve something for myself, too!*"

Sterling took another step back as Yates rounded the desk and advanced on him.

"What are you going to do, Dad?" Sterling demanded as Yates drew near. "Are you going to hit me?"

"I'm going to *kill* you if you don't give me that fucking—" Yates lunged, and Sterling dodged sideways, eeling out of Yates's grip lightning fast.

He held up the thumb drive, betrayal and horror coating his throat, and dropped it into his pocket. "Tomorrow," he said. "Tomorrow, we're going to sit down and renegotiate my *employment* here."

He ducked away from Yates's outstretched hand again and ran, out of the office and past Donna as she stood beside her desk, phone to her ear and shock on her face. Sterling kept going, running blindly down the stairs to the ground floor as his father's words rang in his ears.

"You're dead, do you hear me? *Dead!*"

Sterling made it to his car in record time and gunned it out of the parking lot, heart hammering so hard he thought vaguely that it might leap right out of his chest.

He drove fast and careless through the streets of downtown Vancouver, weaving in and out of traffic until he was sure his father wasn't following him. Only then did he pull over into an alley and park.

He lifted his hands off the wheel, disgusted at the way they trembled as he held them up.

"Stupid, *stupid*—" Sterling punched the dashboard, hissing at the pain that blossomed in his knuckles. Tears prickled his eyelids, and he blinked them fiercely away. *You will not cry.*

Sterling rubbed his face, swallowing hard, and pulled the thumb drive from his slacks. It lay in his palm, a small oblong with the ability to ruin lives hidden within its plastic casing.

Sterling closed his fingers over it convulsively. What had he been thinking, threatening to blackmail his father so he didn't have to work a job he hated? In a long history of selfish acts, this one had to reign supreme.

He couldn't keep this information secret. The board of directors at the very least needed to know, and the police would have to be involved. His father had to answer for what he'd done.

Sterling caught his breath on a sob. "I don't want to," he whispered, his voice thick, but no one answered.

Tomorrow. Tomorrow he'd call Ainsley Rose, the head of the board of directors, and tell her what had happened. *First thing in the morning,* he decided, and put the car in gear.

15

Sterling was relieved to see Adam on duty in the foyer of his apartment building. Adam was the most discreet, the most trustworthy, and the one least likely to be bribed or threatened into anything. He was also, Sterling suspected, who had kept letting Sanyam up into the building.

He was half propped against the desk, perusing a magazine, but he perked up as Sterling came inside. "Evening, Mr. Reynard! Working late tonight?"

Sterling nodded. "Adam, listen—if I tell you something, can I rely on you to keep it to yourself?"

"Of course, Mr. Reynard," Adam said, his shoulders subtly squaring and head going up.

"My dad and I had a fight this evening," Sterling said. He waved off the look of concern on Adam's face. "I'm fine. I just… don't want to be disturbed. Can I trust you to keep *anyone* from knocking on my door tonight?"

Guilt flickered over Adam's expressive face, confirming Sterling's hunch. "Doesn't your father own your apartment, Mr. Reynard?"

Sterling peeled off three hundred-dollar bills from his roll and pressed them into Adam's hand. "I think you'll find that the lease is in my name. In the morning, you'll get the same if I'm not disturbed tonight."

Adam bobbed his head. "Yes sir, Mr. Reynard. No one gets up. You'll have the place to yourself."

"I knew I could count on you," Sterling said. "Buy your little girls something nice." He turned and headed for the elevator, steps suddenly dragging as the adrenaline of the evening wore off.

He wanted to sleep for a *month*.

Sterling leaned his head against the glass of the elevator, remembering how Sanyam had ridden up with him that night, what felt like forever ago.

"I fuck everything up."

He'd been warning Sanyam, too drunk and exhausted to better articulate what he was trying to say, and in the end, it hadn't mattered. Sanyam had touched him and Sterling's resolve had fled like shadows at dawn, fleeting wisps under Sanyam's gentle hands.

The elevator dinged, startling Sterling out of his restless doze. He straightened and dragged his keys from his pocket as he stumbled for his apartment. His bed sounded like the best idea in the world.

He plugged in his phone, set it to silent, and fell face-first across the bed.

Somewhere around 3:00 a.m., Sterling was jerked out of sleep by a heavy pounding on the door.

Swearing, he nearly fell off the bed in his haste to get up, and he was halfway through the apartment before he realized he was still wearing yesterday's clothes, rumpled and wrinkled.

The knocking sounded again, even louder and more insistent.

"God*dammit*, Adam!" Sterling snarled as he jerked the door open.

Adam was on the other side, wringing his hands, guilt and misery all over his face. Standing behind him were two men in greatcoats.

"I'm sorry, Mr. Reynard," Adam said. "But they have *badges*."

Sterling stared at the ID that the first man held out. It took him several tries to focus on it.

Gulden, it read in small script at the bottom, below *Royal Canadian Mounted Police.*

"You don't have a horse," Sterling said before his brain caught up.

Gulden didn't smile. He was short, barrel-chested, and in his midforties, with a face that had seen its share of sun, judging by the fanning of lines around his eyes.

"Mr. Sterling Reynard?" he asked. "Detective David Gulden, this is Detective Reece Laplante. May we come in?"

"If you must," Sterling said. He stepped aside to let the officers into the apartment but caught Adam's arm as he tried to slip away and pressed several more bills into his hand.

When he turned, the officers were facing him, their eyes sober.

"Sir," Gulden said. "Have you checked your phone recently?"

"I've been asleep," Sterling said. A thought struck him, his brain still foggy with sleep-deprivation, and he straightened. "Is this about the thing?"

Gulden and Laplante exchanged a glance.

"Thing, sir?" Gulden said.

"The thing," Sterling said. "You know, the thing with my father. Is that what this is about?"

"It is safe to say there is indeed a thing with

your father that we need to discuss with you," Gulden said carefully. "Could you elaborate on what that thing might be?"

Sterling rubbed his face, still half-asleep. "The… fight. This evening, at work—did Donna call you?"

"No, sir, Donna didn't call us," Gulden said. "What fight are you referring to?"

Sterling flipped a hand. "It's not important. If that's not why you're here, then why don't you stop playing games and *tell* me?"

Laplante nodded.

Gulden spoke. "Sir, we are very sorry to report that your father was killed in a car accident this evening. Take all the time you need to process this information—we understand how much of a shock it must be."

Sterling's world tilted on its axis. Gulden's lips were still moving, but all sound had been replaced by a dull buzzing noise.

Sterling shook his head, trying to clear it.

"That's—that's impossible. I saw him a few hours ago."

Gulden glanced at Laplante again and inclined his head a fraction. "Yes, sir, so we have been led to understand. If I may, where were you this evening between the hours of seven and midnight?"

Sterling reeled, catching himself on the mantelpiece. "You think *I*—you think I had something to *do* with it? But—wasn't it an accident?"

"There were several things about the scene that raised… questions. We just need your whereabouts so we can remove you from suspicion," Gulden said smoothly.

Sterling tightened his grip on the mantelpiece, until his knuckles protested the strain. "I was—I was here. I worked late. I came straight home."

"And can anyone corroborate that?"

"Adam—" Sterling pried his fingers free and sank into the nearby chair. He looked up. "Adam saw me when I came in. I talked to him."

"And before you left the office?" Gulden asked, settling on the couch opposite and resting his elbows on his knees. His hands dangled between his legs, big and strong and square, and Sterling suddenly missed Sanyam with a desperation that bordered on a physical ache.

He struggled to marshal his thoughts. "I—we fought. At the office."

Gulden's face told him this wasn't news. "Perhaps it's time to tell us what you fought about, sir."

"Money," Sterling whispered, his lips numb. "He was stealing it. Embezzling from the company. Millions of dollars over time, in fractions of percentages, that no one would ever miss, apparently, unless they knew what they were looking for."

"And how did *you* know?" Gulden asked.

Sterling shrugged helplessly. "Donna gave me client databases. Said to familiarize myself with them, learn the numbers, get comfortable with them. She said something about… looking for patterns. I didn't know what she meant, but I've known her all my life. She knows I like puzzles; I figured she was just trying to keep me engaged." He glanced up. "Why are you asking me about this now? Do you think this was more than an accident?"

"What happened to your hand, sir?" Gulden asked.

Reminded, Sterling glanced down. His knuckles were bruised, he realized with faint surprise. "I—punched my dashboard."

"Do that a lot, do you?" Laplante asked. "Lash out in anger, I mean."

"Only on days I find out my father's an embezzling bastard," Sterling snapped. He pushed himself upright and stumbled for the bedroom. His phone was on the charger, still set to silent. He'd missed twelve calls and several dozen texts, he realized, his stomach sinking.

Cricket had called at least five times, leaving three messages. Dorian had called twice and left one. His mother had only called once. No messages from her.

Sterling couldn't seem to make his legs work properly, but somehow he made it back to the living room, where Gulden and Laplante were waiting.

"How did it happen?" Sterling asked. He couldn't feel his fingers. He wiggled them experimentally.

"We don't have all the details yet," Gulden said.

Sterling made an impatient motion. "Tell me what you *do* know, then."

"He was driving on the freeway," Laplante said, his voice matter-of-fact. There was no sympathy in his tone, and Sterling was dimly grateful for that.

Laplante continued. "From what we can gather, he lost control or his brakes failed. Either way, the end result was the same. He was involved in a collision at approximately 95 kph, although we'll know more when the troopers finish processing the scene."

The scene. The scene where my father died, crushed in a mangled heap of bloody, twisted steel.

Sterling's knees buckled, and Gulden lunged, guiding him to the chair.

"Easy, son," he said. "Head down, deep breaths."

"I want to see him," Sterling managed.

"Your mother identified the body," Laplante said. "I would recommend you wait a day. If you still want to see him before he's interred, we can arrange that."

"Mom," Sterling whispered. "I need—where is she? I have to see her."

"She's… sedated," Gulden said.

"Cricket," Sterling said. "And Dorian—are they okay?"

"They're understandably very shaken," Laplante said. "We can take you to the house if you would like."

Sterling nodded and stood, pausing as a thought hit him. "*Am* I a suspect?"

Laplante and Gulden shared a glance, silent communication passing between them in the lift of Gulden's eyebrow and the tiny shake of Laplante's head.

"Not at this time," Gulden said finally. "It appears to have been an accident. But you understand we have to rule out all other possibilities."

"Let's go," Sterling said. "I want to see my family."

16

─────

One month later

"What do you mean, it's all gone?" Alice said, her voice shrill. She was all in black, a handkerchief held to her face and the tip of her nose pink from crying.

Noble Whittier squirmed in his seat. They were in the Reynard library, gathered to hear the reading of the will. Sterling was sitting on the couch beside Cricket with Dorian on her other side, unable to quite believe what he was hearing.

"Your husband siphoned millions of dollars from hundreds of investors, Alice. They all want their money back. In addition, he left behind staggering amounts of debt that must be paid."

Alice waved the handkerchief. "So sell some of the antiques. They're worth a fortune."

"Believe me, they'll have to be sold," Noble said. He was a stuffy man, short and stocky, with square fingers and a pugnacious jaw. "As will the house, the vehicles, the yacht, and Sterling's apartment. From my calculations, if you liquidate 95 percent of your physical assets, you'll be able to pay off the debts."

Cricket gasped, and Dorian swore viciously under his breath. Sterling didn't move, frozen to his seat. This couldn't be happening. Bad enough he'd killed his father. Now this? He stared at Noble, whose lips were still moving, but Sterling couldn't hear over the buzzing in his ears.

Alice was openly weeping into her dainty linen handkerchief. "There has to be *something* you can do!"

Noble shifted his weight again. "I'm doing everything I can, Alice. I promise. But you need to start making arrangements to sell your valuables and contact a Realtor to put the house on the market."

"What about the trust funds?" Alice asked, lifting her head. "Couldn't we use those?"

"The trust funds are tied up in so much red tape that they're basically untouchable," Noble said. "I suppose it's possible that once they're freed, you could use the balances to pay off the bulk of the debts, but that'll be *years*, Alice, there's no telling how long it will take."

Dorian patted Cricket's knee. "You can stay with me and Tatum. It's a one-bedroom, but if you don't mind sleeping on the couch, it'll work."

Sterling stood up, and everyone turned to look at him. "I have to—I can't—" He swallowed around the lump in his throat. "I have to go."

"*Good*," Alice said, the sudden venom in her voice shocking. "This is your fault anyway. I can't believe you *did* this. We were doing fine, and you went and rocked the boat. How *could* you?"

"Mom!" Cricket protested, reaching for Sterling's hand, but he pulled away.

"She's right," he said. "I fucked it all up." He hesitated, looking at his mother, her slim shoulders bowed and shaking as she wept. "I'm sorry, Mom."

Alice didn't answer, and after a moment, Sterling nodded and left.

In his Lamborghini, he called Colby.

"Hey, man!" Colby's voice was too loud, overly cheerful in that way he had when he knew his friends weren't. "Been too long! How you holding up?"

"Can I sleep on your couch for a couple of weeks?" Sterling asked abruptly.

Colby hesitated. "You losing your apartment?"

"Have to sell it to pay Dad's debts," Sterling said. "Can I?"

"Maybe for a week or so," Colby said, doubt in his voice. "But you know how my girlfriend is, man. She—"

"She doesn't like me, I know," Sterling said. *I don't much like her either.* "A week would be fine. I'll be there tonight, okay?"

"Sure, sure," Colby said, clearly relieved that Sterling wasn't going to make it difficult. "I'll throw some steaks on the grill. We can have some beer; be like college again!"

"Sounds good," Sterling said. "Thanks, Col, you're a good guy."

"Hey, I just wish I could let you stay longer. But get your skinny ass over here. Let's get shitfaced!"

Sterling hung up and dropped the phone on the passenger's seat. He smoothed a reverent hand over the rich red leather. He'd had the Lamborghini almost exactly a year, a twenty-third birthday present from his father. It felt like a lifetime, but not long enough, either.

"I'll miss you," he said aloud, touching the dent he'd put in the dashboard. Sighing, he put the car in gear and headed for his apartment.

Halfway there, he changed directions and

went to the office instead. He'd left several things there that he wanted, if they hadn't been seized as evidence.

He was startled to see Donna at her desk when he walked in.

Donna's eyes welled with tears, and she dashed around the desk to hug him.

"I'm so sorry," she wept into his neck. "I'm so sorry, Fox, *so sorry*. If I'd known, I never would have—"

Sterling froze in the act of patting her gingerly on the back. "What?"

Donna pulled away, her face blotchy and nose running. "When I gave you those files," she said through her sniffles. "I didn't *know*—"

"What are you *talking about?*" Sterling demanded. "Gave me the files?"

Donna nodded, plucking a tissue from the box on her desk and wiping her nose. "I suspect-ed," she said, her voice muffled. "I thought—I mean, I didn't have any *evidence*, but I had this feeling… like maybe your father wasn't playing by the rules, you know? And when he told me to give you some client files so you could get comfortable with the database, I thought—"

"You thought maybe I'd figure it out," Sterling whispered, blood running cold.

"I swear, if it had been anything more than a

gut instinct, I would have *said* something!" Donna cried. "I just thought, if there *was* something there and you found it, then well and good, and if you didn't, then no harm done, right?"

Her eyes beseeched him to understand, but Sterling couldn't move, couldn't reassure her that it was okay. He didn't blame her. All he could see were the photos someone had leaked to the press of his father's mangled car, the lurid headline that screamed *Yates Reynard Dead After Embezzling Millions.*

"I have to… I was just picking up some stuff," he managed.

Donna nodded again, more tears running down her face, and Sterling fought through the shock to reach out, grab her, and pull her into a hug.

She clutched at his shirt as another sob shook her slim frame.

"It's not your fault," Sterling said, blinking back his own tears.

"Not going to s-stop me from b-blaming myself," Donna managed, hiccupping.

"I know," Sterling said. He patted her on the back and let her go. "You'll come to the funeral, right?"

"I wasn't sure you'd want me there," Donna said.

"You're practically family," Sterling told her. "Of *course* we want you there."

"Okay," Donna whispered, giving him a watery smile. "I'll come, then."

WHEN STERLING GOT BACK to the apartment, he packed everything he couldn't live without. It made a depressingly small pile, he realized, staring at his two suitcases filled with clothes and very little else. He rolled them to the door, wrote a note explaining the situation for Astrid and a letter of recommendation for future employers, and went back for the box of broken glass.

Finally he took one last look around the spotless apartment. He'd eaten curry at the table with Sanyam, fallen asleep on the couch beside him, slept with his face pressed to Sanyam's hip after the second sub drop—Sterling shook himself. Maybe someday he'd examine why his only real memories of the place were when Sanyam was with him, but his cab was waiting for him. He left the keys in the bowl and closed the door behind him.

Colby bounded outside when Sterling's cab pulled up. He lived in a Spanish-style villa, stucco roof glowing in the setting sun. His girlfriend,

Annaliese, stood in the door as Colby helped him haul the suitcases up the sidewalk.

Sterling smiled at Annaliese, unable to shake her hand with his arms full of Cricket's glass. "Thanks for having me."

Annaliese shrugged, unsmiling, a tall, slim girl with blue eyes too big for her face and brown hair pulled back in a messy ponytail. "It's Colby's house." She stepped aside and let them enter.

Sterling hid his flinch and followed Colby down the dark hall to the guest bedroom, where Colby set the suitcases down and took the box of glass fragments from him.

"What's in here?" he asked curiously as it clinked.

"Broken glass," Sterling said. "Is staying here going to be a problem?"

Colby waved his question away. "Nah, man. Liese'll come around. She just likes to have me to herself. Honeymoon phase, or whatever they call it when you're not actually married." He grinned and flopped onto the bed, his blond hair a bright contrast to the purple-and-blue quilt spread out under him.

Sterling moved into the room, trailing a finger across the desk in the corner. "I won't stay long. Just have to... find a job. Maybe Tatum and Dorian will let me sleep on their floor for a bit."

He forced a smile as Colby propped himself on his elbows, looking worried. "I'll be fine," Sterling said. "Really. This is just temporary."

"I'll talk to Liese," Colby said. "Maybe I can bring her around to you staying two weeks. Hey, your birthday's coming up, isn't it?"

Sterling stopped and thought. "Yeah, actually."

"Perfect," Colby said. "I'm gonna throw you the best birthday bash ever."

"Oh God," Sterling said, cringing. "Please don't."

Colby sat up and cocked his head. "The Sterling I know and love was an attention-hog. Where'd he go, and how do I get him back?"

Sterling sat down on the bed beside him, running his hands through his hair. "I'm… I'm just feeling kind of raw, Col. Nothing personal."

"Are you seeing anyone right now?"

Dark, slanted eyes that saw too much and judged me for none of it. A neatly cropped beard, curly black hair, and teeth that flashed white when he smiled.

"Every time I turn around," Sterling said.

"Huh?"

"Nothing," Sterling said, plastering another fake smile on his face. "Not seeing anyone right now."

Colby was watching him closely. "You think you'll ever be okay with being openly gay?"

Sterling stiffened. "Can I help with dinner?"

"Sure," Colby said, accepting the redirection and bouncing to his feet. "How are you at tossing a salad?"

That surprised Sterling into genuine laughter as he stood, making Colby punch the air in victory.

17

Sanyam was having a bad day. It had started with a couple that had claimed to be experimenting with dominance and submission, and wanted him to show them the ropes. That had been fine—Sanyam genuinely enjoyed showing baby Doms how to take control and teaching them to explore their subs.

But he'd realized quickly that the "Dom" was nothing more than a petty abuser, getting his kicks by hurting his girlfriend, who clearly wanted him to stop but was afraid to safeword.

Sanyam had thrown the man out and dried the woman's tears as he did his best to explain the difference between dominance and abuse, but she was too worried about her boyfriend's feelings to listen to him and bolted soon after to find him.

After that, the evening had quickly gone downhill, with several subs wanting things that were hard limits for Sanyam. He hated having to explain why he wouldn't touch certain kinks, and it rarely went well.

So when there was a timid knock on his door, Sanyam was grumpy. The irritation dissolved immediately at the sight of Eleanor on the other side, though, a hopeful smile on her round face.

Sanyam smiled back, surprised and delighted. "Hello, Eleanor. How are you?"

"I'm doing so great," Eleanor told him, clutching her purse as Sanyam stepped back to let her in.

"What would you like to do this evening?" Sanyam asked.

"Oh, I'm not here to scene," Eleanor said earnestly. "I just… I wanted to thank you. Since I saw you last, I've signed up for speed dating and I'm going on dates and having fun and I don't blame myself anymore for my husband leaving me. I know you didn't 'fix' me, but you started me on the path, and I just…." Her eyes filled with tears. "Thank you so much."

Overwhelmed, Sanyam gathered her into a hug. "I'm so glad," he said into her hair. It smelled like honeysuckle. "Take care of yourself, won't you?"

"I will," Eleanor said as she stepped back and smiled up at him.

Sanyam's phone buzzed.

"I have to go anyway," Eleanor said. "Nanette—you remember Nanette? She's taking me out tonight. We're celebrating my divorce being finalized."

She smiled at him again and left, and Sanyam picked up his phone.

Kimi: *You might want to get out here.*

Sanyam swore and ran for the front. It was the usual cacophony of music so loud it was impossible to be heard over, but there didn't appear to be any disturbances. He headed for the bar, where Kimi was talking to Delfia, her mouth close to Delfia's ear.

They both looked up when Sanyam got near, and Kimi dropped a kiss on Delfia's cheek before turning to him.

"What's going on?" Sanyam asked over the music.

"Table just seated, far corner," Kimi said. "One of them is blindfolded—I think it's a surprise party for him, but he looks like… well, just see for yourself."

Sanyam turned to look in the direction she indicated. He recognized Colby instantly, the slim girl beside him unfamiliar, but on his other side,

Fox's long throat and perfect jaw were unmistakable even with the blindfold that covered his eyes.

Sanyam watched, unable to look away, as Colby pulled the blindfold off and made a grand gesture, grin stretching his mouth.

Horror flashed over Fox's face, and he said something.

Colby looked confused and shook his head, asking a question.

Fox slid from the booth in one fluid motion but froze in place when he caught Sanyam's eyes across the room.

Sanyam moved toward him, winding between the tables as he held Fox's gaze. Fox seemed trapped, his fingers twitching spasmodically against his leather pants as Sanyam drew steadily nearer.

Sanyam stepped right into his space, bodies almost touching. Fox's eyes were wide and scared, his lips wet and a flush creeping up his neck.

"I didn't know," he said hoarsely.

Sanyam couldn't stop looking at him. He'd missed Fox more than he'd even realized, the fear and guarded wariness on Fox's mobile face only serving to make Sanyam ache to touch him, soothe away the pain that was written all over Fox's slender frame.

"Is there a problem?" Colby asked from

behind Fox. "Hey, I know you. You were the guy who kicked Jacks out that time."

"I'm leaving," Fox said, tipping his chin up as a hint of defiance crept into his eyes. "I know you don't want me here. I'm gone."

Sanyam caught his wrist, Fox's pulse fast and thready under Sanyam's fingers. "You're not going anywhere," he said below the music, just loud enough for Fox to hear. He glanced at Colby and the strange girl. "I need to speak to Fox alone. Your drinks are on me for the night."

He turned and pulled Fox through the crowd before Colby could speak, weaving his way around drunken patrons until they were in the back hall.

Fox balked briefly. "What—"

"Privacy," Sanyam said, not breaking stride. "We have things to talk about."

He wasn't holding Fox tightly, and Fox could have pulled away at any time, but instead he followed him into the room and wrapped his arms around his ribs as Sanyam closed the door behind them.

"I didn't know what Colby had planned," Fox said when Sanyam turned back to him. "If I'd known, I wouldn't have—"

Sanyam put a finger to Fox's lips, drinking in the sight of him. "You look *terrible*," he said. Fox had lost weight he couldn't afford, his cheeks almost hollow and his skin waxen and pale under the warm light of the room.

Fox's face shuttered and he turned his head away. "I'm fine."

Sanyam caught his chin and gently pulled his face around. Fox's lips parted, and he took a shaky breath and swayed into Sanyam's touch.

"What happened?" Sanyam said.

"I lost—I lost everything," Fox whispered. "My dad—" To Sanyam's horror, Fox's face crumpled, and he jerked away, swiping at his eyes.

"Sofa." Sanyam pointed. Fox followed him to it and sank onto the cushions, drawing his knees to his chest. Sanyam settled opposite him, carefully not touching. "Tell me," he said gently.

"My dad was embezzling," Fox said in a tone so low Sanyam had to lean forward to hear him. "I—found out. I threatened him—told him I was going to tell everyone. And then he died. We lost the house. The yacht. My apartment. My *car*."

"I read about his death and the embezzlement in the papers," Sanyam said, fighting the impulse to touch Fox's knee.

Fox stiffened. "If you knew, then why the fuck did you make me say it?"

"Because it's eating you up inside. I could see that the moment I laid eyes on you," Sanyam said.

"You needed to say it, understand it's not your fault."

Fox gave him a scornful look. "I know that."

"Perhaps with your head," Sanyam said. "But this is not something cool logic can explain away. Your father did bad things, and you were the one to uncover them. He died shortly thereafter. Of course you blame yourself. Where are you staying?"

Fox closed his eyes. "I was staying with Colby, but his girlfriend doesn't like me—my two weeks are up tomorrow, and I have to find somewhere else. I told them I had a place. I lied. Dorian and Tatum don't have room for me—they're in a studio apartment, and Cricket's already staying with them. I don't—" His voice cracked. "I don't know what to do."

"You'll come home with me," Sanyam said. He hadn't thought before he spoke, but somehow he knew immediately it was the right thing to say.

Fox jerked upright, his eyes widening. "*What?* No, I can't."

"Why not?"

"Because… because… I barely know you!"

"Do you trust me?" Sanyam asked.

Fox hesitated and nodded reluctantly.

Sanyam stood and held out his hand. "Stay as long as you need, leave whenever you want, once you've found a job and a place. Let me help you, Fox."

Fox swallowed hard and took his hand, unfolding himself, and followed Sanyam out the door.

THEY CAUGHT A CAB QUICKLY, and the ride to his apartment was silent. Fox sent a text and after, kept his hands neatly tucked together in his lap.

"Did you let Colby know?" Sanyam asked.

Fox nodded. "He said to text me your address and he'll drop my things off tomorrow." His profile was starkly outlined in the lights they passed beneath, tension evident in his muscles.

Sanyam scooted away to put more room between them and keep Fox from feeling crowded. It worked—Fox relaxed in increments as they rolled through the streets of downtown Vancouver, until they pulled up in front of Sanyam's building and Fox stiffened again.

"You can leave whenever you want," Sanyam repeated, holding Fox's gaze.

Fox nodded again, chewing on his lip, and climbed out of the cab.

18

Sterling followed Sanyam up the stairs to the apartment. Sanyam was quiet as he unlocked the door and ushered Sterling through, flicking a switch that illuminated running lights set into the floor.

It was a big, open space Sterling stepped into, the kitchen on his right and the living room in front of him stretching out with a view over the waterfront.

From somewhere in the building, tiny feet hit the floor. The cat was meowing before she turned the corner, ears pricked and plumed tail in the air as she welcomed Sanyam, who laughed and bent to scoop her up.

"Hello, my darling. We have a visitor. Fox, this is Polly. Polly, meet Fox."

Sterling eyed the cat skeptically and made no move to pet her.

"You're not allergic, are you?" Sanyam asked.

"No idea," Sterling said. He wandered farther into the room. A long, low couch sat under the window, and Sterling ran a finger along the leather upholstery. "Will I be sleeping here?"

"If you really want to," Sanyam said, amusement in his voice as he set Polly down and put a kettle on the stove. "But I thought perhaps you'd prefer my guest bedroom. Do you drink tea?"

Sterling shrugged. His nerves were besting him, making him uneasy and off-balance, and he couldn't figure out what to do with his hands. Finally he shoved them into his pockets and hunched his shoulders.

"Have a seat," Sanyam said without looking. His long fingers were quick and deft as he put teabags in cups and got out milk and sugar from the fridge. "I hope you like PG tips." He poured the water over the bags and set the cups on a tray before carrying it to the coffee table and setting it down.

"Don't know what those are," Sterling admitted as he accepted a cup.

Sanyam feigned shock. "Haven't you ever been to England?"

"Sure." Sterling shrugged. "Mostly it was just

layovers on our way to Europe. Dad didn't like the weather." He set the cup down, and sympathy flashed across Sanyam's face.

"Do you want to tell me more about how he died?" he asked quietly.

"Car crash," Sterling said, glancing up. "He— was upset. My fault. He rear-ended a semi, died instantly."

Sanyam made an abortive gesture, as if he wanted to touch Sterling's hand, but checked himself. Polly hopped up into his lap and curled into a tight donut, purring so loudly Sterling could hear her, and Sanyam stroked her back absently, eyes on Sterling's.

"You said Cricket was with Dorian, yes?"

Sterling nodded.

"And your mother? Where is she?"

Sterling lifted a shoulder. "I didn't stop to ask, to be honest, after what she said to me at the reading of the will. I think she's with some friends until the estate gets settled." Grief prickled his eyelids again, and he blinked viciously until it receded.

"May I ask what she said?"

This is your fault anyway. I can't believe you did this. We were doing fine, and you went and rocked the boat. How could you?

"The truth," Sterling said.

Sanyam looked sad and Sterling wanted to snarl.

"*Don't*," he said.

"Don't what?"

Sterling pushed himself to his feet and took two long strides away, putting distance between them. "Don't *pity* me," he hissed, clenching his fists.

Sanyam didn't move, still stroking Polly's small frame. "But I don't. I'm sorry you suffered this catastrophic loss, Fox, of course I am. But you are not and never have been an object of pity."

"Why am I *here*?" Sterling demanded. "You— we had sex a few times. You don't even *like* me. Why would you invite me into your home like this?"

Sanyam dislodged Polly, who protested loudly, and stood up fast. Sterling flinched backward, but Sanyam was on him before he could move, crowding right up into his space as he snaked an arm around Sterling's waist to keep him still.

"I have never said I didn't like you," Sanyam said. His breath was warm and sweet on Sterling's face, his arm an iron bar holding him where he was. Sterling went limp, his brain fuzzing.

"Do you think I scene with people I don't like?" Sanyam continued. "That I have *sex* with people I don't like?" He leaned in and brushed the tip of his nose along Sterling's cheek. "Trust me, kit, you infuriate me, you annoy me, you do any number of things that make me *ache* to punish you, and I like you *very much*."

Sterling fought the whimper that wanted to slip from his mouth. He turned his head just enough to catch Sanyam's lips, tongues meeting in a soft, wet slide. Sanyam tasted like black tea and cinnamon, and Sterling could have stayed there forever. But with an iron force of will, he managed to tear himself away.

"Is that—" He stopped and swallowed. "Is that how I'm paying my rent?"

Sanyam let go so fast Sterling nearly went down. He caught himself as Sanyam took a step back, eyes angry.

"There it is," he said, running his hands through his hair. "You can't make anything easy, can you?" He sighed and the anger in his eyes faded to something closer to exasperation. "I want you, Fox, of course I do. I've never pretended otherwise. But you are under no obligation to me. If you choose to stay in my home, I will not ask anything of you but perhaps your friendship. I *am* lonely, and whatever you believe of yourself, I enjoy your company." He smiled, tilting his head. "And if you choose to come to my bed, well… that will be your choice as well."

Sterling floundered, unsure what to say, and Sanyam's eyes softened.

"It's late, and I'm tired," he said. "Let me show you where you'll be sleeping."

Sterling followed him silently down the hall to the guest bedroom. It was small and cozy, looking out over the alley.

"I took the room with the waterfront view," Sanyam said, eyes creased with amusement. "But you should be comfortable here nonetheless."

Sterling wrapped his arms around his ribs, feeling suddenly lost. "I—" He took a deep breath. "San, I need to—" How did he apologize for the horrible things he'd said last time they were together? How *could* he? Why had Sanyam even let him back into his life after the way Sterling had treated him?

His breathing shortened, and he squeezed his eyes shut, helpless to stop the panic clogging his throat. "I'm sorry," he blurted. The words burned his mouth, acrid and bitter, and he opened his eyes to Sanyam regarding him sympathetically.

"For what?"

Sterling groped for words. "For—everything, I guess. But... for what I said to you. That... time. I was angry and hurt and I didn't mean—"

Sanyam moved closer and traced the line of

Sterling's jaw. "It's forgotten," he said quietly, and fitted their lips together.

It was slow and sweet, no expectations or urgency to it, and Sterling allowed himself to melt against Sanyam's frame with a shaky breath. Sanyam held him still, hands on Sterling's shoulders, but finally drew away, bringing a hand up to thumb Sterling's dimple.

"I'm just across the hall," he said. "Help yourself to anything in the refrigerator. Cook if you like. Treat this like it's your home. All I ask is that you pick up after yourself. The bathroom is down the hall on your left. Good night, Fox."

He left, leaving the door cracked behind him, and Sterling sat down on the bed. After a minute, he tilted sideways until his head was on the pillow. It smelled like laundry detergent and crisp linen, and he drew a deep, comforting breath.

He was nine years old, the joy of life fizzing in his chest and almost impossible to contain.

"'Paro, 'Paro, come see!"

Amparo turned from the sheets she was putting on Sterling's bed and caught him in midair as he launched himself at the mattress.

"Oh no you don't," she said, tickling him as he

squirmed and giggled and kicked. "I just made that bed. You don't get to mess it up just yet!"

Sterling flailed as she danced her fingers up and down his ribs and made him convulse in helpless laughter.

When she finally stopped to let him breathe, he collapsed against her, smelling warm cotton and soap as she held him.

"What did you want to show me, esterlina?" she said, letting him stand up.

"I made something," Sterling said, grabbing her hand and pulling to urge her to her feet. "I wanna show you!"

Amparo followed him out of his bedroom and down the stairs to the main floor.

Sterling had brought in great, heaping armfuls of dried leaves and twigs, using the stark white of the marble floor to accentuate their golden and russet hues as he arranged them in a swirling vortex of color. The leaves were even arranged by shades of brown, going from dark all the way to sandy tan in a rippling curve, hemmed in and framed by the branches.

Amparo gasped. "Oh, oh Sterling, it's lovely, but your mother—"

Sterling shrugged that off. "She's busy. It took me a long time, and I made it for you. Do you like it?"

"I love it," Amparo told him, taking his hand.

"But it can't stay on the floor in here, you know that, yes?"

"I know," Sterling said. "I just made it 'cuz it was pretty. And so are you." He knelt by one of the sections of dark brown leaves. "Look, 'Paro, it's the color of your eyes."

Amparo smiled at him as footsteps sounded from above them, and someone gasped sharply.

"What have you done?"

Amparo's smile slid off her face as Sterling straightened.

"I made 'Paro something pretty, Mom!" he said.

"I'll clean it up right now, Mrs. Reynard," Amparo said. She sent Sterling a private smile as she hurried off to find the broom and dustpan, and Alice descended the stairs.

"Do you like it?" Sterling asked.

Alice's mouth was pursed, the skin around her eyes tight with contained fury. "The Wings of Courage ladies will be here any minute, Sterling, and you've turned my house into a—a pigsty!"

Sterling flinched. "I'm sorry," he whispered. "I thought it was pretty."

Amparo came back with two brooms, and stepped between Sterling and Alice. "Querido, why don't you start on that side and I'll work on this one, and we'll sweep it out together?"

Alice made an annoyed noise. "Honestly,

Amparo, we've talked about you using Spanish around the children."

"I'm sorry, Mrs. Reynard," Amparo said, sweeping industriously and dropping Sterling a wink where Alice couldn't see.

Sterling caught on and began to wield the broom vigorously, leaves and twigs flying everywhere as he "swept."

Alice coughed in the ensuing cloud of dust and beat a hasty retreat.

As soon as she was gone, Amparo and Sterling slowed down, and she smiled at him again.

"You have such an eye for color, mi amor.*"*

Sterling grinned at her and helped sweep the leaves out of the house and back into the yard where they belonged.

<hr>

HE OPENED HIS EYES, staring up at the ceiling that soared twenty feet above his head, and wondered idly where Amparo was. He'd barely even thought of her in years, not since—

Sterling rolled to his side and gazed into the hall. Sanyam's door was shut, but a light showed beneath it. Sterling wanted suddenly, desperately, to get up and pad across the hallway, to open Sanyam's door and slip inside, crawl into his bed, and let Sanyam gather him into his arms.

You're pathetic, a tiny voice jeered. *Be a man. Men don't cry. They don't need to be* comforted *like babies. What is wrong with you? Useless, weak—*

Sterling buried his face in his arm and took a shaky breath as something landed on the bed with a soft *whump*.

He propped himself on his elbows to behold Polly sitting by his feet, regarding him curiously.

"No," Sterling told her. "Go away."

Polly opened her mouth, and a tiny squeak came out.

Sterling's eyebrows climbed. "You call that a meow? You disgust me. Come back when you sound like a real cat."

Polly squeaked again and stood up to cross the bedcovers on silent feet and climb onto Sterling's stomach, where she sat down again.

"You have *got* to be kidding," Sterling said.

Polly yawned and began to purr, crystal-blue eyes half-closed. She flexed her front paws, and Sterling yelped as tiny pinprick claws kneaded his shirt rhythmically.

"I know I'm not a *nice* person," Sterling told the ceiling, "but what did I do to deserve this?"

Polly curled up and closed her eyes. The purring was surprisingly soothing, Sterling had to admit, and after a minute, he cautiously touched her with a finger. Her fur was cloud-soft, cream melting into beige into seal brown on her ears, legs, and tail, and Sterling sighed and put his head back on the pillow as he relaxed for the first time in weeks.

* * *

HE WOKE UP WITH A WARM, furry weight draped across his chest and the noise of a shower running. Ordinarily the thought of Sanyam in the shower, water droplets glistening in his hair and beard, that bitable brown skin wet and sleek, would have been more than a little diverting. But Sterling was not a morning person, so he snarled and rolled over, dislodging Polly to bury his face in the pillow.

He drifted in and out as the sun stole across the bed, and came back to consciousness when Sanyam knocked lightly on the open door.

"I made breakfast."

Sterling lifted his head and rubbed his eyes. "Not hungry."

Sanyam's lips twitched. "The shower's free. You can jump in while I set the table."

Polly *mrrp*ed at Sanyam and hopped off the bed.

"You made a friend," Sanyam observed, bending to pet her as she rubbed against his leg. "Polly usually takes a while to warm up to strangers."

Sterling made a muffled noise that could have meant anything and rolled off the bed, going up on his tiptoes to stretch. He dragged his shirt off over his head and dropped it on the floor, scratching his stomach absently as he shuffled for the bathroom. There was dead silence behind him, and it wasn't until Sterling got to the bathroom that he remembered he'd taken his pants off at some point in the night and was naked except for his silk boxers.

Serves him right for waking me up, he decided, and turned on the water.

He took his time, enjoying the heat that turned his muscles to taffy. When he stepped out, he was more alert, and hesitated when he realized he didn't have any clean clothes.

Sterling wrapped a towel around his waist and shook his damp hair out of his eyes as he opened the bathroom door and nearly tripped over a neatly folded pile of clothes on the floor. He bent and picked them up to discover a soft royal-blue T-shirt with the Canucks logo emblazoned across the front and a pair of sweatpants.

Sterling curled his lip but retreated back into the bathroom to get dressed.

When he emerged, damp and rumpled, he followed his nose to the kitchen, where Sanyam was setting out a plate of french toast next to a platter piled high with bacon.

"I thought you weren't allowed to eat pork," Sterling said, before his brain caught up to his mouth.

Sanyam's eyes creased in amusement. "I don't eat halal," he said, gesturing to a seat. "I see you found the clothes."

"It was that or eat breakfast naked," Sterling said. He sat down and stole a piece of bacon off the plate.

Sanyam made a disappointed noise. "Clearly, I didn't think that through."

Sterling fought a smile and took a bite.

"Colby will be here today with your things, correct?"

Sterling shrugged with his mouth full. "Prob'ly."

"You're not sure?"

"Colby kind of… isn't reliable," Sterling said. "If he says he's going to do something, he'll *try* to do it, but he's just as likely to get distracted by a butterfly as he is to actually follow through. He's kind of like a big, dumb puppy."

Sanyam sat down opposite him and made a motion indicating Sterling should dig in.

He did so, realizing as he filled his plate that he *was* hungry, and heaped thick slabs of french toast on top of each other.

"But he took you in," Sanyam said as Sterling took a bite. "He sounds like a good person."

"He is," Sterling said, surprised into looking up. "He's the best." *Better than me, that's for sure.*

"Are you thinking of getting a particular job?" Sanyam asked, cutting his own piece of toast into neat squares.

Sterling hunched his shoulders. "I'm—I don't know. I *need* to, but I'm not… good at anything."

"That's clearly not true," Sanyam said. "You went to college, didn't you? Got a degree?"

"In finance," Sterling muttered. "I *hate* finance. But I didn't have a choice—it was what Dad wanted, and he was paying for it. Anyway, I barely scraped through."

"Because it's not your passion." Sanyam nodded and handed Polly a tiny piece of bacon. "Well, you'll need to figure out what you're doing at some point, but it can wait. There's no rush."

"I'm not going to fucking freeload off you," Sterling snapped as fury suddenly flooded him and he threw his fork down. "I'll pay you back, okay? As soon as Dad's estate settles, I'll have a little bit. Not much, not enough to live on, but I can pay for my food at the very least, I'm not going to just be a sponge!" He pushed his chair back and stood.

"Sit down," Sanyam said flatly.

Sterling hesitated and sank back to his seat.

Sanyam's eyes were tight with irritation. "Fox, I understand that you have a multitude of issues on your mind right now. You blame yourself for your father's death, if not his misdeeds. You hate yourself, and you can't understand why anyone would ever help you, because you don't *deserve* help, in your mind. Still, that doesn't give you the right to lash out like that."

Sterling stared at his plate, and Sanyam sighed.

"I'm sorry, kit. I shouldn't have snapped. We'll figure this out, all right? Fox, look at me, please."

Sterling lifted his gaze. Sanyam was smiling, affection in his eyes.

"You can stay as long as you need," he said. "Perhaps the club is hiring. Would you be willing to work there as a server?"

"I—I don't know *how*," Sterling admitted, hot shame flooding his face.

"They would train you," Sanyam said. "If you have me recommending you, I'm sure Ava would give you a chance. You'd have to promise to work hard, though. Are you interested?"

Sterling drew in air. *Was* he interested? He had no idea what serving entailed. Surely it couldn't be too difficult, and he needed the money. He nodded.

Sanyam smiled. "I'll talk to Ava tonight."

Sterling opened his mouth and closed it again. Polly tapped his knee with one tiny paw, and he handed her a piece of egg as Sanyam picked up his own fork and took another bite.

19

"Have you lost your fucking mind?" Ava demanded before Sanyam was even through the door.

"Probably," Sanyam said calmly. "It's always been a possibility. Why do you ask?"

Ava glared, bristling with outrage. "You—you want me to hire your… your *boyfriend!* The one you were seeing after I explicitly told you not to? The one you got written up over?"

"He's not my boyfriend," Sanyam said, clearing a chair to sit down. "And yes."

Ava's jaw sagged. "You have a *nerve*," she sputtered. "Tell me why I shouldn't just fire you right now and have done with this entire nonsense."

Sanyam arched an eyebrow. "Because I'm the highest-earning performer you have, barring

Trinity on the pole. I've nearly doubled your club's revenue in the few months I've been here. You're not going to fire me. But if Fox doesn't work out, you're more than welcome to fire *him*. All I'm asking is that you consider taking him on. He's in a bad place right now. And he wouldn't be a client of mine or anyone else's here, so there'd be no conflict of interest."

"The big brass balls on you," Ava said, almost admiringly.

Sanyam smiled. "I'll take that as a compliment. So is that a yes?"

"I'm not going to go easy on him just because you think he's cute," Ava warned.

"I wouldn't expect you to," Sanyam said. He inclined his head. "Thank you. I will impress on him the importance of working hard."

"Whatever," Ava said. "Get out of here, you moneymaker."

Sanyam obeyed, smiling.

Fox had stayed behind at the house, and Sanyam was distracted all through his shift, thinking about the wounded look in his eyes, the way he didn't know what to do with his hands, or how to thank Sanyam for helping him.

He was relieved when he was done for the evening and able to catch the bus home. There was a light on in the living room when he climbed the stairs, but he eased the door open to see Fox sprawled on the couch, fast asleep, Polly snoozing on his chest.

Sanyam toed his shoes off silently and tiptoed nearer.

Fox's face was soft, his mouth lax, and he looked young and vulnerable, a piece of porcelain poised to shatter.

Perhaps he already has, Sanyam thought. He brushed Fox's hair off his forehead as Polly squeaked at him.

"Shh," Sanyam whispered.

Fox turned his face against Sanyam's hand and sighed, opening his eyes. He froze when he realized where he was, and Sanyam pulled away to pick Polly up and put her on the floor.

"It's nearly three," he told Fox, who pushed himself to a sitting position. "You should go to bed."

Resentment flickered across Fox's face. "I'm not a child."

"No, of course you're not," Sanyam said, taking a step back. "I talked to Ava. She's willing to give you a chance, but you'll have to work for it."

Fox stood and stretched, going up on tiptoe like he had that morning, and Sanyam was just as helpless against it as he'd been earlier.

He cleared his throat and turned away, stopping when he caught sight of what was spread out on the coffee table.

"Did you *make* that?" he asked, staring at the pieces of glass forming an ornate letter *C* in a rainbow kaleidoscope.

"I was just dicking around," Fox said. He bent to sweep the fragments back into the box, and Sanyam caught his arm.

"Leave it," he said, still looking at the glass. "It's lovely, Fox. I had no idea you had such an artist's eye."

Fox jerked away from Sanyam's grasp. "I don't." He stalked away, his back stiff, and Sanyam was left wondering what he'd said.

Polly followed Fox down the hall, and Sanyam suppressed a pang of envy.

"You start tomorrow," he called after Fox.

HE WOKE at his usual early hour the next morning and did his stretches under the window, warming up until his muscles were loose and easy. Stepping into his running shoes,

Sanyam bent and tied them, then crossed the hall.

Fox's door was cracked just enough that a small cat could slip through, Sanyam noted, amused.

He pushed it open a few more inches and put his head through. Fox was draped across the bed, facedown and one arm dangling off the mattress, in nothing but his boxers.

"It's a beautiful morning," Sanyam said.

Fox jerked and rolled over with a muffled grunt, presenting his sharp shoulder blades.

"Would you like to go for a run along the waterfront with me?" Sanyam asked.

Fox turned and fixed Sanyam with one bleary, baleful eye. "Burn in hell forever," he said, and rolled over again.

Sanyam managed not to laugh, biting the inside of his cheek. "I'll make us breakfast after," he persisted.

Fox threw a pillow at him and pulled the remaining one over his head.

"Suit yourself," Sanyam said, grinning, and left him to it.

When he came back from his run, sweating

and pleasantly exhausted, Fox was stumbling out of his bedroom, still in only his boxers, his eyes squeezed shut against the light.

Sanyam stopped dead to avoid bumping into him, but Fox didn't seem to notice. He made a weaving line for the bathroom, the thin silk showing the curve of his ass as the sun haloed him.

Sanyam just managed to keep his groan internal as the bathroom door closed. He wasn't going to survive this.

20

———

That night, Sterling stood in front of the mirror in the bathroom, glaring at his reflection. "This is going to end horribly," he mumbled, smoothing his pants. He jumped as Sanyam knocked on the door.

"We need to go, or we'll miss the bus, Fox."

Sterling growled silently but opened the door.

Sanyam's eyebrows went up. "Well. I approve."

Sterling fought the urge to smooth the leather pants again. His shirt clung to his frame, and he felt exposed suddenly, rethinking every life decision he'd had.

"You look very nice, Fox," Sanyam said. The heat in his eyes made Sterling swallow, but he said nothing, running a hand that shook only a little through his hair as he scowled at Polly, who was rubbing against his ankle.

"Come on," Sanyam said, stepping aside. "The bus will be here in just a few minutes."

"Why are we taking public transportation again?" Sterling asked, giving Polly a furtive scratch behind the ears before following him down the hall. "What's wrong with cabs?"

"They're prohibitively expensive," Sanyam said over his shoulder. "It makes no sense financially. The bus is far less costly."

Prohibitively expensive, Sterling mouthed to himself, rolling his eyes. Sanyam turned, and Sterling jerked, trying to look innocent.

"Unless you still have your Lamborghini," Sanyam said.

Sterling glared. "Fuck you."

Sanyam just shrugged and opened the door for him. "Be good, Polly," he called, and locked the door.

"Oh my God, you say goodbye to your stupid cat," Sterling said, snickering as he jogged down the stairs. "That is the *nerdiest* thing I've ever heard."

THE BUS RIDE WAS TORTURE, smelling vaguely

of sauerkraut and the seats small and cramped. The one upside was that Sterling was squeezed in against Sanyam, his muscled thigh hard against Sterling's nervously jiggling one.

A baby was crying farther up the aisle, and Sterling squeezed his eyes shut as the reality of the situation rushed over him and panic swamped him. He couldn't, he *couldn't*, why had he thought he could, he was going to fuck everything up yet again—he tensed to bolt, and Sanyam pulled Sterling's head around and kissed him, hard and filthy, until Sterling was gasping against Sanyam's mouth, hand tangled in the placket of Sanyam's coat.

Sanyam slowed and gentled the kiss, his tongue sweeping between Sterling's lips, tilting his head so that their mouths fit together perfectly.

When they separated, someone applauded from behind them, but Sterling didn't even look, still trying to catch his breath.

Sanyam pressed their foreheads together, smelling warm and sweet and comforting. "Deep breaths, kit," he murmured. "You're going to be fine." His eyes creased. "It's not like they're going to ask you to strip for the patrons."

"The bartender already doesn't like me," Sterling managed. "After everything with Jacks.... And the serving drinks, and balancing all those glasses on a tray and trying to remember every-one's orders, I'm going to screw up, I'm going to be shit at this, I can't do anything *right*, San—"

"Stop it," Sanyam ordered, gripping his shoul-ders and giving him a gentle shake. "You do a lot of things right, kit."

"Like what?" Sterling hated himself the second the words were out, but he couldn't snatch them back.

Sanyam smiled and thumbed Sterling's dimple. "You submit so beautifully, for one."

"I do not," Sterling said. "I fight you every step of the way."

Sanyam hummed, their lips only a few inches apart. "But when you *do* surrender, kit, it's the most glorious thing." He ran a thumb along Ster-ling's cheekbone, and Sterling leaned into it, under his spell.

"When you mess up, you put things right as best you can," Sanyam continued. "With your father, with the glass of Cricket's that you broke— you try to fix things, even when they can't be put together again the same way as before."

Tears prickled Sterling's eyes, and he blinked them away viciously, concentrating on Sanyam's voice.

"You're gentle with Polly, even when you pretend to hate her," Sanyam said.

"I *do* hate her," Sterling said.

Sanyam laughed, breath warm and sweet on Sterling's face. "You do not. You're as gone for her as—" He hesitated. "As she is for you," he finished.

Sterling narrowed his eyes, but the bus was pulling up to their stop, and Sanyam withdrew gently, his warmth fading from Sterling's skin as he stood and wrapped his scarf around his neck.

INSIDE THE CLUB, Sanyam settled a hand on Sterling's lower back and guided him through the room, stepping around patrons already settled in for a night of entertainment as music played through the speakers.

"Trinity's our top performer," he said into Sterling's ear. "She'll share tips if you keep the perverts away from her. Once you're done talking to Ava and signing the paperwork, I'll turn you over to Kimi for training."

Sterling balked. "You're not staying with me?"

"I can't," Sanyam said, clearly startled. "I have my own duties, and you're a server. I work in the back—I *can't* train you. I'll come check on you during breaks, and we can eat together on our lunch, all right?"

Sterling nodded reluctantly and allowed Sanyam to navigate their way through the crowded space to the back hall. Instead of turning left to get to Sanyam's room, he turned them right, and they went all the way down to the end, where Sanyam knocked on a door.

"Come in!" came a brisk voice.

———

AVA TERRIFIED HIM, Sterling decided. She was tiny and fierce and bristly, like a porcupine ready to stab him with her pointy quills if he put a foot wrong.

He signed what she set in front of him without arguing, still off-balance and unsure of himself.

When he was done, he set the pen down and folded his hands in his lap as Ava fixed him with a sharp look.

"You take care of those who need it, you get me? Kimi doesn't, but Delfia, she's not tough like our Kimi. You keep an eye on her, and if anyone bothers her in any way, you get them tossed out on their ear. The bouncers are here to help; don't hesitate to use them."

Sterling nodded. Sanyam was quiet beside him, listening but saying nothing.

Ava leaned forward. "Sanyam's risking his own job for you, kid. Don't make either of us regret it."

Sterling swallowed resentment at the suggestion in her tone that he *would*, and simply nodded again.

"Out," Ava said, and flicked a finger like shaking off water. "Get to work."

IN THE HALL, Sterling caught Sanyam's eye. "She's delightful. I see why you like working for her."

Sanyam snorted a laugh. "Come on, smartmouth, time to turn you over to Kimi."

Sterling braced himself as Sanyam ushered him to the bar, where Kimi was busy mixing and pouring drinks. But Kimi's face lit when she saw Sterling, and she opened the bar hatch to grab him and pull him into a hug.

"Um," Sterling said, tentatively patting her back.

Kimi drew away and grinned up at him. "San told me you were joining us. Welcome to the Honeytrap. You ready to work?"

"I... guess," Sterling said. "I have no idea what I'm doing, though."

Kimi shrugged that off. "We'll teach you. I'm

putting you with Delfia; you're going to shadow her for this shift."

"Is she okay with that?"

"Del couldn't hold a grudge to save her life," Kimi said. "Plus you tried to protect her last time. She'll be fine."

"I'll leave you to it, then," Sanyam said. He touched Sterling's shoulder. "Come find me on your break."

DELFIA PROVED true to Kimi's words, dimpling at Sterling when Kimi called her to the bar.

"I move fast," she warned him. "I hope you can keep up. Come on. I'll give you the tour." She led him around the room, showing him the doors to private rooms scattered along the walls. "Trinity does private showings between her sets. Most of our strippers do, but she's our headliner—you'll get a lot of people asking about her. Part of your job will be to keep the pervs off the stage and their hands to themselves. Generally the dancers will share tips, especially if you're able to keep the customers happy and the drinks flowing."

She walked rapidly, pointing out things he'd need to keep an eye on.

"Do you guys serve food?" Sterling asked.

"Finger foods, chips, cheese sticks, and stuff," Delfia said. "The busboys will clean the tables, but any pitching in is always appreciated."

Sterling was getting the message. *Pull your weight.* He nodded.

"You're going to get hit on," Delfia warned him. "Like, a lot. Laugh it off. Don't get offended. Try not to let them touch you, but I'll tell you right now, your ass is going to be pinched so often you'll probably have permanent bruises."

"Awesome," Sterling mumbled.

"General rule is, flirting is allowed. Touching is not encouraged, but we try to play it down so we don't lose customers. If someone persists, though, you're allowed to get Logan to toss them out. When you're on your own, you'll have mostly female tables, or openly gay customers. Gotta give the clientele what they like, after all."

Sterling nodded again. "I can handle it."

"Your... friends," Delfia said, a shadow crossing her face. "They're not coming back, are they?"

"Not as far as I know," Sterling said. "But I haven't spoken to Jackson since I punched him, and Braden was always attached to his hip. And they're not my friends, okay? Not anymore."

"Okay," Delfia said. She patted his arm. "I just

had to ask. Come on, I'll show you the kitchen, and you can meet the chef and busboys."

By the end of his shift, Sterling's head spun. Delfia had told him the truth—he'd been flirted with ruthlessly, groped and felt up so often he'd lost count, and his feet hurt so much he was surprised they weren't swollen to twice their usual size.

"How do you do it?" he asked her, sprawled in one of the booths as she closed out the register. "I'm dying. Like actually, literally dying."

Delfia laughed. "It gets easier. You're not used to being on your feet for so long, for one thing. And you'll get better at fending off the horndogs."

"I'm not sure I want to," Sterling muttered, rubbing his ass. He glanced up as Sanyam came into the main room and threaded his way through the tables toward them with a smile on his face.

"I see you survived," he said as he stopped in front of Sterling's limp form.

"Matter of opinion," Sterling mumbled. "I think I'm actually undead at this point." He held up his arms. "Carry me."

Sanyam laughed. "Not a chance, you spoiled

brat. Get up. Let's go home. I'll make you a cup of tea and Polly will cuddle your woes away."

Sterling groaned and waved an arm until Sanyam caught it. He pulled him easily to his feet and steadied him as Sterling swayed.

Delfia snickered. "Put your poor boyfriend to bed," she told Sanyam. "He worked hard."

"He's not my boyfriend," Sanyam said.

"Not his boyfriend," Sterling agreed, letting his head droop until it was resting on Sanyam's shoulder.

"Right," Delfia said in tones of deep disbelief.

Sterling followed Sanyam out of the club and onto the bus, sagging with exhaustion.

"Why did I ever think this was a good idea?" he muttered.

Sanyam laughed quietly. "Because you need a job, and as hard as it is, the club pays well. Besides, this is good for you."

"How, exactly?"

"Builds character," Sanyam said, smiling at him. "Everyone should work menial labor at some point. My children certainly will."

"You have kids?" Sterling asked, stiffening.

"Hypothetical future children," Sanyam said,

smile widening. "No need to look so panicked, kit, I don't have plans to settle down anytime soon."

Sterling relaxed and shoved a fist against his mouth to stifle the yawn.

"Put your head on my shoulder," Sanyam said. He shifted as Sterling obeyed and then wrapped an arm around Sterling's waist. "We have a thirty-minute ride ahead, you might as well rest."

"You need a car," Sterling slurred, and closed his eyes to the steady *thump-thump* of Sanyam's heart.

SANYAM WOKE him when the bus pulled up to their stop, and Sterling followed him down the aisle and up the stairs of the apartment, muffling another yawn.

Polly came running, greeting them both with great excitement, and Sterling was too tired to do more than run a hand over her back as she squeaked at him.

"Go to bed," Sanyam told him. "Unless you'd like some tea?"

Sterling shook his head. "Prob'ly fall asleep in it."

There was affection in Sanyam's eyes, and it

scared Sterling. Sanyam shouldn't like him. There was nothing *to* like, and Sanyam was just going to end up horribly disappointed with him, like everyone else in Sterling's life.

But he was too exhausted to address it.

"Night," he muttered, and headed for his room.

21

Sanyam was dying. Fox had been with him for two weeks, and so far, it was nothing but unadulterated torture.

Fox woke up grumpy, and his temperament didn't improve much until close to noon. Sanyam soon gave up on trying to get him to go running, coming home every morning to find Fox in various stages of undress as he came to and from the shower.

The worst day was when Fox came out of his bedroom completely naked as Sanyam was walking down the hall. He didn't notice Sanyam stopping dead, his own eyes still mostly closed against the morning sun as he shambled toward the bathroom.

His long, long legs and perfect ass nearly

glowed, haloed by the sun, the muscles in his back sliding under his skin with every movement, and Sanyam pressed a heel to his groin, fighting the moan.

He *wanted*, so much, to take Fox apart again, reduce him to a whimpering mess, make him *beg*, but it had to be Fox's idea. No matter what, Sanyam wasn't going to make sexual advances on a guest in his home.

So he kept his mouth shut and suffered silently and jerked off a lot in the shower, fast and quiet as his legs trembled and lightning rippled through him.

At the end of Fox's second full workweek, Sanyam came out of the back to discover him with his shirt off, a towel draped around his neck and his hair standing up in damp spikes, his eyes molten with fury.

"What happened?" Sanyam demanded.

"Patron didn't like it when I didn't want her number and refused to give her mine," Fox said through his teeth. "Let's go."

"She dumped a pitcher of margaritas on his head," Delfia said in a low tone as Fox dragged a spare Honeytrap T-shirt on.

"That's a lot of alcohol to waste," Sanyam observed.

"She *really* wanted his number," Delfia said.

There was sympathy and amusement mingled in her eyes.

Fox flipped a hand at her and gave Sanyam an impatient jerk of his head. "Can we go?"

He was tense and irritated all through the bus ride home, responding to Sanyam's comments with terse monosyllables. Finally Sanyam gave up, and they rode silently the rest of the way.

Fox stomped up the stairs and waited, bouncing on his toes, for Sanyam to unlock the door.

"I need to get you a key," Sanyam said, pushing it open.

Fox hesitated in the act of brushing past him but said nothing as he stalked into the loft and yanked his clothes off. He left the shirt in a crumpled heap on the floor, kicking his shoes off and leaving them and his pants in a trail that led to his bedroom door.

Sanyam stifled a sigh. "What happened to picking up after yourself?"

"Maybe when I smell less like tequila and triple sec," Fox shot as he stormed back out of the bedroom, still naked, and made for the bathroom.

Sanyam gritted his teeth and made himself some tea as he listened to Fox banging around in the bathroom.

"How much harm can he do?" he asked Polly,

sitting at his feet.

She blinked up at him.

"Yes, you're right. Best not to ask." Sanyam carried his tea to the sofa and sat down, stretching his legs out with a relieved sigh.

When Fox came stomping back through, damp and rumpled but dressed, Sanyam was sipping his tea and reading, Polly on his lap.

Fox ignored the clothes on the floor to root in the refrigerator, coming up with a piece of cheese and a beer.

Sanyam tsked, turning the page. "That's not a meal."

"Bite me," Fox snapped. He flopped into a chair at the table and glared at his beer, tapping the tabletop with a fingernail.

"Don't forget to pick up your clothes," Sanyam said mildly.

Fox blew an irritated breath and said nothing.

Silence fell as Fox drank his beer and sulked, and Sanyam pretended to read, focused on Fox's brooding figure.

"I have to go shopping tomorrow," he said after a minute. "Would you like to go with me, so I can get food I know you'll eat?"

Fox shrugged. "Whatever." He pushed himself to his feet, leaving the beer bottle on the table. "I'm going to bed."

"Fox," Sanyam said.

Fox stopped at the entrance to the hall. "What."

"Pick up your mess," Sanyam said.

There was a tense moment as Fox stared at him. Sanyam's pulse sped up as he turned another page, not even seeing the words.

"No."

Sanyam nearly dropped his book, turning the fumble into setting it down on the coffee table. Fox's eyes were still hot with anger when he looked up, but there was something else there too —a hunger, a *need* that Sanyam knew he couldn't make himself express.

He set Polly on the sofa beside him and stood. He crossed the living room and moved right into Fox's space.

Fox swallowed hard and licked his lips but didn't budge.

"Pick up your mess," Sanyam repeated.

"I won't," Fox said flatly, but his eyes begged for Sanyam to keep pushing.

Sanyam leaned in close. "If you do not, I will… punish you."

Fox brought his chin up. "I'd like to see you try."

Sanyam caught Fox's shoulders and slammed him against the wall, pinning him there. "You infuriating *brat*," he growled, and Fox surged up and kissed him before he could say anything else.

Fox tasted like beer and Manchego, salt and cream and the tang of hops, pressing in on a shaky moan.

Sanyam pushed back, cupping Fox's groin in one hand and thumbing his rapidly hardening shaft through his soft sweats.

"Safeword," he demanded when he broke away.

Fox's eyes were dazed, lips wet and swollen. "I —Calypso. What are you waiting for?"

"Clearly not manners from you," Sanyam jibed, and turned away. "Be naked when I get back."

"Or what?"

Sanyam swung back, and Fox flinched. "Don't test me, kit." He bent to pick Polly up and stalked for his bedroom without looking. There, he deposited her on the bed and came up with a few items from the nightstand drawer before closing the door behind him and returning to the living room.

Fox was kicking his pants into a heap with his shirt, bare except for his socks.

Sanyam scooped up the sweatpants and caught Fox's arm to pull it behind his back. "Grab your elbows," he ordered. Fox obeyed, breath catching in his throat, and Sanyam made short work of binding his forearms against each other with the pants, making sure Fox couldn't pull free, before moving around in front of him.

Fox twisted, his skin darkening as a flush crawled up his chest. His eyes were huge, pupils blown so wide only a thin strip of green remained, and Sanyam wrapped one hand around his throat and squeezed lightly.

Fox's mouth fell open as he struggled to breathe, and Sanyam took a moment to appreciate how lovely he was, dark hair falling into his unfocused eyes, before he eased the pressure, letting Fox suck in air.

"No breath play tonight," he said. "That needs more time and preparation. But one day, kit…." He thumbed Fox's dimple. "One day. For now… you need to be punished." Sanyam stepped back and sat down on the sofa, gesturing to his lap. "Facedown."

Fox nearly tripped over the shirt on the floor as he moved to obey. He lowered himself awkwardly until he lost his balance and ended up sprawled on his stomach across Sanyam's knees.

Sanyam caught and steadied him with a hand smoothed over the curve of Fox's ass. "Do you know what you've been doing to me the past two weeks?" he murmured.

Fox was silent, tension in every muscle.

"You've been driving me *crazy*." Sanyam trailed a finger along Fox's spine, feeling the bumps of the vertebrae one at a time. "Was it on purpose, kit? Were you deliberately wandering around naked just so you could send me out of my mind?"

Fox said nothing, and Sanyam smacked his ass, hard enough to sting.

"Answer me."

"I—yes," Fox gasped. "Not… at first, but I—I wanted you. I w-wanted—you wouldn't even *look* at me, and I—"

Sanyam stroked the handprint that had formed on Fox's skin, making him shiver. "You don't know how to ask for what you need. That's all right, kit. I can give it to you anyway."

Without further warning, he began to hit him, hard enough that he knew Fox would be feeling it the next day but careful to preserve his strength and save his hand. He didn't have many toys at home, preferring to keep his professional and personal lives separate, so he was improvising as he went.

Fox jerked, and Sanyam caught his thigh with his free hand, holding him in place. He could feel Fox's erection pressed against his leg, and Sanyam struck several more blows before stopping to give his hand a rest and admire the cherry red of Fox's ass.

He rubbed his palm across the handprints and, when Fox didn't move, used his fingernails to scrape light welts along them. That got a flinch and muffled groan, and Sanyam smiled to himself.

"Are you clean, kit?"

Fox hesitated. "I—what?"

"STDs," Sanyam clarified. "I have something in mind for you, but—"

Fox sagged, hips moving in tiny, unconscious circles as he looked for friction. "I'm—clean. Haven't—*ah*"—as Sanyam smacked him again —"I'm clean," he repeated. "It's been *years*—"

"Good," Sanyam said. "So am I." He patted Fox's thigh and pushed until Fox got the hint and slid sideways to land on his knees in front of him. His hair was in his face, and he already looked wrecked, debauched, and *wanting*.

Sanyam unzipped his pants and lifted his hips to push his slacks down and off as Fox watched, lips parted and eyes hungry.

Naked from the waist down, Sanyam arched his back, sighing as his cock fell against his belly.

"Between my feet," he ordered, and waited until Fox shuffled into position. "Now… watch." He closed a hand around his shaft and began to stroke as Fox's mouth fell open and outrage flashed across his face.

"I want to—"

"You want to what?" Sanyam asked, hand steadily moving. "You want to taste me? Suck me off? You want me to come in your mouth?"

Fox nodded jerkily, and Sanyam grinned.

"Now you know how I've felt the past two weeks." He twisted his wrist on an upstroke and groaned. "*Mashalla*, that's good." Fox looked furious, glancing between Sanyam's cock and his face, but he said nothing.

Instead, he pulled on his bonds, shoulders straining, but Sanyam didn't even lose his rhythm. He'd done his job well. Fox wasn't getting out until he safeworded or they were done.

He sped up, catching his breath, and Fox leaned forward, whining deep in his chest, and rubbed his cheek against Sanyam's inner thigh, his mouth just an inch from Sanyam's cock.

With his free hand, Sanyam caught a fistful of Fox's hair, yanked his head back, and came with a punched-out groan all over Fox's face.

Fox closed his eyes and opened his mouth as creamy globs splattered his skin, trying to catch them with his tongue, and Sanyam swore under his breath as he shuddered through the aftershocks.

Wrung dry, he sagged backward, releasing his grip on Fox's hair and taking a deep breath. He lifted a hand, trembling still, and used his thumb to swipe through the come on Fox's face, gathering it.

"Open," he said, and Fox obeyed so that Sanyam could push his come into Fox's mouth. Fox's eyes fluttered shut and he sucked on Sanyam's thumb, tongue working to clean it thoroughly, and Sanyam hissed.

He pulled away with a soft *pop* and drew in air. Fox watched him, hunger stark on his face, and Sanyam smiled at him.

"You're afraid even to ask, aren't you? Afraid I won't let you come again."

Fox hesitated and finally nodded, shame and want chasing each other across his mobile features.

Sanyam stroked his cheekbone, affection and exasperation flooding him. "I'm not *that* heartless, kit. On your back. Spread your legs."

Fox scrambled to obey, squirming in an effort to get comfortable on his bound arms as Sanyam slid off the couch onto the floor between Fox's splayed knees. He stroked the soft skin of Fox's inner thigh, admiring the desperate hardness of Fox's shaft as it strained against his stomach, leaking in slow, heavy drops, and Fox's puckered hole, flexing and twitching as he waited.

"So beautiful," Sanyam murmured, and reached for the lube he'd brought from the bedroom.

He coated his finger and pressed inside Fox's body in one smooth motion, silken heat enveloping him as Fox grunted, planting his feet on the floor as his hips bucked up.

"When's the last time you did this?" Sanyam asked in a conversational tone as he slid in and out, movements slow and even.

Fox couldn't seem to concentrate enough to find words. His mouth was open, eyes dazed, and finally he swallowed and managed, "C-college."

Sanyam hummed. "It *has* been a while for you. Push into it when I add another finger."

Fox moaned as Sanyam pulled out and pressed back in with two fingers. "I need—" His hips canted, seeking friction for his neglected erection.

"You're not getting it," Sanyam said.

Fox jerked his head up, staring at him in disbelief. "But—you said—"

"I said you could come," Sanyam said. "I never said I was going to touch your cock. You need punishment, kit, someone to take you in hand and discipline you." He crooked his fingers up sharply, and Fox's back bowed, heels scrabbling against the floor. "So you'll take what I give you, and you'll come untouched or not at all."

Fox sobbed for breath but said nothing, bearing down on Sanyam's hand.

Sanyam smiled as he bent to his task, and silence fell, broken by Fox's harsh breathing. After a few minutes, Sanyam added lube and a third finger, sighing as Fox's body stretched to accept him.

"So lovely," he murmured. "So responsive. How are you feeling?"

"Dying," Fox spat. "Need to be *touched*."

Sanyam raised an eyebrow and pulled his fingers out. "I was under the impression that I *was* touching you."

Fox moaned, jerking again at his bonds. "I—I need—you know what I *meant*."

Sanyam took pity on him and pushed back in with a slow, steady slide. He bent and kissed Fox's inner thigh, nosing along the soft skin, and latched on over the tendon to suck.

Fox twisted, another sob falling from his mouth, but Sanyam ignored him, driving his fingers in deep with sharp, cruel precision. He found Fox's prostate and began to rub in smooth strokes as he sucked a livid bruise into Fox's thigh.

He could tell when Fox was close by the tightening of his muscles, and Sanyam redoubled his efforts, pushing him relentlessly up the hill to the edge.

Fox clamped down on his hand, his entire body seizing up as he came soundlessly, mouth open in helpless ecstasy.

Sanyam eased away from his thigh, admiring the mark he'd made, still wringing the last dregs of pleasure from Fox's body in slowing thrusts.

Finally Fox collapsed back to the floor as tiny tremors rippled through him, eyes dazed, and Sanyam pulled out, careful to move slowly.

With his clean hand, he gathered up the come on Fox's belly and crawled up his body. Fox sighed, turning his head toward him, and Sanyam smiled down at him.

"Open," he said, and fed him his own come.

Fox lapped it off Sanyam's hand obediently, tongue kitten-soft and willing as he licked at the web of Sanyam's fingers. When he was done, Sanyam bent and kissed him, tasting beer and the sharp bite of come on his tongue.

"So good," he whispered, cupping Fox's jaw.

Fox's eyes closed, and he turned his face into Sanyam's palm.

Sanyam helped him upright and kept him steady as he released his arms, then drew him down onto the couch, Fox sleep-loose and pliant against him as he curled up. They needed to get clean, but it could wait.

22

___

Sterling had no idea how long he'd been asleep when Sanyam nudged him awake.

"Time for bed, kit."

Sterling made a muffled noise against Sanyam's thigh and tried to melt into the couch.

Sanyam laughed quietly. "Come on, you. Wouldn't you prefer your comfortable bed?"

"Nnnn," Sterling said, but Sanyam ignored him, gently pushing and pulling until Sterling was upright.

Sterling glowered at him, and Sanyam's lips twitched.

"So grumpy. Up you get."

He hauled Sterling to his feet and chivvied him down the hall to his bedroom. Sterling crawled between the sheets as Sanyam disappeared, but he was soon back with a warm, wet rag and cleaned Sterling up in quick order.

Sterling caught his wrist as Sanyam straightened. "Am—am I going to drop?"

Sanyam smoothed Sterling's hair off his forehead. "Did you hit sub space particularly hard?"

Sterling shrugged. "I don't… know. Don't think so."

"Then maybe it won't be too bad," Sanyam said. "Sleep well, kit. We'll go shopping tomorrow, and I'll stay with you all day, make sure if you do drop, I'll be there to help you through it."

Sterling opened his mouth, but he couldn't make the words come, couldn't thank Sanyam for his kindness when Sterling had done nothing to deserve it.

Sanyam's eyes creased. "See you in the morning, Fox."

STERLING AWOKE to the sound of the shower running, the early sun slanting across his feet. He stretched, enjoying the slide of the sheets against the skin still tender from Sanyam's attentions the night before. He felt good, warm and relaxed and comfortable, and he didn't particularly want to get out of bed.

The shower stopped, and Sterling rolled over to face the door. Sure enough, Sanyam appeared a few minutes later, his hair curling and damp, a towel wrapped around his waist and drops of water still glistening on his chest.

Sterling made an appreciative noise and beckoned, but Sanyam just laughed. "Oh no you don't. We have things to do today. The shower's free; I'll make breakfast while you're in it."

Sterling pouted but threw the sheet off and stood up. He went up on his tiptoes to stretch, groaning in appreciation as his spine popped.

Sanyam took a sharp breath. "You little *shit*," he muttered, and crossed the room. Sterling hid his laugh as Sanyam yanked him close. Instead he wrapped his arms around Sanyam's neck, pressing up against his body.

"Much more like it," Sterling murmured, and rubbed his nose along Sanyam's damp beard.

Sanyam turned his head and caught Sterling's mouth in a kiss, tasting like peppermint, and Sterling sighed into it, melting appreciatively.

When he tried to sink back to the bed, though, pulling Sanyam with him, Sanyam stepped away.

"Shower and breakfast," he said, adjusting his towel. "There's time for… that… later, if you still want it then."

"You're no fun," Sterling mumbled, but he headed for the bathroom.

Sanyam slapped his ass as he walked by, making Sterling yelp and glare at him. "Sure about that, kit?"

They ate breakfast together at the kitchen table, Sanyam reading the news on his phone and Sterling sneaking bits of pancake to Polly.

"So are we taking the bus again today?" Sterling asked, putting his elbows on the table and resting his chin on his hand.

"Were you raised by wolves?" Sanyam said mildly.

"Yes," Sterling said. "Bus? Or by some miracle are we using some other form of transportation that maybe *doesn't* smell like sauerkraut and contain creepy guys who undress me with their eyes?"

Sanyam laughed. "We'll take a cab."

"Thank Christ for small mercies," Sterling said, stealing a piece of bacon off Sanyam's plate. He shared it with Polly, who was sitting on his knee, and Sanyam sighed.

"You're spoiling my cat."

"Bitch, please," Sterling retorted. "This cat was spoiled before I ever walked in the door. You sicken me, by the way," he told Polly, who squeaked at him. Sterling gave her another tiny bit of bacon fat and looked up to see Sanyam watching him, his eyes warm.

"Is Cricket still at Granville Island on the weekends?" he asked.

Sterling flinched, breath catching. "I don't—I think so. She had a lot of stuff that she could sell, she's probably there."

"Would you like to go see her?"

"Yeah," Sterling said as his chest eased. "I— yeah, I would."

THEY RODE to Granville Island in companionable silence, and Sterling let his hand rest on the seat between them, close to but not quite brushing Sanyam's thigh.

At the island, he was the first out, bouncing on his toes as he waited for Sanyam to catch up.

He ignored the crowds, ducking around knots of shoppers and throttling back his impatience so he didn't leave Sanyam behind.

"Go on," Sanyam said. "I'll catch up." He was looking at a booth full of vintage clothes, but Sterling didn't wait to see what had caught his eye.

He dashed through the throngs, slithering in between clumps of tourists until he was on Cricket's aisle. He could see her in the booth, handing a bag to someone with a smile on her face, and tears prickled Sterling's eyes. He hadn't even realized how much he'd missed her until that moment.

Cricket brushed her hair out of her face, looking up, and caught his eye. *Fox*, she mouthed, and bolted out of the booth straight for him.

They collided in the middle of the aisle, the impact knocking the air from Sterling's lungs as he wrapped his arms around her.

"Oh my God, *Fox*, oh thank God, I'm so glad you're okay!" She pushed him to arm's length and gripped the lapels of his coat to inspect him, tears in her big green eyes. "Why haven't you texted me?" she demanded. "You look *good*; are you finally taking care of yourself? Your skin is glowing, and your hair's all shiny, and I think you've gained weight!"

Sterling laughed and pulled her back into another hug. She smelled like jasmine and coconut. "I'm good," he said into her hair, surprised to realize it was true. "I'm… yeah, I'm doing good. How're you? Still with Dorian and Tatum?"

Cricket nodded and tugged him toward the booth, where Tatum was sitting in Sterling's camp chair, one leg slung over the arm. They glanced up and grinned at the sight of Sterling, raising one hand in a laconic wave. Their nails were bright orange with red stripes today, Sterling noted.

"Good to see you," they said. "Where've you been keeping yourself?"

"I'm… staying with a friend," Sterling said.

Sanyam arrived then, a bag hanging from his arm. He smiled at Cricket, who gasped at the sight of him.

"*You?*" she said. "Are you the friend he's staying with?"

Sanyam slanted a glance at Sterling, his smile widening. "I suppose I am," he said, bowing slightly.

Cricket flung her arms around him. Sanyam's eyebrows shot up, but he hugged her back, patting her gingerly.

"Hello," he said to Tatum when Cricket released him. "I'm a friend of Fox's."

Tatum waved again. "Tatum. Dating Dorian."

"I'm staying at their place," Cricket said. "Fox, you know you could have stayed with us until you had your own place, right?"

"Four's a crowd, Cricky," Sterling said. He sat down on the trunk and looked around the booth, full of Cricket's glassware. "How's the gig? Selling a lot?"

"Actually, yeah," Cricket said. "This is my second haul of the morning—I had to restock about an hour ago."

"That's awesome!" Sterling said, grinning at her. "Where's Dorian?"

"At work," Tatum said as they scrolled through their phone. "He's working at the aquarium."

"I've actually got a job there too," Cricket said as she turned to greet another customer. "We usually carpool. He's picking up another shift today, last-minute. He'll be sorry he missed you."

"Sure he will," Sterling said under his breath.

Cricket rounded on him, her eyes fierce. "He *will*, Fox—he's been worried about you!"

"She's right," Tatum added, apparently absorbed in whatever was on their phone. "He talks about you a lot. Wonders how you're doing. He even asked me if there was any way we could get a bigger place so you could stay with us."

Sterling opened and closed his mouth, stunned. "I—"

"I know you guys have your differences," Cricket said, voice soft, "but he loves you, Fox."

"Tell him I'm okay, would you?" Sterling managed. "I've got a job too. I'll try and check in with you guys more often, but I'm okay, I prom-ise." He hesitated. "Have you heard from Mom?"

"She's still with the Whittiers," Cricket said. "She's in their guest house, doesn't seem to have any plans to find a place of her own."

"Has she—" Sterling was unable to finish.

Cricket's eyes were unhappy. "We don't see her that often, but… she hasn't asked about you. I'm sorry, Fox."

Sterling hunched his shoulders and nodded, unsurprised.

Cricket turned to Sanyam, who'd said nothing. "If you need anything—"

He smiled. "I won't hesitate. Fox, would you like to stay with your sister and friend while I do the shopping, or come with me?"

"Come with you," Sterling said, standing. He kissed Cricket's cheek and gave Tatum a parting wave. "I'll see you soon, Cricky."

"You'd better," Cricket said. She waved as they left, and Sterling fell into step beside Sanyam.

"Um… thanks," he said after a minute. "That was a good idea."

"Of course," Sanyam said. He stopped to examine a block of cheese on display. "Family is important, Fox, and I'm glad you're close with yours."

"The twins, anyway," Sterling said, shoving his hands in his pockets. "Mom wouldn't care if I dropped dead tomorrow. She'd probably be happy, somewhere, because then she wouldn't have to pretend to care about me anymore."

Sanyam stepped close, and Sterling turned his head away from the sympathy in his eyes.

"She's wrong. Do you understand me?" Sanyam said. He touched Sterling's wrist, and Sterling flinched. "I don't know why your mother is like that, Fox, but I *can* tell you it's not your fault."

"Right," Sterling said. "Are we going to get groceries or not?"

"In a minute," Sanyam said. He moved in until they were flush together, and caught the back of Sterling's neck, drawing him into a kiss.

It wasn't hard or filthy this time. Sanyam held him still, tongue caressing Sterling's lips delicately until Sterling opened and let him in with soft, gentle sweeps, scouring away the hurt and leaving Sterling feeling light and somehow almost... hopeful.

When they separated, Sanyam cupped Sterling's face. "*Now* we're getting groceries."

Sterling cleared his throat and nodded, dizzy, following him down the aisle toward the produce.

"So what did you buy at that one booth?" he asked as they debated the merits of fresh pasta over frozen. "Fresh pasta is so much better, you can *taste* the difference."

"You'll see," Sanyam said. "I agree that fresh is

better, but it's also much more expensive. Smarter to go with the frozen."

"It's not *that* much more expensive," Sterling argued. "Besides, you have a waterfront apartment in *Vancouver*, you're not exactly hurting for money."

Sanyam gave him a level look. "I am comfortable but I did not get that way by spending in a profligate manner."

Sterling rolled his eyes and groaned. "*Profligate*. Who even talks like that? What's in the bag?"

"You'll see," Sanyam repeated. "Frozen."

"*Fine*," Sterling said, dropping the pasta into the cart. "You're definitely no fun."

"If you think I won't smack your ass again just because we're in a public place," Sanyam warned, and Sterling laughed, leaning against Sanyam's solid shoulder.

A child ran by, her mother in hot pursuit, and Sanyam smiled, his eyes softening as he watched. Sterling sobered and drew away.

"What else is on the list?"

Sanyam consulted it. "What vegetables won't you eat?"

"Most of them," Sterling said. "But especially peas." He shuddered. "Little evil green balls."

Sanyam snickered and started walking again, heading down the aisle as Sterling kept pace, sneaking curious peeks at the innocuous brown paper bag still in Sanyam's hand.

"Is it something for me or you?" he persisted.

Sanyam gave him an irritated look. "Were you like this on Christmas and birthdays too?"

"Of course," Sterling said cheerfully. "I knew all the good hiding places, and I always found the presents beforehand."

"That's half the fun!" Sanyam pointed out. "The surprise and anticipation is part of the gift-giving process, and you took that away from yourself."

Sterling shrugged. "Still got the presents—it wasn't a big deal."

"Well, you're waiting this time," Sanyam said firmly.

Sterling groaned again and followed him.

BY THE TIME they got back to the loft, Sterling was dying with curiosity. Sanyam kept the bag tucked close to his hip, apparently oblivious to the way Sterling's fingers were twitching.

They lugged the groceries inside, and Sanyam disappeared into his bedroom with the mysterious bag as Sterling fumed and put the groceries away and Polly wound around his feet, squeaking at him.

When Sanyam came back out, Sterling had folded the grocery bags and was stowing them in the pantry.

Sanyam came up behind him and wrapped a piece of what felt like silk over Sterling's eyes. The world went black.

Sterling froze, taking a startled breath, and Sanyam nipped at his ear and tied the blindfold in place. All Sterling could see was a strip of the floor at his feet, and his breathing was harsh in his ears.

"San—" His voice was unsteady.

Sanyam guided him out of the pantry and through the kitchen, one hand on Sterling's shoulder and the other on his waist.

"You're safe, kit," he said in Sterling's ear. "Trust me?"

Sterling nodded, relaxing into Sanyam's body. He felt Sanyam fumble for the doorknob and the rush of cool air as it swung open, and they stepped forward over the threshold.

He'd never been in Sanyam's bedroom before, and any other time, he'd have been looking around as soon as Sanyam pulled the blindfold off, but Sterling was instead transfixed by what was on the bed.

It was a *dress*, sunshine gold banded in olive

green at the flaring hem, in what looked like a vintage '50s housewife style, with its wide skirt and fitted bodice. Next to it lay a pair of sheer stockings, garters, and white satin elbow-length gloves.

Sterling swung around to Sanyam, who hadn't moved. "You—you're going to wear this?" *Please be for you, please say it's for you, please don't—*

Sanyam's lips quirked. "Not me, kit. You."

Sterling swallowed hard and looked back at the bed, at the dress staring silently back. "I—I don't—"

"I didn't know your shoe size," Sanyam said, touching his waist. "But if you like, we can look into getting you some later."

Sterling jerked away from his hand. "*Calypso.*" He bolted from the room before Sanyam could respond. He ran for his own bedroom and the door slammed behind him.

HE WAS TWELVE YEARS OLD, coltish with adolescence, more guarded with his heart but still hopeful. Amparo had brought her daughter's dress to mend during the day, and Sterling was on the floor beside her as she made tiny, neat stitches in the hem. He was touching the fabric with one finger, feeling the satin and the dark red embroidered roses that were scattered across it in a careless tumble, when Amparo made a satisfied noise and held it up.

"Finished!" she said. "Stand up, querido, you're the same size as Beatriz. I want to make sure it will fit her."

"Me?" Sterling said, startled. He scrambled to his feet. "But… I'm a boy."

Amparo smiled as she stood and pointed to the chair. "So? You can still put on a dress. It won't make you any less of a boy. Take your shirt off, mi amor."

Sterling took his shirt off and climbed onto the chair, bending so Amparo could settle the silk of the dress over his head. It fell in soft chuffing folds, nipping in at his waist and flaring out in pale pink satin petals.

"I feel like I'm standing in the middle of a rose," he said, awed, and moved his hips to make the fabric sway.

Amparo laughed and put several pins in her mouth as she knelt in front of him. "Be still, corazón, let me make sure the hem is even."

The sharp gasp in the doorway was the only warning, and Sterling's blood turned to ice when he looked up and saw his mother standing there.

"What do you think you're doing?" she hissed.

Amparo scrambled to her feet, pins tinkling on the marble floor as she flung out a hand to stop Alice's *forward charge. "Please, Mrs. Reynard, he was just helping me make sure the hem was even!"*

"Yates!" Alice shouted, her eyes dark with fury.

Sterling shrank away as she reached for his arm, and his father nearly fell into the room, horror and outrage flashing across his face.

"Get out of that dress!"

Yates yanked him off the chair, and the fabric ripped, catching on Sterling's arm and making him cry out in pain as he was hauled sideways and the dress jerked off over his head.

Amparo was weeping openly, trying to pull Sterling away from where he dangled from one of his father's big hands. "Leave him alone, it's my fault, it's not his fault—please, Mr. Reynard, please—"

Alice rounded on her. "You're fired," she spat. "Get out of my house right now."

"Mommy, no!" Sterling sobbed, twisting away from Yates's grip and bolting for Amparo. He flung his arms around her waist, burying his face in her shirt, and clung to her, his thin shoulders shaking. "I'm sorry, 'Paro. I'm so sorry—"

Yates caught him by the arm and dragged him backward as he kicked and screamed, and Alice hustled Amparo from the room.

Yates shook him. "Stop crying, goddammit. Be a man. You're not a baby. Men don't cry. Stop it, I said!"

Sterling gulped back his tears, the sobs still shaking his frame, craning to see where Amparo had gone.

"Only girls wear dresses. Do you hear me?" Yates continued. His grip was painful on Sterling's arms, his eyes cold with rage. "You're a boy, about to be a man. You do not wear dresses. Ever."

"I'm sorry," Sterling whispered, his vision blurred. "I didn't mean to—"

Alice came back in, heels tapping rapidly on the marble, and Yates straightened, turning to her.

"Is she gone?"

"Of course," Alice said. "Sterling, go to your room."

Sterling swallowed more tears and fled for the safety of his bedroom.

He curled up in the bed, face in the crook of his elbow, and fought the tears. *So stupid, useless, pathetic*—the door creaked as it opened, and Sterling went still.

"Fox." Sanyam's voice was low and full of nothing but concern. "May I talk to you?"

Sterling said nothing, staring at the wall, and listened as Sanyam approached the bed and sat down on the edge of it.

"I'm sorry," he said after a minute. "I didn't realize—no." He cleared his throat. "It's my fault, Fox. I should have talked to you first. Instead I just sprang it on you without warning. That's not what a good Dom does. Can you forgive me?"

Sterling closed his eyes, and Sanyam touched his hip, warm and comforting.

"I'm going to be in the living room," Sanyam said. "If you need anything, anything at all, don't hesitate, all right?"

He was almost to the door when Sterling rolled over. "San?"

Sanyam turned, and Sterling stood and pulled his shirt off. Sanyam's intake of breath was audible, but he didn't move.

Sterling held out a hand. *Don't make me beg, San, please don't.*

Sanyam took a step toward him, then another, and Sterling met him halfway, bodies colliding as hands grappled and lips met in a hot, hungry slide.

"Are you—*sure*," Sanyam managed to say. "Fox—"

"I'm sure," Sterling husked. "I need you to fuck me, San. I need—"

"All right, *kamsin*," Sanyam whispered. He walked Sterling backward to the bed and pushed him onto it, swarming up his body and kissing him breathless again.

Sterling arched up into it as Sanyam caught his wrists and pinned him to the bed, holding him down. Sanyam broke the kiss and slid down a few inches, nudging until Sterling got the hint and tilted his head to give him better access.

He gasped as Sanyam latched on and sucked, pulling blood to the surface, scraping his teeth across the delicate skin under Sterling's ear.

"This throat of yours is still criminal," Sanyam murmured, and moved to another spot. "Still begging to be marked up." His breath was hot on Sterling's skin, and he took his time as he picked the next place to claim.

Sterling twisted under him, breath hitching, but Sanyam's hands were implacable where they held him down, an immoveable force, and Sterling had never felt safer.

This wasn't a scene. Sterling had safeworded, ended the scene, and they hadn't restarted. Sanyam's mouth was hot on Sterling's skin, and Sterling shivered beneath him. Something had shifted in their relationship, but he was afraid to look at what it was.

It was quiet in the bedroom, the early afternoon sun haloing Sanyam's curly hair, and there was a decadence to what they were doing in the middle of the day, a sense of the forbidden being flouted. Sanyam kept going, laying claim to every inch of Sterling's helpless body, until Sterling was fighting tears, his eyelids pricking.

Please. The word was on the tip of his tongue, poised to fall, when Sanyam looked up and caught sight of his face.

"Fox?" He crowded close, cupping Sterling's jaw in one big hand, worry in his eyes. "*Gulbadan*, are you okay? Talk to me."

Sterling turned his face into Sanyam's palm, swallowing back the tears. "I'm—fine," he managed. "I just… I need you to fuck me, San."

"All right, *maahi*," Sanyam murmured. "Don't go anywhere."

He rolled off the bed and disappeared out the door, and Sterling took the opportunity to push his pants down.

Sanyam was back before Sterling had them over his ankles, and helped him tug them the rest of the way off. He'd taken his shirt off in the living room, and he set the lube on the bed to push his own pants down.

Sterling propped himself on his elbows to watch. Sanyam was beautiful, his brown skin nearly glowing in the sunlight, the tiny black hairs on his broad chest crisp and curled, thickening on his stomach and melding into his happy trail, and

Sterling crossed his arms over his own almost concave stomach, fish belly–white and almost hairless.

But Sanyam was looking at him with wonder in his eyes, stiff cock a silent testament to just how much he wanted him, and Sterling caught his breath. He held out his hand again and drew Sanyam down on top of him, his full weight pressing Sterling into the mattress.

They kissed leisurely for a while, but it wasn't long before Sterling deepened them, running his hands up and down Sanyam's body, over his satin skin and along his sides.

He planted his foot on the bed and pushed to roll them over, until Sanyam was spread out beneath him, his eyes soft as he gazed up at him.

"I want—be still," Sterling whispered.

Sanyam was motionless as Sterling lowered his head to worship. He pressed his lips to the chevet of Sanyam's inner elbow, tasting the velvet soft skin there and delighting in the shiver that ran through Sanyam's frame.

The wings of his collarbones spread above the cathedral of his ribs, and Sterling worked his way along each one, his mouth soft as he placed each reverent kiss and then moved lower, letting his lips drag over each rib until he'd reached the delicate skin stretched over Sanyam's hip bone.

Sanyam seemed to have been turned to marble beneath him, hardly even breathing as Sterling followed the arches of his hips, slow and deliberate in his worship.

"*Tum mujhe barbaad kartey ho*," Sanyam managed, his voice unsteady.

Sterling glanced up and Sanyam met his eyes.

"You ruin me, kit," Sanyam whispered, and held out a hand.

Sterling took it and slid onto Sanyam's broad chest so their erections were rubbing together and lowered his head to kiss him again as Sanyam traced intricate patterns on Sterling's skin, thumbs deft and gentle.

Finally, though, Sanyam shivered and drew away. He rolled Sterling off onto his back and went to his knees between Sterling's splayed thighs.

"Shouldn't take much," he murmured as he picked up the lube and coated his fingers. "Considering last night."

Sterling tilted his hips up so that Sanyam could put a pillow under them, and folded his arms behind his head as Sanyam focused on his task.

A thought occurred to him as Sanyam slipped the first finger in. "You're not going to make—*ah*—me come… untouched again, are you?"

Sanyam's smile lit the room. "No, *mastana*, I'm not."

"Not that that wasn't—*fuck*—fun," Sterling said, forcing himself to relax as Sanyam added a finger and scissored them. "But—oh God —San...."

"I've got you," Sanyam said, his voice low and ragged. He was up to three fingers, Sterling realized with dim surprise, and he bore down against it, panting.

"Come on," he said. "Come *on*, San, come on come on, I—"

Sanyam pulled his fingers free and replaced them with his cock, sliding in so swift and sure that he punched the air right out of Sterling's lungs.

"One day, kit," Sanyam said through his teeth. "One day you'll beg."

Sterling half laughed and hooked a heel around Sanyam's hips, squirming beneath him. "*Move.*"

Sanyam bent to kiss him as he obeyed, pulling out and driving home in quick, hard thrusts, establishing a rhythm that made Sterling's eyes roll back as Sanyam pounded in.

It didn't take long for the familiar sparks to gather under his skin, rippling along his nerves with each movement of Sanyam's hips, and Sterling reached up, grabbing desperately at the bed frame to brace himself.

"I'm close," he managed. "*Close*, San, I'm—"

Sanyam wrapped one big hand around Sterling's shaft and stroked once, twice, and Sterling spilled on a choked sob between their bodies, every muscle seizing in the ecstasy that lit him from the inside out.

He was dimly aware of Sanyam driving deep and stiffening, forehead pressed to Sterling's chest as he rode out his own orgasm, but Sterling didn't even have the strength to raise his hand and touch Sanyam's hair, which was tickling his nose.

Instead he closed his eyes and drifted, safe and protected by Sanyam's body wrapped around his.

23

―――――

He woke up with Sanyam's arm draped across his waist, heavy with sleep. Sterling lay quietly, watching Sanyam's face, just a few inches from him on the pillow, but finally the needs of his bladder asserted themselves, and Sterling sighed and freed himself in careful stages.

He tiptoed to the bathroom and, after, padded out to the living room. Polly was asleep in a ray of late afternoon sun, and she stretched and rolled over, exposing her fluffy belly, as Sterling sat down on the couch beside her.

Sterling rubbed her stomach absently, and she purred, closing her eyes again, as he bent forward and sorted through the box of glass fragments on the floor beside the coffee table.

The *C* was still laid out where he'd put it, and Sterling touched one of the pieces. It needed to be set in some sort of foundation, something that would showcase the colors and the simple elegance of it, but he didn't have the faintest idea what would work.

Sanyam's laptop was off to the side in sleep mode, and Sterling hesitated, chewing on his lip. Surely Sanyam wouldn't care if he used it.

WHEN SANYAM CAME out of the bedroom, hair rumpled and eyes sleepy, Sterling was deep in a dozen opened tabs, making a list on a scrounged piece of paper. He glanced up at the sound of Sanyam's footsteps.

"Oh," he said. "Um… is this okay?"

Sanyam smiled and sat down beside him. "Of course, kit. What are you looking up?"

"Mosaic shit," Sterling said, putting the pen between his teeth. "Trying to figure out how to make this secure so I can give it to Cricket."

Sanyam half laughed and leaned his head back against the couch. "Every time you mention your sister's name, I think you're talking about the sport."

Sterling glanced at him, diverted. "Oh yeah, cricket's big in India, isn't it?"

"Mm. And Britain, of course."

"How long were you in England?" Sterling asked.

Sanyam ran a hand up Sterling's spine, making him shiver. "For university. Four years. I went home for school holidays, of course, but the rest of the time I was at Oxford."

"Did you date while you were there? How did you figure out you liked BDSM stuff?"

Sanyam smiled, his head still back against the couch. "You remember my boyfriend, the one I mentioned?"

"Yeah, the homophobic one."

Sanyam hummed, slipping his hand under Sterling's shirt to caress his backbone. "Vivek. He wanted to try it with me, said our sex life was getting boring. It was too much for him, too intense, but I discovered that I—well." He lifted a shoulder. "I liked it very much indeed."

"Have you ever…?" Sterling struggled to remember what he was trying to say as Sanyam's finger danced up his vertebrae. "Have you ever fallen for a client before?"

"You are a first for me in many ways, kit," Sanyam murmured, splaying his hand warm across Sterling's shoulder. "Come back to bed. Perhaps we can explore some more firsts together."

Sterling snorted and put the computer down. "That wasn't me fishing for compliments," he said as he stood and extended a hand.

Sanyam took it. "Not going to stop me from giving them," he said, and towed Sterling toward the bedroom.

"I WANT to go to the craft store," Fox said when they were lying in bed after, spent and breathless.

Sanyam traced the hairs on Fox's arm where it lay across his stomach. "Is that an invitation, or do you prefer to go alone?"

Fox shrugged. Other than his arm, they weren't touching, lying side by side on the bed, and Sanyam tried not to want more.

"You can come if you like," Fox said. "Gonna be pretty boring, though."

FOX SEEMED to know exactly what he needed. He made a beeline for the adhesives aisle as Sanyam followed more slowly.

A perky sales associate appeared, blonde ponytail bouncing. "I'm Courtney. Can I help you gentlemen find anything?"

Sanyam smiled at her as he unwound his scarf. "Hello, Courtney. We're just here for my—" He faltered. What *was* Fox to him? Were they boyfriends?

"Do you have Weldbond?" Fox asked abruptly.

"Yes, of course!" Courtney chirped. "Follow me." She set off down the aisle, and Fox hurried to catch up, Sanyam taking his time and inspecting anything that caught his attention.

When Fox found him, Sanyam was admiring a display of watercolor paints and canvases.

"Do you paint?" Fox asked.

"I've always wanted to," Sanyam said, and touched a fine brush. "But somehow I've never had the time. Other things occupying me, I suppose. Do you have what you need?"

Fox glanced at his basket, heaped high with various frames, backing, and adhesive supplies. "I don't know," he admitted. "Guess I'll find out."

It was dark by the time they set out for home, and Sanyam wanted to take Fox's hand, but something in the way Fox held himself told him not to try.

So he walked beside him, their shoulders brushing, and described life in Mumbai, working as a Dom there, and why he'd decided to immigrate to Canada.

"I miss it," he admitted, smiling as they passed a little boy holding his mother's hand. "The noise, the smell—all of it. India is so colorful, so bright and cheerful, wealth and abject poverty cheek by jowl. No one thinks anything of the slums right up against the skyscrapers. And the street food!" He kissed his fingers, and Fox's lips curved.

"I'm not a fan of Indian food," he admitted.

Sanyam feigned horror. "Not a fan of the best food in the world? What am I going to do with you, kit?"

Fox's smile widened. "It's too spicy."

Sanyam clicked his tongue. "For shame. I'll take you to a good restaurant and teach you the error of your ways soon."

"Oh, that reminds me," Fox said. "Colby invited us over for dinner next month. It's his birthday, and he was hoping we could come."

"We?" Sanyam said. "Not you?"

Fox shrugged. "I told him we were... involved. He wants to meet you properly, I think. Dorian and Cricket are invited too. It's gonna be a whole... thing."

"I'd like that," Sanyam said as they climbed the steps to his apartment. "Colby seems to be a good person. I'd like to get to know him better. What do you think he'd like as a gift?"

"He's big into, like… wrestling and shit," Fox said as Sanyam unlocked the door. "That and Formula 1 racing. Give him a chance, he'll talk your ear off about either."

"Sounds devastatingly boring," Sanyam said, stepping aside for Fox to enter. "But I will endeavor to look interested. What would you like for dinner?"

"I don't care," Fox said. "As long as it doesn't involve peas." He took his purchases to the coffee table and settled in as Sanyam huffed a laugh and turned to see what he had in the refrigerator.

They ate spaghetti carbonara by candlelight, Sanyam watching the play of shadows on Fox's face as he shoveled pasta in.

"Have you ever had subs fall in love with you?" Fox asked.

Sanyam lifted a shoulder, playing with his fork. "I've had subs believe they were in love with me. I don't think they were, but scening creates very intense emotions and can form strong bonds. It has to be handled with care."

"Who's the worst sub you've ever had?" Fox said around a mouthful.

"There was a man a few weeks before I met you, actually," Sanyam said. "He claimed he wanted to submit, but he… fought me. Ended up punching me, actually."

Fox winced.

"Why do you ask?" Sanyam said.

"Just curious," Fox said, shrugging. "Interested in what it entails, what you do during a scene, everything that goes into it. Do you usually follow up with subs when you're afraid they're going to drop badly?"

Sanyam smiled. "You really are special, kit." Fox ducked his head, a blush staining his cheeks, as Sanyam continued. "Although there was one sub, in India—he intrigued me."

Fox glanced up. "What do you mean?"

"A friend of mine asked me to take him on. His name was Micah, and he was getting over a really bad breakup. My friend—Kali, the one who connected me with Ava here—said that Micah needed to sub, but he couldn't do it for her, since they'd been involved in the past. So I said of course that I would."

"What happened?"

"Nothing much, really," Sanyam said, toying with the pasta on his plate. Micah's face was vivid in his memory, even though it had been over a year ago—lost eyes filled with bottomless grief, a bold nose, and sensitive lips. "He was obviously not new to subbing, and we did some spanking, a little punishment, but he safeworded before we went further. Ran out of the club." He smiled at Fox, listening intently. "Kali told me later that he was actually Canadian, when I called her to ask after him. But he lived in Toronto, so I don't imagine we'll ever run into him."

"Were you… interested in him, romantically?"

"I think I could have been," Sanyam admitted. "But he was very obviously in love with someone else. Kali told me, later, that he went back to Toronto and got back together with his ex."

Fox just nodded and fed Polly a piece of pasta.

"Kimi says you're doing well," Sanyam said when they were done. "About ready to be turned loose on your own."

Fox shrugged. "I guess," he said, putting his plate in the sink and going back to clear the rest of the table. "It's not exactly rocket science."

"Don't downplay it," Sanyam said as he started the water. "It's your first real service job, and it's hard as hell to do it well."

Fox didn't answer, but his shoulders eased subtly, and he brushed against Sanyam's fingers as they began the washing up.

The rest of the evening passed with Sanyam reading and Fox working on the mosaic for Cricket, muttering under his breath and occasionally out loud to Polly, who watched with rapt attention.

"Stop squeaking," he told her at one point. "You're an embarrassment to cats everywhere."

Sanyam laughed to himself and turned the page.

Later, it was "Maybe I should teach you to play fetch."

"She's a cat, not a dog," Sanyam said without looking up.

"Doesn't mean she can't be trained," Fox said.

"She's a *cat*," Sanyam said, glancing up this time. "Pretty sure that's exactly what that means."

"Your owner knows nothing," Fox told Polly. "We'll show him, won't we? Do you have any bouncy balls, San?"

"Why on earth would I have bouncy balls?" Sanyam asked, startled.

Fox waggled his eyebrows, and Sanyam laughed out loud.

"No, kit, I don't have bouncy balls. Sorry to disappoint."

It was peaceful, relaxed, and Sanyam found himself pleasantly tired, yawning before it was midnight.

He closed his book and stretched. "I'm going to bed. Joining me?"

"Not done," Fox said without looking up.

Sanyam stood and bent over Fox's curved back to look at what was taking shape. He had sketched the outline on the board and was placing the pieces carefully, tongue caught between his teeth in concentration.

"It looks beautiful, kit," Sanyam murmured, and kissed the shell of Fox's ear.

Fox shivered but said nothing, putting another piece into place.

"Don't stay up too late," Sanyam said.

Fox grunted something that might have been acknowledgment, and Sanyam smiled and went to bed.

But Fox never crawled in next to him, and when Sanyam woke up the next morning, Fox was sound asleep in his own bed across the hall.

24

Sanyam went running alone, trying to figure out what to do. Perhaps it was a flaw in himself, but he needed to know what they *were*, if there was a label they could apply to their relationship. But something warned him that Fox would likely push back if Sanyam tried to get an answer from him, and the last thing he wanted was to spook an already fragile Fox into either bolting or saying something they both regretted.

When he got back to the apartment, muscles loose and warm, he'd decided that he wouldn't make any more moves. Fox clearly didn't want to pursue anything resembling a real relationship. Maybe he didn't even want to have sex again, and Sanyam would respect that.

But when he walked in, the shower was running and the bathroom door was open. Sanyam kicked his shoes off and put his head in the bathroom just as Fox looked around the shower curtain, shampoo in his hair and suds on his nose.

"What took you so long?" he asked, holding out a hand. "Get in here."

Shower sex with a slippery wet and very enthusiastic Fox was definitely excellent, Sanyam decided, and something that should be repeated as often as possible.

OVER BREAKFAST, Sanyam regarded Fox as he slipped Polly tidbits. Fox glanced up and saw him.

"What?"

Sanyam spread his hands. "I can't admire the view?"

Fox snorted rudely and took another bite.

"There actually was something I wanted to talk to you about," Sanyam said.

Fox tensed but said nothing.

"I don't know… what we are," Sanyam began, feeling for the words. He didn't miss the thunderclouds gathering on Fox's brow, but he forged on.

"I'm not sure if there's even a name for us, but I wanted to ask—"

"No," Fox said flatly.

"You don't even know what I was going to say!" Sanyam protested.

Fox stood. "Doesn't matter, the answer is no. I'm not your boyfriend. We're not dating. We're just having sex occasionally. Why can't you just let it be that? Why can't we just be having some fun? Why do you have to box me up and slap a label on me?"

Sanyam's voice cracked like a whip. "*Stop.*"

Fox froze in place.

Sanyam took a deep breath, forcing the irritation down. "Fox, please sit down and let me say what I need to say."

Fox sank mutely into his chair, every muscle taut, face utterly still.

"Prickly as a hedgehog," Sanyam muttered. He ran a hand through his hair and blew out the frustration. "Regardless of how you view our 'relationship,' Fox, the fact remains that we *are* having sex more than occasionally. I need to know if it will bother you if I continue to Dom at the Honeytrap. Obviously, as long as you and I are… involved, I will not be having sex with anyone else, but do you have a problem with me dominating others?"

Fox looked up, startled into letting the mask slip. "*That's* what you were going to ask?"

"*Yes,*" Sanyam said, exasperated. "Will it be an issue?"

Fox considered. "Nope," he finally said.

"Are you sure?" Sanyam pressed.

Fox lifted one elegant shoulder. "You said it yourself. You're not having sex with them. It's a— psychological thing, I guess, not physical, right?" He met Sanyam's eyes, and his mouth quirked. "You come home with me. I'm not worried."

Sanyam searched Fox's face, but there was nothing but truth there. The tension in his shoulders eased, and he settled back in his seat.

"All right," he said. "Thank you for your honesty, Fox."

"Whatever," Fox said, and took another waffle. "Anything else?"

Sanyam dropped his head into his hands and laughed, half-despairing. "Since you asked, yes— I'd like to get us both tested, just to make sure we're clean."

"God, you're fussy," Fox muttered.

Sanyam brought his head up at that. "STDs are no laughing matter, Fox."

Fox rolled his eyes. "Fine. Whatever." His expression softened at whatever was showing on Sanyam's face. "I mean—okay. You're right."

"Thank you, kit." Sanyam resisted the impulse to touch him, and Fox ducked his head, avoiding his eyes.

THEY SETTLED INTO A ROUTINE, Fox sleeping in while Sanyam went running, eating breakfast together, going shopping or to the island to see Cricket, who loved her gift.

Sanyam didn't push to put a label on what they had, as much as he wanted to. Fox flatly rejected any hint of intimacy that wasn't a lead-up to or aftermath to sex, often with a sharp word or worse, a laugh.

But those moments right after they'd finished, when Fox was sprawled in a loose-limbed heap across his bed, ribs heaving and sweat sheening his skin—Sanyam lived for those moments, when he could touch Fox and know that Fox would turn into it, close his eyes and sigh and curl closer to Sanyam's warmth.

Sanyam didn't bring up the possibility of Fox finding another place to live, either. He liked what they had too much, liked knowing that even if Fox wasn't sharing a bed with him, at least he was *there*, he was close, and Sanyam could stand outside his door in the middle of the night and

listen to him breathing if he needed the reas-
surance.

He tried not to do that too often, though,
because that was creepy and he didn't want to
scare Fox away.

25

He waited a while before he brought up the possibility of breath play again. Fox was up for nearly anything Sanyam suggested in the bedroom, possessed of a natural fearlessness of spirit and a love for pain that was an intoxicating combination, but breath play was different. It was *dangerous*, and Sanyam needed to know that Fox was fully informed before consenting.

So he sat him down one day, about a month after they started having sex, and took his hand.

"Are you interested in exploring oxygen deprivation further?"

Fox's eyes went wide and he licked his lips. "*Yes.*"

"You need to understand exactly what it

entails," Sanyam said, rubbing a thumb over Fox's knuckles. "It is one of the most dangerous kinks out there, kit. It could result in brain damage or death if either one of us makes a mistake. Do you hear what I'm saying? It is not something to embark on lightly."

"We're not going to dive in headfirst and put a plastic bag over my head, right?" Fox said, pulling his hand away. "I mean, we'd take it slow."

"Of course," Sanyam said. "And I'm not comfortable with you having anything over your head or restricting your airflow other than my hand, so that I can monitor you as closely as possible."

Fox shrugged. "Then what's the big deal?"

"The big deal is you could *die*," Sanyam said.

"Eh," Fox said. "I'm not worried. Can we try it tonight?"

"You terrify me," Sanyam said, sitting back.

Fox tilted his head and smiled at him. "Is that a yes?"

"I wouldn't want your arms to be bound this time," Sanyam said. "That way you can physically signal if you need to stop."

Disappointment crossed Fox's face, but he nodded.

"I mean it," Sanyam insisted. "You have to

promise me right now that you *will* tap out if you need to."

"I promise," Fox said. "Can I at least be blindfolded?"

"Yes, kit," Sanyam said. "You can be blindfolded. Go in your bedroom and get naked."

26

Sterling hurried to obey, but Sanyam wouldn't be rushed. Sterling stripped as Sanyam circled him, watching his every movement closely, but he didn't touch him until Sterling was naked and had conquered his jitters, forcing himself to take a deep breath and settle on his heels as he clasped his hands behind his back.

Only then did Sanyam step in close and draw a finger down Sterling's bare chest. Sterling shivered at the contact and leaned forward, but Sanyam drew away.

Sterling thumped back onto his heels, glaring, but Sanyam just smiled.

"In due time, kit. Kneel."

Sterling went to the floor, fighting the tremors running through him, and Sanyam stepped over his legs behind him, so close Sterling could feel his body heat on his shoulders.

He settled the silk blindfold in place and tied it snugly, his fingers gentle. Sterling sagged as his world went dark, tension draining from him like water out of soil.

Sanyam caressed his jaw, sliding a finger down over Sterling's dimple. "So good," he murmured. "Keep your hands clasped behind your back. Don't let go for any reason except to tap out."

Sterling tightened his grip and nodded.

Sanyam moved away, warmth fading, and Sterling listened to his heartbeat thundering in his ears, straining for any sound.

There was nothing but silence, and Sterling shifted his weight. Still nothing. He couldn't see anything but the floor just in front of his knees, his chest and belly and half-hard cock, and he fought the desire to let go of his hands, to rip the blindfold off and see where Sanyam had gone, what he was doing.

Sterling bit back a whine, tightening his grip on his wrist. *Don't leave me, San, please, I know I deserve it but—*

It felt like an eternity before a soft noise came from behind him, and Sterling just barely kept in the relieved whimper.

"Look at you," Sanyam murmured, footsteps

drawing nearer and a warm hand running over the nape of Sterling's neck. "So good for me."

I'm good, I can be so good, please, I'm good for you…. Sterling's thoughts swirled, fragmenting and dissolving as he swayed toward the sound of Sanyam's voice. He recognized the feeling of sub space now, the drifting of his awareness like being suspended in honey, movements slow and every sensation unbearably sweet.

Sanyam's hand settled around Sterling's throat, thumb stroking his pulse, and squeezed, slow and steady.

Sterling choked, and Sanyam eased off, but Sterling shook his head.

"More."

Sanyam resettled his grip, took a deep breath, and squeezed again.

Sterling's mouth fell open and he labored for air, lungs heaving. Sparks danced across the backs of his eyelids, and he gripped his own wrist so tightly his bones ached, a distant pain that only served to send him spiraling farther down the slope into deep sub space.

He was only dimly aware when Sanyam let go, lost in his head, but he opened his mouth dreamily at Sanyam's urging and hummed when Sanyam fed him his cock.

Sanyam pressed in deep until his shaft was

buried in Sterling's throat, soft curls tickling Sterling's nose at the base of his cock.

"*Mastana*," Sanyam whispered. "You intoxicate me."

He pulled back and pumped in and out in slow, even thrusts, pinching Sterling's nostrils shut with one hand.

Sterling was drowning. The only air in his lungs was what he was able to draw in when Sanyam retreated. His head spun, and he'd lost feeling in his fingers and toes. He was a receptacle for Sanyam's touch, a vessel to be filled, and he wanted nothing else. He was at peace, serenity settling over him like a silken mantle.

Sanyam hissed through his teeth, losing his rhythm as his thrusts turned needy and desperate, and then salty, bitter liquid flooded Sterling's throat.

Sterling swallowed again and then again, eyes closed as Sanyam shuddered above him through the last of his orgasm and finally withdrew. He wiped the corner of Sterling's mouth with his thumb, and Sterling dragged in sweet oxygen.

Sanyam pulled the blindfold off and cupped his face. "How do you want to come, *jaaneman?*"

Sterling blinked, unable to form words, Sanyam blurry in his vision. He'd been crying, he realized, but he couldn't muster panic at that—he felt wonderful, swept clean and purified.

Sanyam helped him up and to the bed, settling him on the mattress with careful hands before he straddled Sterling's legs.

"Lie back and enjoy this, kit," he murmured, and lowered his head.

Wet heat engulfed Sterling's cock, and he closed his eyes again as sensation rushed over him. It was no time at all before he stiffened, toes curling and lightning rippling across his nerves as he emptied soundlessly in Sanyam's mouth.

Sanyam took every bit, thumbs stroking small circles on Sterling's thighs as he eased him through it with skillful touches.

Finally he slid off and wiped his mouth. Sterling barely noticed him leaving the bed, still lost deep in his head, but he cooperated as best he could when Sanyam returned with a warm, wet cloth and cleaned, then dressed him.

Cool sheets were pulled over his shoulders, and Sterling turned on his side, rubbing his cheek against the pillow.

Sanyam touched his hair. "Sleep well, kit," he whispered, and left the room.

Sterling frowned, fighting his way back to awareness. This wasn't right. It wasn't—he needed—

He sat up, movements loose and uncoordinated, and managed to make it to his feet, swaying dangerously. The floor was uneven beneath his feet, shifting treacherously as he tried to walk, and Sterling staggered and fell against the wall.

"Fox?" Sanyam sounded worried. "*Kamsin*, what are you doing? You should be in bed!"

Sterling grabbed his arm, and Sanyam steadied him.

"Bed," Sterling rasped.

"Yes," Sanyam said. He swung him up into his arms and turned to carry him back into Sterling's bedroom.

Sterling clung to him when Sanyam tried to put him down, though.

"*Your* bed," he managed. "You."

Sanyam froze. "You want—you want to sleep with *me*?"

Sterling closed his eyes, burrowing into Sanyam's warmth, and Sanyam took a shaky breath.

"All right, *meri jaan*," he whispered, and carried him back out, through the hall, and into his own bedroom.

Sterling moaned happily when Sanyam put him down, and nestled into the pillows that smelled delightfully of vanilla and sandalwood.

Sanyam crawled in behind him, pulling him close and dropping a kiss on the nape of his neck.

"*Now* will you sleep?" he asked.

"Mm-hmm," Sterling said, and sank into the black.

THEY DIDN'T TALK about it. Sterling still flatly refused to discuss anything emotional, distracting Sanyam with hands and mouth and teeth whenever Sanyam tried, until he got the message.

But after that scene, Sterling slept in Sanyam's room, waking up as often as not tangled in Sanyam's arms and legs, his nose buried in Sterling's hair and his breathing steady and warm on Sterling's neck.

Sometimes Sterling would stare at the ceiling while Sanyam slept, fighting panic. *Why are you doing this? He'll see you for who you are soon enough. Why are you trying to convince yourself it'll work? Besides, remember what he said? You're not actually falling in love with him—it's just because you're subbing for him that you feel this way.*

Sterling always slipped out of bed when those thoughts came, curling up on the couch with Polly or taking a long, hot shower, arm braced on the glass as he tried not to listen to his brain.

Often Sanyam would join him, slipping an arm around Sterling's waist or kissing his wet shoulder, and Sterling would turn to face him, plastering on a smile as he wrapped his arms around Sanyam's neck.

NEARLY THREE MONTHS into his stay with Sanyam, Sterling was back at Granville Island with Cricket. She didn't need him or Dorian there, but Sterling enjoyed her company more and more these days, and found reasons to spend time with her when he wasn't working.

He was playing a game on his phone, tongue caught between his teeth in concentration, as Cricket spoke to a customer.

"—My brother, Fox," she said, and Sterling glanced up, startled, to see her gesturing at him.

"What?"

The man smiled at Sterling. He was in his sixties, silver-gray hair swept neatly off a high forehead, trim and compact, with a friendly face. "I'm Navin," he said. "You made that mosaic?"

Sterling nodded, glancing at the *C* that Cricket kept prominently displayed above her wares.

"Do you have any other pieces?" Navin asked.

"Not really," Sterling admitted. "I was just fooling around."

"Well, if you do, I'd be very interested in displaying some of them in my gallery," Navin said. He held out a business card. "My partner and I have been looking for some new talent. You have a bold eye for color and style that I think would sell well."

Sterling stared at him, lost for words, and Cricket took the business card.

"The gallery is downtown," Navin said. "You're more than welcome to come by anytime."

Cricket met Sterling's eyes as Navin walked away. "Fox," she whispered. "Do you know who that is?"

"He said his name was Navin," Sterling said. "So?"

"*So*, that's Navin Arya," Cricket hissed. "He and his partner run one of the top-rated art galleries in Vancouver, how do you not know who he is?"

Sterling shrugged. "I don't run in art circles, Cricky. How the hell would I know him?"

Cricket rolled her eyes. "You should make some more mosaics, is what I'm saying. He can probably sell anything you make, and it would help your income, wouldn't it?" She held out the card.

"I guess," Sterling said doubtfully, accepting it. "I'm just… not an artist."

"You make art," Cricket said. Her tone brooked no argument. "That makes you an artist."

Sterling stared at the card and finally tucked it into his pocket. "I'll think about it."

27

The night of Colby's party, Sterling dashed around the apartment in a frenzy, hunting for his shoes.

"I left them in the living room, didn't I?" he shouted. "When you wanted to suck me off last night after work?"

"I put them in your bedroom," Sanyam called from the bathroom.

"Right, of course," Sterling muttered. He found them tucked neatly under the end of the bed and stepped into them, tying the laces carelessly. "Are you ready? We're going to be late. Bus'll be here any minute!"

Sanyam stepped into the hall, looking dapper and elegant in a long-sleeved T-shirt so dark brown it was almost black. He smiled at Sterling as he pulled on his cabled sweater.

"I like that shirt," he said. "It's the color of your eyes."

Sterling smoothed the front of the olive-green silk T-shirt. "I wore it to the club once, didn't I?"

Sanyam's smile widened. "Indeed you did. Are you ready?"

Sterling grabbed Colby's present and followed him out to the front door, where Sanyam picked up his own bag.

"Bye, Polly!" Sanyam called. Sterling snickered, and they clattered down the stairs to the bus stop.

Spring was fully underway, the trees blossoming with color and birds calling to each other in their branches. Sterling took a deep breath of cool salt-scented air, filling his lungs.

On the bus, he leaned against Sanyam slightly. "I should warn you, Annaliese is… prickly."

"She was with Colby that night at the club, wasn't she?" Sanyam said.

Sterling nodded. "She's never liked me. Feeling's mutual, believe me. I think Colby can do better. She resents me for telling him that."

"You *told* him that?"

Sterling hunched his shoulders. "It wasn't personal. I just… he's been my best friend for ten years. We met in high school, and he hung out at my house all the time growing up. I felt like Annaliese wasn't right for him, and I should've kept my mouth shut, but I didn't, and she's never forgiven me."

Sanyam touched his knee. "Regardless of how you did it, your reasons were motivated by caring."

"Yeah, well, I'm just letting you know," Sterling said.

"Thank you," Sanyam said gravely. He hefted the bag he'd brought. "Perhaps she'll be appeased by the wine I brought."

Cricket opened the door for them. She flung her arms around them both in turn and then pulled them into the house, which smelled enticingly of fresh-baked bread and apple pie.

Dorian and Tatum were on the sofa, arms around each other. Dorian scrambled up and hugged Sterling, who returned it, and then held out his hand to Sanyam.

"I'm Dorian. We've never actually been introduced, but I've heard a lot about you."

Sanyam took his hand. "It's very nice to meet you, Dorian. Your brother speaks of you often."

"He does?" Dorian slanted a look at Sterling, who rolled his eyes.

"He's exaggerating for effect. I might have

mentioned the troll that lived in our basement growing up. Maybe he inferred something from that. Hi, Tatum, still with this slob?"

Tatum grinned and hugged him. Their nails were yellow, white, purple, and black, pairing perfectly with their black cargo pants and yellow shirt.

"I like the polish," Sterling said.

Tatum held up a hand. "It's the nonbinary pride colors."

Colby bounded in. "Break it up, break it up, you guys aren't supposed to be having fun without me!"

He engulfed Sterling in a hug and stood back to look him over.

"Man, you look *good!* Introduce me to the guy responsible so I can give him a big ol' kiss for taking such great care of you."

Sterling snorted and pulled Sanyam forward. "Sanyam, this is Colby. Colby, Sanyam. Do *not* kiss him or I'll have to punch you."

Colby laughed, a deep belly laugh that vibrated his muscled frame, and shook Sanyam's hand. "It's great to finally meet you, dude. Thanks for looking out for my boy here."

"It's been my pleasure," Sanyam said. "Happy birthday, and thank you for inviting me to your celebration."

"Thanks!" Colby said. He accepted the gifts that Sterling and Sanyam handed to him and put them on the table behind him.

Sanyam lifted the bottle of wine. "I brought something for dinner, as well."

"*Liese*!" Colby bellowed. "Guests!"

"I'm here," Annaliese snapped, coming out of the kitchen and drying her hands on a towel. "No need to bring the house down, Colby. Hello, Sterling." She accepted the air-kiss he offered, turning her head away enough that he didn't make contact, and held out her hand to Sanyam. "Thank you for coming."

Sanyam bowed over her hand. "Thank you for having us."

Annaliese was spoiling for a fight, Sterling realized with a sinking sensation. It showed in the way her blue eyes sparked, the set of her jaw, and the tension in her shoulders. Colby could see it too, from the uneasy looks he was giving her.

Don't do this, Sterling thought. *Don't ruin Colby's night.*

"Gotta go check the steaks," Colby said, and disappeared out the back door.

"Can I help you with anything?" Sanyam asked Annaliese.

She gave him a dubious look but shrugged. "You can set the table."

"I'll show you where everything is," Sterling said.

Annaliese didn't say much in the hour leading up to dinner, busy in the kitchen and not coming out very often, and Sterling spent the time talking to Cricket, Dorian, and Tatum.

"I hear you liked your gift," Sanyam said to Cricket.

Cricket lit up. "*So much*. I had no idea he was such an artist! Fox, did you tell Sanyam about Navin?"

Sanyam lifted his eyebrows, turning to Sterling. "Who's Navin?"

"He's some guy who runs an art gallery, apparently," Sterling muttered. "He said he liked my stuff. It's not a big deal."

"It is *too*," Cricket said. "He could get you so much exposure. Dori, did you even know Fox was an artist?"

Dorian shook his head. "Other than his puzzles, it's not like he's ever really shown that side of himself before," he said, but he was smiling.

"Too interested in partying and telling his friends who to date," Annaliese said, setting a bowl of chips and salsa on the coffee table and stalking out again.

Sterling stiffened.

"Fox, do you really tell your friends who to

date?" Cricket demanded as she leaned forward to grab a chip.

"Not in years," Sterling said, forcing a smile.

"But you have!" Cricket said. "That's such a Fox thing to do. Dori, do you remember that time you brought that girl home—sorry, Tatum—and Fox made her cry?"

"Oh yeah," Dorian said. He patted Tatum's knee and took a chip. "That was a fun day."

"Wait, when was this?" Sterling demanded. "When did I make a girl cry?"

"I think I was in ninth grade," Dorian said. "What was her name, Crick?"

"Tiffany Cooper," Cricket said, sighing. "She had the most *fantastic* breasts."

The room fell silent as everyone turned to look at Cricket, who went red.

"She did! Stop looking at me, this is about Fox and his tendency to make Dorian's partners cry."

"What did you say to her?" Sanyam asked. He was next to Sterling on the couch, warm thigh pressed against Sterling's and his dark eyes alight with curiosity.

"Does it really matter?" Sterling muttered. "I was a dick."

"Was," Dorian echoed. "Sure, Fox. We'll go with that." He turned to Sanyam. "He asked her if her breasts were real, and when she said they were, he said he could recommend a great plastic surgeon who could, and I quote, 'perk them right up.' She ran out in tears." He snorted a laugh and took another chip.

Sterling squirmed as Sanyam turned and looked at him, a quizzical smile in his eyes.

"Like I said, I was a dick."

"And it wasn't even true," Dorian told Tatum. "Like Cricket said, she had great boobs. Fox was just in a bad mood that day."

"How was that day different from every other day?" Cricket asked, laughing. "Oh man, Dori, do you remember that play in third grade, the really awful one with the singing elves?"

Dorian chortled and explained to Tatum and Sanyam, "Fox was so bored that he announced at the top of his lungs during the second act that he was going to wait in the car, where everything sucked less."

"I was thirteen!" Sterling protested. "Everyone's a jerk at thirteen." Sanyam was just looking at him, a smile on his lips, but Sterling wanted to crawl into a hole and die of the embarrassment that choked him.

Cricket patted his knee. "Dori, did I tell you that the day I met San here, he'd bumped into Fox and spilled his coffee on him?"

"No!" Dorian exclaimed. "What'd he do?"

"Charged him two hundred dollars for a new T-shirt!" Cricket managed through her giggles.

Sanyam's lips were twitching, and Sterling's face felt like it was on fire as Colby came back inside. He was being flayed alive, strip after strip pulled away from his core. Sanyam was going to see him for who he really was, any minute now.

"What are we talking about?" Colby asked, flopping down in the chair at the end of the couch and accepting a beer from Annaliese with a smile of thanks. She sat down on the arm of the chair, and Colby wrapped his arm around her waist.

"My flaws as a human," Sterling snapped.

Colby perked up. "I can play this game! Did I ever tell you guys about the time in college when he got a professor fired because he didn't like the grade he'd gotten?"

Heads swiveled, and Sterling flinched.

"He was sleeping with his TA," he said feebly.

"This other time, he didn't like his roommate," Colby continued. "But the dude refused to be reassigned, because he liked the room and where they were on campus. So Fox—" He stopped to laugh. "Fox basically made the guy's life a living hell. He got up at 5:00 a.m. and made tons of noise every morning—"

"You, an early riser?" Sanyam interrupted, his eyebrows going up.

"When he has to be," Colby said, grinning. "He had parties every weekend in the room, and when that didn't work, he resorted to bringing home a different guy every week and having sex with him in front of his roommate."

Cricket gasped and Annaliese rolled her eyes.

He bragged about hitting his girlfriend when she "stepped out of line," Sterling thought miserably. He'd tried reporting him, but he'd had no evidence and the girl had refused to testify. Sterling hadn't been able to stomach looking at him after that and he'd resorted to drastic measures.

Colby had already moved on to another story, and everyone was laughing except for Tatum, who was watching Sterling's face silently.

He caught their eye and tried for a smile. *Nothing more than I deserve.*

Tatum said nothing, but there was sympathy on their face.

"That's our Fox," Colby said cheerfully. "He's an asshole, and we wouldn't have him any other way."

Sterling forced a lighthearted shrug and popped a chip into his mouth. "Good, because I don't plan on changing."

Dinner was more of the same, lighthearted ribbing of Sterling's failings interspersed with anecdotes from their childhood. Sterling tried to join in, his smile pasted firmly in place. He'd brought this on himself, after all. He had no one else to blame. Better that Sanyam see it now than that he keep trying to make Sterling into a decent person. He was working with flawed material, after all.

Toward the end of the meal, Colby cleared his throat and stood up, tapping on the empty wineglass in front of Annaliese's plate.

"I'd like to make an announcement," he said loudly. He beamed around the table. "Thank you all for being here and celebrating my birthday with me. It means the world to us both that you guys could come." He took Annaliese's hand. "On that note, we have something to say." Annaliese ducked her head, a smile blooming, as Colby grinned down at her. "We're expecting!"

The room exploded with congratulations as Annaliese blushed and Colby preened, and when it finally quieted, Colby looked at Sterling.

"Fox, man. Would you be the godfather?"

Sterling's mouth fell open. "*What?*" He snuck a look at Annaliese, who didn't look pleased but just nodded.

"We've talked about it," Colby said earnestly. "You're my best friend. I love you like a brother, and I'd just—I'd be so honored if you'd be the godfather of my kid."

Sterling struggled to remember how to speak. "But—you—doesn't the godfather raise the child if something happens to the parents?"

"Yeah, but nothing's happening to us," Colby said cheerfully. "It's just a title, man, you're not going to have to actually adopt my kid. What do you say?"

"I—" Sterling's head was spinning. "Can I… think about it?"

Colby's smile slipped, but he nodded. "Sure, dude, take your time."

"Use your bathroom?" Sterling said.

"'Course," Colby said. "You know where it is."

Sterling nodded and rose. The guest bathroom was at the other end of the house, through the kitchen and down the hall. When he was done, he braced his hands on the sink and stared at himself in the mirror.

His reflection gazed back, eyes sullen and mouth downturned.

"You would be the worst father in the world," Sterling told it.

His reflection didn't argue.

When he came out of the bathroom, he heard soft voices in the kitchen. Sterling stopped in the doorway at the sight of Colby and Annaliese, her arms around his neck and their foreheads pressed together.

Sterling ached at the tenderness in the way Annaliese cupped the back of Colby's head, a smile curving her lips. He wanted that. He wanted to let Sanyam touch him like that, to sink into his warmth and never let go. But he didn't get what he wanted.

Why not? a tiny voice whispered. *Why can't you have that?*

Sterling stomped hard on the voice. *Because I fuck everything up. Everything I touch breaks.*

He faded back into the hall and waited a few seconds before making his footsteps loud and coming back in.

Colby bent and kissed the end of Annaliese's tilted nose and picked up the apple pie on the counter. "I'll carry it, babe. Don't want you straining yourself."

Annaliese rolled her eyes and gathered the plates. "It's a pie, Colby, not an anvil."

Sterling followed them back into the dining room as Annaliese handed out plates around the table.

Cricket leaned forward. "When are you due?"

"February," Annaliese said.

The talk turned to pregnancy symptoms and woes, and Sterling sat silently, his shoulders hunched, feeling sick.

"What about you?" Cricket said, turning to Sanyam. "Do you want kids?"

Sanyam smiled at her and took a sip of wine. "Oh yes. Very much so. At least one, but possibly two, I think."

Cricket clasped her hands and sighed. "I love babies, especially if I can give them back after I'm done holding them."

"Do *you* want children?" Sanyam asked.

"I don't know," Cricket admitted. "I don't think so, but I think they're adorable." She nudged Dorian with an elbow. "Can you imagine Fox as a father?"

Dorian shuddered dramatically, and everyone but Sanyam and Tatum laughed.

Sterling had abruptly had enough. The constant jibes, no matter how laughing the tone, had worn him to the bone. He was an exposed nerve, raw and sensitive, and he couldn't take another second of it.

He dropped his napkin on the table and stood. "I'm sorry, but I'm not feeling well. I have to… go. Col, happy birthday. I'm—I'll catch you later." He turned to Annaliese and forced a smile. "Congratulations, I'm sure you'll be a great mother."

He bolted before anyone could say anything,

away from the table and out the front door as he pulled his phone from his pocket and called a cab.

"Fox!" Sanyam sounded out of breath and alarmed as he pounded up behind him. "What happened, Fox, what's wrong?"

Sterling swung to face him. "Nothing's wrong. Everything's fine. Go back inside and trash me to my friends and family some more."

Sanyam's eyebrows shot up. "Is that what you think we were doing? *Jaanam*, it wasn't like that."

"No? Because it sure as shit felt like that from where I was sitting," Sterling snapped. The cab pulled up and he yanked the door open. "Get your own ride home."

He couldn't do it. Why had he ever thought he could? *You ruin everything.*

WHEN SANYAM ARRIVED HOME, Sterling was already half packed, throwing clothes into his suitcases and stalking around the apartment to gather his personal items.

"*Fox*," Sanyam said. "What are you doing?"

"What do you think I'm doing?" Sterling said, not looking at him as he packed his mosaic supplies into the box. Polly squeaked, clearly bewildered, from the couch beside him, but Sterling couldn't bring himself to touch her.

"*Stop*," Sanyam said as Sterling stood.

Sterling froze in place and then snarled and spun. "*You* stop. You don't get to *do* that anymore. You don't get to boss me around. You get off on it, on telling me what to do. Well, I'm done. I've had enough."

"I thought you *liked* it when I bossed you around," Sanyam said.

"In the bedroom, sure!" Sterling said. He headed down the hall to pack his other suitcase as Sanyam followed him. "But you're always doing it. You're telling me to eat. To exercise. Take care of myself. 'Go to bed, Fox. Eat your breakfast, Fox. Come running with me, Fox.' I need a minder, remember? You can't stand not being in control of every little detail of my life, can you?"

Sanyam stood in the doorway, eyes full of shock and hurt. "I didn't—Fox, it wasn't like that."

Sterling sneered. "It was for my own good, is that it?"

"It *was*!" Sanyam exclaimed, clutching at his hair. "You're *terrible* at taking care of yourself, Fox. You need someone to look out for you. Well, I *like* looking out for you, so why won't you let me do it?"

"Because I'm not a child!" Sterling shouted as he whirled. "I'm a grown man, and I can take care of myself!"

Sanyam nodded, standing his ground and holding out his hand. "Okay, Fox. I'm sorry. I shouldn't have assumed. Can you forgive me?"

Sterling shrugged and turned away again. "There's nothing *to* forgive. I'm done. I'm done freeloading off you. I'm done experimenting with BDSM. I'm done."

"No," Sanyam said, his voice low. "Don't say that, Fox."

"I told you when I met you," Sterling continued as he shoved the last of his shirts into the suitcase and zipped it up. "I'm not a sub. I was just having some fun, okay?"

"Is this about dinner?" Sanyam asked. "I didn't realize—I should have put a stop to it. Of course it hurt you. But you were laughing—I thought you were okay with it."

Sterling scoffed. "I wasn't hurt. But it did make one thing perfectly clear. We want different things. You want kids. I don't, in a *big* way. Like, a deal-breaker way. So I'm doing you a favor and I'm getting out now, before this goes any further and we both end up doing something we regret."

"No." Sanyam's eyes were wet, and Sterling

fought the stab of pain at the sight. "Fox, we can talk about this."

"We're done talking." Sterling carried his suitcase down the hall and set it by the front door, then went back for the other one.

Sanyam was standing in the kitchen, grief and frustration on his face. "*Sterling.*"

Sterling stopped, his back to him.

"*Mein tumse pyaar karta huun,*" Sanyam said. There were tears in his voice.

"I don't know what that means," Sterling said without turning.

"Look it up," Sanyam managed. "I'm not going to stop you if you feel you have to go, but I needed to say that."

Polly rubbed against Sterling's ankles, and he fought the tears that blinded him suddenly. He stooped and ran a hand down her back.

"Bye, baby," he whispered, and fled.

28

———

Sterling ended up at a hotel halfway across town, a step down from his preferred tastes, but the room was clean and the door locked.

He dropped his bags, closed the curtains, and crawled into the bed, hugging a pillow to his stomach as he stared at the wall. Tears prickled his eyes, and he blinked them away.

His father's voice echoed in his head. *Boys don't cry. Be a man. Crying is weakness.*

"Fuck you, Dad," Sterling said out loud, buried his face in the pillow, and let the tears flow.

He wept until he was exhausted, frame limp from the sobs that wracked him, and finally, wrung out and hiccupping, he rolled off the bed and stumbled to the shower.

He stood under the spray until it ran cold, eyes closed.

"Mein tumse pyaar karta huun. Look it up."

Sterling had a feeling he knew what Sanyam had said, but when he was done, he dragged on clean clothes and picked up his phone. Google Translate confirmed his fears, and he put the phone down and drew his knees to his chest.

You can't love me, San. There's nothing here to love.

His phone rang, and he jerked his head up, wiping his face. It was Cricket, he realized, his heart sinking, but he answered anyway.

She sounded like she'd been crying. "Fox—"

Sterling sat up straight. "What is it, Cricky, what's wrong? What happened?"

Cricket took a gulping breath. "Sanyam called. He—"

Sterling's chest seized. "Is he okay?"

"He was angry," Cricket said, hiccupping. "He —he said we should be ashamed of ourselves, that he was ashamed of *himself,* that we treated you terribly at dinner. I'm sorry, Fox, I'm so sorry. That's just how we always talk, and I didn't *think* —did we hurt you? We shouldn't have said those things, I'm sorry—"

Sterling sank back to the bed, stunned.

"Are you still there?" Cricket asked.

"I'm here," Sterling said.

"Tatum agreed with him. Said they could tell you were hurt, even though you tried not to show it. *Fox—*"

"It's okay, Crick," Sterling said. It was hard to breathe. No one had ever done that for him, and he had no idea how to process it. "I'm—it's okay. Thank you."

Cricket sniffled. "I know we don't say it, but I love you, Fox."

Sterling closed his eyes. "I—I love you too, Cricky. I have to go."

He hung up and rolled onto his stomach, pushing his face into the pillow. He needed… advice, someone to tell him what he should do. The notion of talking to his mother was discarded before it fully formed.

Amparo.

Sterling sat up again.

Maybe she wouldn't even want to see him. She probably blamed him for getting her fired, all those years ago.

Sterling set his jaw. If she did, he'd just have to keep apologizing until she forgave him. He slid off the bed and stepped into his shoes, dialing for a taxi as he left the room.

A quick Google search confirmed that, by some miracle, Amparo still lived in the same house she'd been in when she'd worked for the Reynards. Sterling gave the driver the address and sat tensely on the edge of the seat as they rolled through town and fetched up in front of the house.

Sterling paid the taxi driver and climbed out, staring at the neat yard and little picket fence that surrounded it. A child's bicycle was parked by the porch, a pair of skates nearby.

As he stood there, unsure what to do, the front door blew open, and two girls tumbled out, shrieking and laughing. Sterling froze, but it was too late—they'd spotted him.

The older one stepped forward. She was about thirteen, Sterling estimated. Maybe older, from the predatory way she was eyeing him.

She can probably smell fear. Small movements.

"Um. Is Amparo here?"

The younger girl turned and dashed into the house, yelling at the top of her lungs. "*Grandma! Visitor!*"

Sterling winced. The older girl was still looking at him.

"I'm Sophia," she said.

"Hi," Sterling said.

"And you are?" she prompted.

"*Sterling?*" Amparo's voice was unchanged, but physically—Sterling's heart ached. She had silvery gray hair, and her face was lined, crow's-feet around the beautiful brown eyes he'd always loved so much.

Sterling managed a smile even as she blurred in his vision. "Hi, 'Paro," he managed. "Can I, um… come in?"

Amparo hurried forward and opened the gate to pull him into a hug. Sterling clutched the back of her shirt and his knees nearly buckled as the tears overwhelmed him yet again.

"My sweet boy," Amparo said as he tried desperately to keep from breaking down in her arms. "Oh, precious *mijo*, what's happened? Come on, inside with you." She guided him up the walk and inside the house, dim and cool and spotless, where she sat him down on the sofa and clutched his hands.

Sterling couldn't speak for the tears that choked him. "I got you fired," he finally blurted. "I'm so sorry, 'Paro."

"No," Amparo said sharply, squeezing his hands. "No, *querido*, I got me fired. I should have known better than to do that. I'll never forgive myself for putting you in that situation."

Sterling shook his head wordlessly.

"I heard about your father," Amparo continued. "I'm sorry. I know that had to be hard on you, no matter what he was like."

"He died because of me," Sterling whispered. "I—he was stealing, and I threatened to expose him. He had a wreck and died. It was my fault—"

"It's *not* your fault," Amparo said, grabbing his face and forcing him to look at her. "Sterling, *mi amor*, you did the right thing, and you're punishing yourself for it. Your father's choices were his own, and you had nothing to do with them. Now, let me look at you, *cariño*." She sat back, and Sterling wiped his face as she inspected him.

"How did you even recognize me?" Sterling asked. "It's been, what—twelve years?"

Amparo laughed. "I'd know you anywhere, *esterlina*. You're taller, and sadder, but it's still you." She cupped his face, wiping away another tear. "Tell 'Paro what's wrong."

The door opened and both girls burst inside, giggling.

Amparo said something in rapid-fire Spanish and the older girl turned and disappeared into the kitchen, just off the room they were in. The younger girl stared at Sterling, twisting her fingers in the hem of her shirt.

"Are these your granddaughters?" Sterling asked.

"Sophia and Crystal," Amparo said, clearly proud.

"Beatriz's daughters?"

Amparo laughed. "Bless you, *esterlina*, Beatriz is your age! She'd have to have been pregnant at eleven to have had Sophia. No, these are my oldest boy's little ones. I don't suppose you ever met him."

Sterling shook his head as Sophia yelled something from the kitchen, and Amparo rolled her eyes.

"I'll be right back," she said. "Sophia can't find her head with both hands and a map."

She disappeared, and Sterling was alone with Crystal, who regarded him curiously.

"How do you know my *abuela*?" she asked.

"She was my nanny when I was a little boy," Sterling said.

Crystal's eyes went wide. "You're Sterling?"

"You know about me?" Sterling said, startled.

Crystal sat down on the couch next to him, folding her legs and gripping her ankles.

"Um." Sterling scooted away, but Crystal wasn't fazed.

"*Abuela* talks about you a lot, 'specially after what happened with your papa," she said. "She says you were a very sweet little boy, but your parents were awful. *Abuela* would adopt you if you wanted her to. She loves you very much. She could be your new mama! That would make you my….” She trailed off, frowning.

“Your uncle,” Sterling supplied, smiling in spite of himself. “I still have a mother, though. Besides, I’m grown up. I don’t need to be adopted.”

“You need a *better* mother,” Crystal said firmly. She scooted nearer. “Sophia thinks you’re very handsome, but if you’re our uncle, she can’t date you.”

Sterling couldn’t help his laugh. “There are several problems with me dating her anyway. One being that she’s very underage and that’s *illegal*. Another is that I’m—” He hesitated. “Um. Gay.”

Crystal brightened. “You could date my uncle, then! He’s gay too!”

“You’re very persistent, aren’t you?”

“*Abuela* says it’s one of my best qualities. I’m gonna be a lawyer.”

“Oh yeah, that’ll help,” Sterling agreed.

“My uncle’s very handsome,” Crystal said. She pulled out her phone and scrolled through until she found a picture. “His name is Levi. Look!”

Sterling found himself inspecting a picture of a tall man standing next to a red horse. “Is your uncle the guy or the horse?”

Crystal dissolved into helpless giggles, folding

over, and Sterling's lips twitched unwillingly as she laughed.

Amparo appeared in the doorway, smiling fondly at Crystal. "Go help Sophia in the kitchen, *mija*," she said. "Sterling and I need to talk."

Crystal scrambled off the couch and flung her arms around Sterling, who grunted in surprise. She smelled like lavender and bubblegum, her hair soft where it brushed his cheek, and Sterling patted her tentatively on the back.

Amparo sat down in her place as Crystal dashed into the kitchen. "Sorry about that. I know she can be overwhelming."

"She's cute," Sterling said, startled to realize it was true.

Amparo patted his knee. "Now. Tell me what's wrong. Why did you show up on my doorstep after all these years?"

"I need—" Sterling swallowed. "I needed to talk to someone. I need… advice. I met… there's this guy, and—"

Amparo's eyes were keen. "Did you fall in love, *mijo*?"

"No!" Sterling protested, and then froze. "Wait… how did you—you know I'm gay?" He stifled a half-hysterical laugh. "Of course you do."

Amparo smiled at him. "So… you're in love."

He ran a hand through his hair. "Maybe. I don't know. I can't—I can't love him."

"Why not?"

"Because… he deserves better," Sterling whispered.

"Nonsense," Amparo said flatly. "Whoever he is, he's clearly amazing, if you've fallen for him. You always had good taste. Tell me about him."

"His name is Sanyam," Sterling said. His throat was tight, his eyes burning.

"How did you meet?"

"He spilled his coffee on me," Sterling said. "I was—I was a dick, but he…."

Amparo's eyes crinkled as she smiled. "You and your sharp tongue. But he didn't care?"

"He liked me anyway," Sterling whispered. "I thought it was—physical. You know? I thought he just—but he said he loved me. He can't. He *can't*, 'Paro."

"Why not?" Amparo repeated, eyes steady on Sterling's face. "Tell me why he couldn't love the sweetest boy I ever took care of."

Sterling hunched his shoulders. "I'm not that little boy anymore. I'm…. No one likes me, 'Paro. I'm a dick to everyone. I'm selfish and grumpy and allergic to human emotions. Every time San touches me, I'm rude to him unless we're in bed. I'm—I'm not good enough for him."

Amparo's eyes were sad. "The worst part is you clearly believe that."

"Because it's *true*," Sterling said.

"So don't be like that anymore," Amparo said.

"It's not that easy," Sterling protested.

"I never said it was going to be *easy*," Amparo said. "But you're strong and smart, and you can do anything you put your mind to. So if you decide you want to be better, a better person, someone worthy of this Sanyam's love, then what's stopping you?"

Sterling rubbed his face. "What if—"

"What if what?" Amparo said. She took his hand. "If you love him—and it's obvious you do, judging by the state you were in when you showed up—then you know what you have to do." She tilted her head. "Do you *like* being a jerk, *cariño*? Do you like yourself this way?"

Sterling shook his head. "I—no. But I don't know how to change."

"It's not a switch you flip," Amparo said. "It's a conscious decision, made a hundred, a thousand times a day. It'll get easier over time, but there's always a choice there. The first step is deciding to be better. And then you keep doing that, over and over again, until it comes more easily."

"It sounds exhausting."

Amparo laughed. "All good things take work.

What's the point if it's effortless?" She leaned forward. "Let me make this clear. You don't change for him, do you understand? You change because *you* want to be better. Never change to be someone else's ideal, *esterlina*. Only do it for yourself."

Sterling nodded. "I do want to change," he whispered. "I just... I don't think I'm strong enough."

Amparo laughed out loud. "*You?* Not strong enough? Oh, my darling boy, you can be so dumb." She squeezed his hand again. "You survived your parents, and you did it with your sense of humor and your loving spirit intact. Maybe it's got a few cracks in it, but it's still there. I can see it." She stood up and pulled him to his feet. "Come, Sophia's making tea. You'll have some with me, and we'll talk about the old days. How are Cricket and Dorian? Tell me everything."

It had been a week, and Sanyam was operating on autopilot. All he could see every time he closed his eyes was Fox's anguished face, grief and hurt and fury in equal mixture, right before he walked out the door.

He'd fucked up, and he had no idea how to make it right. There was no way Fox would answer his calls, and it wasn't like Sanyam knew what to say to fix things anyway.

So he went to work, dealing with clients remotely but politely, and came home, where he sat on the couch and stared at the wall.

He missed Fox with a sharpness that sliced to his soul. His apartment seemed empty in a way it never had before, the rooms echoing with his footsteps. Sanyam kept expecting Fox to come running around the corner, looking for his socks or complaining that Sanyam had moved his stuff again.

But if he was dealing badly, Polly was worse. She was clingy to the point of obnoxious, meowing at Sanyam constantly as if he could produce her cuddle buddy from his pocket for her, and under his feet every time he got up to go anywhere, clearly terrified he'd leave her too.

Ava called Sanyam into her office three days after Fox left. Folding her hands, she fixed him with a sharp look.

"I hear Fox quit. What happened?"

"He moved out," Sanyam said.

"You guys break up?"

"We were never officially together," Sanyam protested feebly.

"Sure," Ava said. "Pull the other one. It's got bells on. He picked up his last check today, before you got here, and said he won't be back. Pity—he was actually doing a good job."

Sanyam said nothing, and Ava sighed.

"Take a week off."

"I'm fine," Sanyam said.

"My left asscheek you're fine," Ava snapped. "You're reeling, bucko, and you can't do your job properly when you're this fucked up. Go home and lick your wounds and deal with this, and then come back ready to work."

So Sanyam found himself at home, with absolutely nothing to occupy his time except for a miserable cat that refused to even let him go to the bathroom alone.

Finally, he gave up. Sick of staring at his empty rooms, he dragged on his coat and bolted out the door.

He had no clear idea where he was going, just that he needed to get out, get fresh air, and away from all the memories of Fox.

The bus started rolling, and Sanyam gazed sightlessly out the window, resting his forehead against the glass.

After about an hour of riding aimlessly, a sign for the aquarium caught his eye, and he straightened. Hadn't Cricket mentioned she and Dorian worked there now? Maybe they'd have word of Fox's well-being.

He paid for his ticket and went inside, only half an eye on his surroundings as he looked for Cricket. He went through the entire place and finally gave up and asked a passing employee.

"Oh, they're both off today," the girl said cheerfully. "They'll be back tomorrow."

Sanyam sagged in disappointment and turned for the exit. On his way, he passed the stingrays, and a man leaning over the tank caught his eye. Sanyam looked closer. Why did he look so familiar? He was small-framed, slender, with black hair, dark eyes, and a bold nose—Sanyam's mouth fell open.

"*Micah?*"

Micah—it *was* him—spun and nearly overbalanced, the man with him catching his arm before he toppled into the tank.

"*Sanyam?* What the *hell* are you doing in Vancouver?"

"I could ask you the same thing!" Sanyam said, looking him over. "You look so good! How have you been?"

Micah's smile widened. That was why Sanyam hadn't recognized him at first—a smile seemed perpetually pasted on his face, setting his black eyes dancing. He was a far cry from the sad, haunted man who had tried to scene with him a year before.

"I've been great," he said, reaching out and catching the wrist of the man beside him and drawing him forward. "This is my fiancé, Devon Mallory. Devon, do you remember I told you how I tried to sub in Mumbai when we were apart?"

Devon was a tall man with brown hair and

bright blue eyes, and he held out one big hand to Sanyam. "Of course."

"This is—um… the guy," Micah said.

Sanyam shook Devon's hand. "It's very nice to meet you, and I see congratulations are in order."

Micah ducked his head, somehow smiling even more, and Devon wrapped an arm around his waist, pulling him close.

"What are you doing in Vancouver, though?" Sanyam asked. "I thought you lived in Toronto."

"Dev's mom lives here," Micah explained. "We came out so I could meet her."

"And then of course nothing would do but that we go see the rays," Devon added, grinning. "So here we are."

"What are *you* doing here?" Micah asked.

"I live here now," Sanyam said. "Kali put me in touch with the owner of a club—the Honeytrap—and I moved here about five months ago."

His heart ached, looking at Micah and Devon in front of him, so happy and secure in their relationship. He missed Fox even more, with a sharp, fierce pang. He needed to find him, apologize again, make Fox realize that no matter what had happened, they could work through it if Fox was just willing to *try*.

No. Sanyam knew even as he had the thought

that that was exactly what Fox had been talking about.

"You can't stand not being in control of every little detail of my life, can you?"

He couldn't make this decision for Fox. This had to be something he came to willingly, on his own, or not at all.

"Sanyam?" Micah sounded worried.

Sanyam jerked, recalled to himself. "I'm so sorry. I got lost in my head for a moment. What were you saying?"

"Nothing much," Micah said. "Are you sure you're okay?"

"I'll be fine," Sanyam said. He held out his arms hesitantly, unsure if Micah would want to—but Micah stepped forward and hugged him hard.

"Do you need to talk about it?" he asked quietly.

Sanyam smiled down at him. "Thank you, but there's nothing to be said or done, except to hope—that things turn around."

"Then that's what I'll do," Micah said.

Devon held out his hand, and Sanyam shook it again.

"Take care of yourself," Devon said.

Sanyam watched them walk away and finally turned to go. Polly was probably climbing the walls with both her people gone—the least he could do was be there for her and comfort her as best he could.

When he got back to his apartment, Fox was sitting on the top step, knees drawn to his chest and arms wrapped around them as he waited.

30

───

Sterling scrambled to his feet, his heart in his throat. Sanyam stared up at him, his mouth hanging open, keys half out of his pocket and his foot on the bottom step.

"I—" All Sterling's carefully practiced words fled, everything he'd rehearsed in front of the mirror, the apology he'd honed until it was perfect in its elegant simplicity—gone, scattered on the wind by the look in Sanyam's eyes.

"*Please*," Fox managed, feeling his face crumple. "*Please forgive me, San.*" He began to weep, and Sanyam bounded up the steps to grab him, pulling him into a hard embrace.

"I'm so sorry," Fox sobbed, clinging to Sanyam's shirt. "I've been such a dick, but I want to do better—I want to *be* better, please, San—"

Sanyam's arms were tight around him, and Fox held on desperately as Sanyam crooned to him, until the worst of the tears had passed and Fox was limp and drained. He sagged against Sanyam's chest, face pressed to his wet shirt.

Finally he lifted his head, knowing his eyes were bloodshot and his nose was red, but Sanyam smiled down at him, tears in his own eyes, and tilted Fox's chin up, thumbing his dimple.

"I've missed you so much, *meri jaan*," he whispered. "Will you come inside and talk to me?"

Fox nodded, hiccupping, and Sanyam opened the door.

They were attacked by a small brown cloud the second they stepped inside. Polly climbed Fox like a tree, squeaking in a ferocious volley, and Fox couldn't help his soggy laugh as he caught her.

"She's been *impossible*," Sanyam said, petting Polly as she snuggled in under Fox's chin. "Clingy and whiny and demanding I bring you back."

"I'm here," Fox told Polly, who purred even louder. "I'm sorry I left you, but I'm back now, I promise."

Sanyam took Fox's hand and drew him to the couch. "We have some things to talk about. Is that all right?"

Fox nodded and sat, putting Polly on his

knees. When Sanyam withdrew, though, Fox grabbed his hand.

Sanyam froze, and Fox ducked his head, petting Polly with his free hand, focused on Sanyam's touch but unable to look at him.

"I… looked up what you said," he told Polly's back, afraid to meet Sanyam's eyes.

"I still mean it," Sanyam said, squeezing Fox's hand. "I'll always mean it."

"It scares me," Fox confessed, finally looking up. Sanyam's eyes were full of sympathy. "I'm—I don't deserve it, and—no, please, let me finish"—as Sanyam tried to speak—"but even though I don't deserve it, I still *want* it. I want you to love me as much as—" His throat closed. "As much as I love you."

Sanyam caught his breath on a laughing sob and covered his mouth, eyes filling with tears. "Oh, kit, do you mean it?"

Fox nodded, terror and hope choking him. "I've—never meant anything more."

"May I kiss you?" Sanyam asked.

"Yes *please*," Fox said.

Sanyam leaned forward, and their lips met, soft and tasting like salt, as Polly dug her claws into Fox's thigh to prevent being moved. Fox laughed breathlessly against Sanyam's mouth and deepened the kiss, pressing inside with quick sweeps of his tongue.

Finally, though, he had to break away to loosen Polly's grip. "Sorry," he said to Sanyam. "Your cat's... determined."

"I think she's every bit as much your cat now," Sanyam said, stroking Polly's back.

"I guess it's a good thing I'm not allergic." Fox sobered. "We need to... discuss some other stuff."

"Of course," Sanyam said immediately.

"I don't...." Fox sighed. "I don't like it when you boss me around or try to manipulate me outside the bedroom."

Sanyam nodded. "I'm sorry, kit. At first I didn't even realize I was doing it, and then I justified it to myself that you clearly needed to be taken care of, so I was doing you a favor. It's inexcusable, but I was—no." He shook his head. "I'm doing it right now. It won't happen again."

"Yeah," Fox said, squeezing his hand. "And if it does, I'll call you on it, okay?"

"Good," Sanyam said. "Is there anything else?"

"I—" Fox took a breath. "I don't know if I want kids." He ducked his head and waited for Sanyam to withdraw, to tell him that was too much, but Sanyam didn't move. Finally, Fox glanced up.

Sanyam's eyes were sad, but he smiled,

rubbing Fox's knuckles with a thumb. "I only want children with someone who wants them as much as I do. If you're not ready, or you don't want them, then—" He lifted a shoulder. "You are much more important to me than future, hypothetical children who don't even exist."

The weight on Fox's chest eased. "I'd be a shitty father anyway," he pointed out.

"Agree to disagree," Sanyam said, smiling at him. "But that's neither here nor there. Did you have anything else?"

Fox marshaled his thoughts. "I think that's it."

"I have something too," Sanyam said.

Fox braced himself.

"It's not bad," Sanyam said hurriedly. "I just… I want to be able to call you my boyfriend."

Fox grimaced.

"I'm proud of you," Sanyam said gently, thumb stroking the back of Fox's hand. "I want to be able to introduce you to people as my boyfriend. I want to shout it from the rooftops, but I won't because that might embarrass you."

Fox laughed and gave up. "Fine. Anything else?"

"I want to touch you," Sanyam said. "I want to know I won't be rebuffed when I reach for you when we're *not* having sex. I like touching you, kit, and it hurts when you pull away or make a rude comment. I won't be an octopus, but—"

Fox took a shaky breath and set a protesting Polly on the couch so he could crawl forward into Sanyam's arms. He burrowed close as Sanyam pulled him in and pressed a cheek to his hair.

"I'm sorry," Fox said into Sanyam's shirt. "I've just been so *scared*, and—"

"I know, *kamsin*," Sanyam murmured. "We'll start over, all right?"

Fox closed his eyes and nodded as Polly hopped onto his hip, making annoyed noises at having been dislodged.

31

Three months later

Fox stood in front of Sanyam's closet, staring at the yellow-and-green dress hanging there. He shouldn't have been surprised that Sanyam had kept it, honestly, but somehow he still was. He reached out and touched the silk fabric with one finger. It rustled, and Fox snatched his hand back.

"What's taking so long?" Sanyam yelled from the other room.

"Sorry!" Fox said. "Just… getting something." He lifted the dress off the hanger and carried it to the bed to lay it out. "Hang on a minute, okay?"

It pooled over the bed in folds of liquid sunshine, almost glowing in the late afternoon light. It was gorgeous, Fox had to admit, and he suddenly wanted—he closed Sanyam's door and yanked his clothes off before he could change his mind.

The dress settled over his head with a silken *shuff* and fell in soft drapes to his calves. Fox contorted himself and managed to zip up the back with a triumphant noise before smoothing his hands over the fabric and moving to the mirror.

You can still put on a dress. It won't make you any less of a boy.

His reflection gazed back at him, eyes wide and afraid. His long neck was accentuated by the low neckline, and he looked delicate, almost ethereal, against the vivid gold silk.

Fox took a deep breath. He didn't know where the stockings and gloves were, and he was afraid he'd lose his nerve if he didn't do this now. He moved for the door, the fabric swishing around his legs.

Sanyam was naked on Fox's bed, arms folded beneath his head and ankles crossed as he gazed at the ceiling and whistled a formless tune under his breath.

Fox cleared his throat and Sanyam lifted his head and then sat up so fast he nearly fell off the bed, his eyes going round.

"What are you—*Fox.*"

"Is this… okay?" Fox asked.

Sanyam stood up and approached him, hands outstretched, and Fox took them as Sanyam looked him up and down with wonder in his eyes.

"It's *better*," he said. "My god, Fox, *look* at you, you look… amazing. Incredible. *Divine*."

"Flatterer," Fox said, laughing as warmth spread through his chest.

Sanyam drew him to the bed and laid him down on it, the dress puddling around Fox's thighs. Fox sank onto the pillows, breath sharp and short in his throat as Sanyam straddled him, a gleam in his eyes.

"May I make love to you, Fox?" he whispered.

"We're literally in the bedroom," Fox pointed out. "You don't have to ask."

"We've also never done *this* before," Sanyam murmured as he dropped his head to nibble along Fox's jawline. "I want to make sure this is all right."

Fox turned his face to capture Sanyam's lips, tasting the tea he'd been drinking earlier. "I love you," he said when they broke apart. "I *want* you, please, San, please fuck me."

Sanyam shuddered and pressed his forehead to Fox's chest. "*Mashalla*, I'll never be over you begging, kit."

He pulled away and reached for the lube on

the nightstand, then scooted down the bed and settled between Fox's splayed legs. He didn't lift the dress, though. Instead, he ran his hands up Fox's thighs, caressing and rubbing until he got to his groin.

Fox hissed as Sanyam clasped him through the silk, nerve endings waking as he bucked into Sanyam's fist. "Fuck, *fuck*, San—"

"Feel good, *mastana*?" Sanyam asked.

Fox nodded, eyes rolling back as Sanyam stroked him. "Ah—San, oh God, not yet, *please*—"

Sanyam backed off, and Fox dragged in air, willing his body back from the edge. The look in Sanyam's eyes made him shiver. He pulled his knees up and planted his feet on the bed, the skirt falling back against his stomach, and Sanyam took a startled breath.

"*Gulbadan*," Sanyam murmured, planting a kiss on Fox's knee. "My beautiful *hamraaz*."

"What's—that one mean?" Fox managed as Sanyam coated a finger with lube and ran it around his entrance.

Sanyam smiled up at him. "'*Gulbadan*' is 'rose-bodied,' because you are perfect and lovely, and '*hamraaz*' is someone you love and share secrets with." He pushed his finger inside and waited as Fox gasped and fought to accept the intrusion. "So perfect."

He took his time opening Fox's body, stretching him on two and then three fingers with gentle, inexorable precision, murmuring endearments and encouragement until Fox was shaking all over, clutching at the bedspread.

"*Please*," Fox begged. "Please, San, I need—"

Sanyam pulled out and went to his knees, shuffling into position. Fox was leaking slow, heavy drops that stained the fabric rubbing against his shaft every time he moved, cranking his arousal higher with each brush of silk on skin.

He was already perilously close to the edge, he knew, and a soft breeze was going to push him right over.

Sanyam lined up and pressed inside, Fox's body stretching to take him, and stillness fell over the room.

"*Meri jaan*," Sanyam said when he was hilted. "My life." He began to move in slow, smooth thrusts, his rhythm even and steady, and Fox sobbed for air, running his hands up and down Sanyam's arms. They were corded with tension, taut and ropy beneath Fox's fingers, and Sanyam's eyes were already developing that far-off gaze as he chased his pleasure, lower lip caught between his white teeth.

Fox tilted his hips, *there*, and made a guttural noise as the head of Sanyam's cock dragged over his prostate. He could feel the familiar tightening in his balls, the knot of pleasure in his groin burgeoning until he thought he might crack open, break apart at the seams from the sensations rippling through him.

"C-close," he managed through his teeth.

Sanyam reached between them, gathering a handful of the dress again and stroking Fox's shaft in time to his thrusts.

"Come for me, *jaaneman*," he ordered. "Let me see it."

Fox cried out, his toes curling, and obeyed, soaking the silk in heavy spurts, and Sanyam followed him on a groan, his head falling to Fox's breastbone as he emptied inside him.

They sagged onto the mattress in a sweaty, exhausted heap, Sanyam still buried in Fox's core, his weight heavy and comforting on top of Fox's frame. His breath tickled Fox's skin, and Fox managed to lift a hand to slip it into Sanyam's curls and cup his skull.

"We ruined my dress," he slurred.

Sanyam laughed breathlessly against Fox's collarbone. "I'll buy you another one, *maahi*."

"Good," Fox said, and fell asleep.

32

"Amparo invited us to dinner next week," Fox blurted as Sanyam set the plates on the table. "Cricket and Dorian too."

Sanyam's eyebrows rose. "Is that something you want to do, kit?"

"I guess so," Fox said, affecting nonchalance.

Sanyam put a long finger under Fox's chin and tipped it up, his eyes keen as he searched Fox's face.

"Is it really?"

Fox nodded. "Yeah. I want you to meet her. Plus maybe her granddaughters will hit on you instead of me."

"Then we'll go," Sanyam said, smiling, and

bent to kiss him. "How are the twins, anyway?" he asked when he pulled away.

"They're good," Fox said. "Cricket's business is taking off—she's been talking to some big-deal vintage-glassware collector about apprenticing for him. And Dorian just got a promotion at the aquarium, plus he and Tatum seem really happy together. The trust funds don't give them much yet, but they're doing well."

"I'm glad," Sanyam said, sitting down.

Fox cleared his throat. "So I've also, uh—been looking at colleges."

Sanyam's smile lit the room.

"There are a couple in Vancouver offering mosaic stuff, but more importantly, LaSalle does some great classes, and I'd like to take their graphic design courses, as well as some art theory to help me get a handle on things. I was thinking I'd still work at the 'Trap for as many hours as I need to pay for classes, and—"

"I'll help," Sanyam said.

Fox shook his head. "No." He took Sanyam's hand and stepped close as Sanyam's face fell. "I want—I need to do this myself, San, don't you see? I can't coast by on your help like I did my father's, and I know—I *know*, it's not the same, but—"

"It sort of is," Sanyam agreed, and curved a hand over Fox's hip, fingers warm and intimate. "I'm so proud of you, *gulbadan*."

THEY TOOK a cab to Amparo's house as Fox muttered yet again about the need for a car of their own.

Sanyam just laughed and took his hand. "Maybe we can look at buying one soon."

"Really?" Fox perked up as the cab stopped.

"It's economically viable," Sanyam said as he paid the driver. "I think we could find a nice little used sedan for a reasonable price."

Fox's lip curled, and he slid out of the back seat. *A sedan. Economically viable.* It wasn't until he heard Sanyam's snicker that he realized he'd been had.

"Can you blame me for teasing you?" Sanyam asked, amusement making his black eyes sparkle.

"Fuck you too," Fox retorted, but he couldn't help his own smile as they walked up the path to Amparo's front porch.

Crystal flung the door open and launched herself at Fox, who staggered backward under the weight of her solid little body.

"You're here, you're here!" she cried.

Fox bent to hug her, smelling bubblegum and soap as his cheek brushed hers. "What's up, pickle?"

Crystal giggled. "Is this your boyfriend?"

"Sanyam, meet the rival for my affections. Crystal, this is Sanyam."

Crystal looked Sanyam up and down. "I'm going to marry Fox if you don't," she announced, and Fox choked on a laugh as Sanyam's eyebrows went up.

"It's very nice to meet you, Crystal," he said, his lips twitching. "Thank you for warning me."

Fox poked Crystal in the ribs, making her yelp. "Go tell your *abuela* we're here." Crystal dashed inside, and Fox straightened to see Sanyam looking at him, eyes soft. "What?"

Sanyam held out a hand, and Fox allowed himself to be pulled close.

"For someone who doesn't want kids, you're very good with them."

Fox smiled and tucked his face into the crook of Sanyam's neck as voices rose from inside the house. "Maybe they're not so bad after all."

"—You just *left* them on the porch? Are we *gringos*, Crystal?" Amparo came into view, tucking her gray-streaked hair behind her ears and smiling up at both men. "I'm so sorry about my granddaughter." She tugged Fox down into a lavender-scented hug. "Hello, *mijo*, I'm so glad you came. Introduce me."

Fox performed the introductions and Sanyam bowed over the hand Amparo held out to him.

"I've heard a lot about you," Sanyam said. "It's wonderful to meet you at last."

Amparo dimpled at him. "Come inside. Let's get to know each other."

———

THEY SETTLED on the couch with mugs of hibiscus tea that Crystal brought from the kitchen, her tongue protruding with concentration as she carried the tray to the table and set it down.

She squeezed between Sanyam and Fox then, making herself comfortable and sipping her tea as they locked eyes in amusement above her sleek head.

Amparo laughed out loud but let her stay.

"Where's the rest of the family?" Fox asked.

"They're on their way," Amparo said. "I thought we'd ease you in—no point in throwing you in the deep end. Sanyam, what do you do?"

"I'm a professional—ah—" Sanyam hesitated,

glancing at Crystal, obliviously sipping from her mug. "I work at the Honeytrap."

"And that's where you and Fox met?"

Sanyam nodded, eyes softening as he glanced at Fox. "How long has it been, kit?"

Fox did the math in his head. "Little over a year—almost thirteen months."

Crystal squirmed and tugged on Fox's sleeve. "Fox, *Fox*. Guess what?"

"What?" Fox asked obediently.

"Do you know what 'fox' in Spanish is?"

Fox shook his head.

"Zorro!" Crystal announced triumphantly. "We should watch the movies. You can be Diego, and I'll be Elena."

Sanyam muffled a snort in a hasty swallow of tea as Fox turned to Amparo, whose lips were twitching, but she took pity on him.

"*Cristal*, my love, go set the table for me. There's a good girl."

Crystal pouted but wriggled free and stomped off to obey as Amparo leaned forward, eyes alight.

"Did Fox ever tell you about the time he made me a leaf sculpture?"

"No!" Sanyam said, taking Fox's hand. "How old were you, kit?"

"I don't know," Fox said. "Eight, I think?"

"It was the loveliest thing," Amparo said. "He arranged them by color—it must have taken him *hours* to sort out all the shades—and then created a spiral framed by branches he'd found in the woods."

Sanyam squeezed Fox's hand. "He has an artist's eye, doesn't he? Did he tell you about the gallery?"

Fox ducked his head at the pride in Sanyam's voice as warmth spread through his chest, thick and sweet like honeyed caramel.

"What gallery?" Amparo demanded. "What's this?"

"You know the mosaics I make," Fox said. "Some guy named Navin Arya saw one, and he really liked it and asked me if I had any more. He said he could sell just about anything I made. There's actually going to be a showing in a couple of months—" He hesitated. "Would you… want to come?"

"Of *course*!" Amparo said instantly. "Tell me when and where and I'll be there!"

Fox smiled at her as Sanyam launched into a story about Polly. "—pretended to hate her at first, of course—"

"Of course," Amparo agreed, nodding.

"But within a day, she'd abandoned me for him. Every time he stopped moving, she was there, wanting attention. She knew, right from the start."

Fox looked up. "Knew what?"

Sanyam's eyes were full of love. "That you were a keeper."

Amparo sighed happily as a car door slammed outside and voices rose. "Everyone else is here, sounds like."

Cricket and Dorian bounded inside first and took turns hugging both Fox and Sanyam. Even though they'd both apologized for that disastrous dinner, Cricket still held on a little longer than usual before pulling away to beam up at Fox.

"What were you guys talking about?" she asked.

Sanyam sat back down and tugged Fox into the circle of his arms. Fox melted against him.

"We were telling stories about Fox," Sanyam said. "Good ones."

"I can play this game!" Cricket exclaimed. "Fox, remember the time you bought me six months of riding lessons because I was going through a horse-crazy phase?"

"In my defense, your instructor was ridiculously hot," Fox protested.

"Yeah, but you didn't know that until after you took me there the first time," Cricket pointed out, grinning.

Fox smiled, joy suffusing him until he thought he might drift away, tethered to earth only by Sanyam's strong arms, and let the conversation swirl on over his head.

383

Keep reading for a sneak peek of Broken Trust, the next book in the Beloved Scars series!

ACKNOWLEDGMENTS

Thank you to everyone who read the first draft(s) and asked for more. Special thanks to the lovely and talented Saumya, for the Hindi phrases Sanyam uses and giving me valuable insight into Sanyam's world. Any mistakes are mine.

ABOUT THE AUTHOR

Michaela Grey told stories to put herself to sleep since she was old enough to hold a conversation in her head. When she learned to write, she began putting those stories down on paper. She and her family reside in the Texas Hill Country with their cats, and she is perpetually on the hunt for peaceful writing time, which her four children make difficult to find.

When she's not writing, she's knitting while watching TV or avoiding responsibilities on Tumblr, where she shamelessly ogles pretty people and tries to keep her cat off the keyboard.

Tumblr: greymichaela.tumblr.com Twitter: @GreyMichaela

Facebook: www.facebook.com/GreyMichaela

E-mail: greymichaela@gmail.com

BROKEN TRUST

"You can't leave me." Dominic briefly considered going to his knees to beg but discarded the idea. She'd probably just laugh at him. "I'm serious, Cory, you *can't*. Please, *please* don't leave me. We'll figure this out."

Cory straightened from tidying her desk with a grunt of pain and pressed one hand to her swollen stomach as she tucked dark red hair behind her ear with the other. "Dom, honey, I can't have the baby in your office."

"I'll get you a recliner," Dominic said. "A—a nurse on duty at all times. An ambulance standing by to rush you to the hospital when you go into labor. *Cory*—"

Cory turned to him at the naked desperation

in his voice. Dominic swallowed hard as sympathy flickered across her face.

"You'll be fine," she said gently. She crossed the room to pull him into a hug, going up on tiptoe to wrap her arms around his neck. "I found the perfect replacement," she said against his ear.

"She won't be as good as you," Dominic muttered, hugging her back. "She won't know what I like to eat for lunch and that I'm allergic to pine nuts and to not let Denise corner me when I come out of my office or how I take my coffee. She won't be *you*. Are you sure you can't stay?"

"First of all, that was pretty sexist of you, assuming my replacement's a woman," Cory said. "Second, do *you* want to be the one to tell my wife that I'm not taking maternity leave like I promised?"

Dominic flinched. Melissa was the most beautiful woman Dominic had ever met, and the most terrifying. Six feet tall, with perfect skin and a shaved head, she looked like she'd be right at home leading warriors into battle. Instead, she ran the bakery downstairs in his lobby, and her croissants were the stuff of legend.

Dominic sighed and shook his head.

"That's what I thought," Cory said. She patted his hand. "It's just six months. And you have only yourself to blame for having such excellent health insurance and benefits for your employees." She grunted again, pressing her palm to her stomach. "Little one's getting restless. I think she's hungry."

"I'll get you something," Dominic said instantly. "What do you want?"

"The usual," Cory said as she sank into her chair and Dominic picked up the phone to call the cafeteria. He placed the order—an extra large turkey sandwich with warm pear compote on sourdough bread for Cory and roast beef for himself, cola for her and pomegranate soda for him—before turning back.

Cory smiled up at him. "I'm fine," she said before he could ask. "Baby's just antsy to come out. Can't say that I blame her."

Dominic perched a hip on the edge of her desk and ran his hands through his hair with a sigh.

"Hey, I have an idea," Cory said. "While I'm gone, why don't you see about finding yourself a boyfriend?"

Dominic stiffened. "We've been over this."

Cory cocked her head. "You're lonely, Dom. You can't tell me you're not. You need someone."

"I don't—" Dominic scowled and stood up. "You know I'm not good at that shit." He crossed to the window and gazed down at the traffic twenty-seven stories below. He turned to face her and rested his shoulder blades against the glass.

"There's no way you don't get hit on every time you go outside," Cory said, gesturing at him.

Dominic shrugged. With his height and the tousled brown hair that fell in soft, glossy curls to his shoulders and eyes that had been described by various journalists as "pale gray like a winter dawn," "hard and glinting like steel," and—his personal favorite—"piercing silver orbs, sure to make women everywhere swoon," he knew he caught and held attention. Didn't mean he liked it.

"That's why I stay inside," he muttered. "I don't like people hitting on me. I don't like people flirting with me—I never know what to say, or what they want."

"You, honey," Cory said, suddenly sympathetic. "They want you."

"But I don't want *them*," Dominic said. "I've never—"

"I know," Cory interrupted. "Even in college, you were like this. Remember that time I set you up on the blind date?"

Dominic scowled. "He spent the entire night making innuendos, half of which I didn't even get. And he was handsy."

Cory's eyes were kind. "But he was hot, right?"

"Well… yeah." Dominic hunched his shoulders. "But I didn't want to have sex with him." He looked up. "He called me frigid."

"Yeah, and I snuck into his room and replaced his toothpaste with diaper rash cream." Cory giggled as Dominic fought the laugh.

"We're off-topic, anyway," Dominic said. "What if I give you a raise?"

Cory glanced at him. "How much of a raise?" She held up a hand before he could answer, though. "No. Nope. I promised Mel. She'll kill us both if I break that promise. You're just going to have to do without me."

"I can't, that's the whole point!" Someone knocked, and Dominic jerked. He closed his eyes briefly, praying Cory hadn't noticed but knowing she had, and crossed the room to answer the door. He accepted the basket with a nod of thanks and turned back.

"I hired the best assistant possible," Cory said. "He's got glowing reviews from every employer he's been with, he's responsible for several practices streamlining procedures in a couple of those positions, he's basically going to do my job with one hand tied behind his back."

"It *is* a guy?" Dominic said. His stomach sank

as he handed Cory her sandwich and dropped into the chair on the other side of the desk with his own.

Cory took a huge bite and moaned happily. When she'd swallowed, she nodded. "His name is Farid. And don't worry, I've left him detailed notes on what you'll need and expect, and how to run interference for you. It's gonna be fine."

"I want to see him."

"Of course you do," Cory said. She swiveled her monitor so he could see it.

Farid Qadir, Dominic read. A man about his age gazed solemnly at him, almond-shaped dark eyes startling in their intensity. His nose was big and his lips were pressed together, but Dominic couldn't stop looking at his eyes.

Cory sighed. "God, he's pretty."

Dominic twitched, recalled to himself. "If you're matchmaking, Cor, I swear to God—"

"I'm not!" Cory protested. "Look at his credentials, Dom, he might be better qualified than me."

"Than I," Dominic mumbled, but obeyed. His eyebrows rose as he read down the list. "He worked at Lockheed Martin?"

"And they begged him to stay, but he missed Seattle and his family, apparently," Cory said. She propped her chin on her hand and pointed. "He's got glowing references, too, see?"

"Well, if Jean-Baptiste recommended him, I definitely don't want him," Dominic said. He looked at the picture again, memorizing the shape of Farid's eyes. "Tell him we don't need him, I'll be fine without you."

Cory laughed out loud and nearly dropped her sandwich. "Bitch, please. You can't get *dressed* without me. You're just bitter because Jean-Baptiste made a pass at you."

"No, I'm bitter because he told the press we slept together after I turned him down," Dominic snapped. He set his sandwich on the desk and shoved his hair out of his face. "When does he get here?"

"Tomorrow," Cory said. "That way I'll have two weeks to train him and make sure he's up to speed on your, ah… eccentricities, shall we say?"

Dominic switched his glare to her. "I'm not eccentric!"

"Oh, because normal people are virgins at twenty-seven?"

"Fuck you."

Cory grinned. "That's kind of the problem, isn't it?"

"At least I don't macramé," Dominic tossed back.

"Hey, macramé is very relaxing, and people love it as gifts!" Cory snapped.

"Macramé this," Dominic muttered, startling Cory into laughter. The anxious knot under his breastbone eased, and he took another bite.

He glanced up as a thought occurred to him. "You're not leaving for good, right? You *will* be coming back when the maternity leave is over?"

"Of course I will," Cory said soothingly. "Can you see me as a stay-at-home mom?" She pitched her voice up half an octave. "Little Junior is gluten and soy and sugar free. Why isn't *your* child on a paleo diet? Did you know that vaccines cause autism? Everyone, L.L. Bean is having a sale on children's clothing!" She shuddered. "No fucking way. The best thing for everyone is me going back to work. Melissa will be keeping the baby with her at the bakery."

"No one sane says autism is caused by vaccines these days," Dominic said absently. He'd had an idea for a new code, and his fingers twitched as he sorted through the pieces in his mind.

"Oh, get back to work," Cory said. "You've already forgotten I'm here."

Dominic strode for his office.

He waved Cory away when she put her head in to tell him she was leaving for the day, still deep in code, but caught a glimpse of her indulgent smile as she shut the door.

This was good, he knew. It was going to turn the operating system upside down and inside out, if he could just get the code to *align*—

He fell asleep at his desk somewhere around 3:00 a.m., head pillowed on his arm.

Cory woke him the next morning, and Dominic nearly fell off his chair when she touched his shoulder.

"What time is it?" he demanded.

"Nearly nine," Cory said. She looked tired, Dominic realized, and guilt stabbed him. "Farid is here. I want you to meet him."

The guilt faded, replaced by anxiety, and Dominic pulled away.

"I'm busy," he said.

Cory rolled her eyes. "You're always busy when you don't want to do something I need you to do."

"I mean it," Dominic insisted. "I have to get this program written. Just… show him around the office."

"Don't tell me how to do my job," Cory said. "And now it's time for you to meet him."

"No." Dominic slouched in his chair and folded his arms.

"You do realize that acting like a toddler won't actually make the problem go away, right?" Cory inquired.

Dominic looked up at her and quickly away, but it was too late.

"Oh, honey," Cory said. She took his chin in her cool fingers and turned his head toward her. Dominic closed his eyes, the anxiety battering the inside of his skull until he thought vaguely he might shake apart, crumble into tiny pieces on the carpet, and leaned forward until he could rest his cheek against her round stomach.

"I can't—" He hated this part, the tailspin feeling of his life spiraling out of his control no matter how wildly he grasped at it, tried to glue it back together.

"Yes you can," Cory interrupted. "God, Dom, I'm so sorry, I wish I hadn't done this. Melissa could have carried the baby, then I'd have only been gone a few weeks. Look, I'll come back sooner, okay? I won't take the whole six months."

"*No*," Dominic said, jerking away as horror flooded him. He stood and took her hands. "No, Cor, I'm being selfish and stupid. You wanted this, you *deserve* this. I'm—I'm glad I can give it to you, okay?"

Cory freed a hand and wiped her eyes. "Stupid pregnancy hormones. So will you meet him?"

Dominic sighed. "Yes." His cell phone rang before he could move toward the door, and he answered absently, not looking at the number. "This is Dominic."

"I didn't think you'd take my call!" The voice was breezy, cheerful, as if the last time Dominic had heard it, its owner hadn't been telling Dominic how frigid he was, how he'd never find love because he didn't know how to relax, that Dominic should thank him for sticking around as long as he had.

Dominic stood very still, and alarm flashed across Cory's face.

"What do you want, Lance?" A distant part of Dominic was proud his voice stayed even as horror replaced the alarm on Cory's expression. Low voices floated in from her office, but she stayed where she was, watching Dominic.

"Is that any way to say hello?" Lance chided. "Maybe I just called to catch up with you, see how you're doing."

"I'm fine, and you never do anything unless it

benefits you in some way," Dominic said through his teeth. "So what do you want?"

"I hear Cory's leaving," Lance said smoothly. "Who's taking over while she's gone?"

Dominic lowered the phone and covered the speaker. "I've got this. Go deal with—whatever that is."

Cory hesitated, and Dominic shooed her toward the door. He brought the phone back to his ear.

"That's not news," he said.

Lance's laugh was low and rich, phantom sticky caramel dripping onto Dominic's skin and making him twitch. "Mm, no, but who's replacing her is, isn't he?"

Dominic clenched his jaw. "Really none of your business."

"I'm a reporter," Lance reminded him. "Everything is my business. Even you." His voice dropped. "*Especially* you."

"Not anymore," Dominic ground out.

"Don't let him fall for you," Lance said, malice heavy in the words. "He won't thank you for it."

Dominic stiffened. "I—" Shame scoured his chest and clogged his throat. "I never meant—"

"Whatever," Lance said briskly. "I wanted to see if I could get an interview with your new assistant. I'm doing a piece on 'the power behind the thrones,' as it were, and I want to talk to him about working for Lockheed Martin and the differences between there and here. I knew Cory wouldn't take my call, and I don't have his number, so here I am."

"It's his first day," Dominic managed through his teeth. "There's not much he can tell you just yet."

"I'm sure he knows more than you think," Lance said, and the patronizing note in his voice made Dominic's hackles stand on end. "Give him the phone, there's a good boy."

Dominic stiffened. "No," he said flatly. "What's more, you are banned from the premises, and I'm going to alert every employee that no one is to give you his phone number. You want an interview with him, you're going to have to figure out another way."

He hung up and went straight for his private bathroom, where he dropped the phone into the toilet just as it began to ring again. It gave a forlorn gurgle and stopped ringing, and Dominic tugged his sleeves down and spun. Time to meet the person who would never be as good as Cory.

He stalked through the double doors into Cory's fishbowl office to see a slim man in a perfectly tailored suit gazing with mild curiosity around the room as he sat in the chair by the window.

He rose when Dominic burst in and held out a hand.

"Mr. Spector, it's very nice to finally meet you."

Dominic looked at the outstretched hand and back up into Farid's face until Farid's eyebrows lifted, and he dropped his hand.

"I need a new phone," Dominic said to Cory, still looking at Farid.

"You couldn't just block the number?" Cory said, but she was already pulling out her own phone and tapping on it.

"I'm very busy," Dominic said to Farid. "I didn't want you here. Your job is to be invisible, got it?"

Farid's eyebrows went higher. "You're the one who advertised for a temporary assistant, are you not?"

"Doesn't mean I want you," Dominic snapped.

Farid narrowed his eyes and opened his mouth, but Cory stepped between them before he could speak. "Enough posturing, boys. Farid, I'm the one who advertised for you, not him. Dom, Farid is very impressed with the size of your dick. Now go back to work and let me train him."

Dominic snapped his mouth shut, stymied, as amusement sparked in the liquid depths of Farid's eyes.

Finding nothing witty to say, he spun on his heel and stalked back to his office.

HE COULDN'T CONCENTRATE, though, and after an hour, he ground his teeth and shoved away from the desk. Maybe a change of scenery and some cinnamon tea would shake something loose.

Dominic slipped out the side door so Cory wouldn't see him and strode down the hall to the break room. He froze in the doorway when he realized Farid was there, talking to Denise. Neither noticed him, and Dominic held his breath.

"—her replacement? Well, aren't we lucky! Tell me, Farid, can you sing?"

Dominic deliberated. Should he rescue him?

Farid tilted his head. "I—what?"

"Sing," Denise repeated. "It's a fairly simple question. Can you carry a tune?"

"Not if my life depended on it," Farid said. The kettle whistled, and he turned it off and poured it over the teabags as Denise clicked her tongue in disappointment.

"So the hunt for a new karaoke superstar continues," she sighed.

Farid laughed, and Dominic hated the sound, warm and rich. "You couldn't pay me enough to get me up on a stage anyway," he said. "Sorry. Maybe you should ask Dominic."

Oh, he did not just do that.

"Ask Dominic what?" he said from the doorway.

Denise turned and pounced on him. "Dominic darling, can you sing?"

Farid stirred the tea as it steeped and didn't look in their direction.

Dominic smiled at Denise. She was predatory and intense, but somehow she didn't set off the alarm bells in his head. Maybe because she knew she didn't have a chance with him, and her posturing was just that—for show. "My shower's never complained, but that's the only place I sing."

Denise clicked her tongue again. "I was just telling Farid here that we need someone for karaoke night. Wouldn't you like to join us?"

Dominic couldn't help his laugh at that, and he didn't miss the way Farid's shoulders tightened.

"Don't you have actual work to do, Denise?"

Denise sighed. "I'm not letting this go," she warned.

The door shut behind her, and Dominic was alone with Farid. Farid's back was turned, his head bent as he stirred whatever was in the mugs in front of him.

Dominic shoved his hands in his pockets and took a step nearer, irritation pushing him to speak. "In future, kindly avoid volunteering me out for karaoke or anything else that involves people."

Farid didn't turn.

"It's not your place to sign me up for the office brunch or karaoke or the fucking party that Olivia and Ryan down in R&D throw every month. I want to be left alone. And if you can't get that, you might as well leave now."

Farid's shoulders were bunched with tension, but he still said nothing.

Dominic moved closer. "I don't like people. So part of your job will be keeping them away from me."

"Is there anyone you do like?" Farid interrupted. He turned, irritation simmering in his dark, slanted eyes and his full lips compressed.

"I like Cory," Dominic said. "That's about it."

"Message received," Farid snapped. "No people. Can I go?"

Dominic narrowed his eyes. "What's your problem?"

"I don't have a problem," Farid said, but his mouth was tight, and anger simmered in the taut lines of his shoulders.

"Yes you do," Dominic said. He didn't know why he was pressing, but he couldn't seem to stop himself. "You have a problem with *me*, don't you?"

"My *problem* is know-it-all employers who think their way is the only way and no one else is able to do their job," Farid said. "You rich techies are all alike. You think because you can code, you know the secrets to the universe. Arm candy hanging off you, magazines and papers begging to interview. But without people like me and Cory, you wouldn't be able to get anything done." He took a step forward, and Dominic flinched back before he could stop himself.

"You are way out of line," he managed, but his voice wobbled, and he snapped his mouth shut.

Farid arched a brow and closed the distance between them. "So fire me," he said, dangerously quiet. "But good luck finding a better assistant with *half* my skills before Cory leaves."

He was a good three inches shorter than Dominic, slimly built with fine boned wrists and a delicate throat. His eyelashes were obscenely thick, his eyes dark and unreadable, and a jolt of... *something* fizzed through Dominic's stomach.

He took a quick step back, yanking his coat

sleeves down, and spun on his heel. He was fleeing the field of battle, he knew, but he didn't care. Farid's low, triumphant laugh followed him as he bolted from the room.

Order Broken Trust now!